THE SONS OF JUDE

The Sons of Jude

Brandt Dodson

MONARCH
BOOKS

Oxford, UK & Grand Rapids, Michigan, USA

Published by Monarch Books
an imprint of Lion Hudson plc
Wilkinson House, Jordan Hill Road, Oxford OX2 8DR, England
Tel: +44 (0)1865 302750 Fax: +44 (0)1865 302757
Email: monarch@lionhudson.com
www.lionhudson.com

Published in conjunction with MacGregor Literary

ISBN 978 0 85721 205 4 (print)
ISBN 978 0 85721 345 7 (Kindle)
ISBN 978 0 85721 346 4 (epub)

A catalogue record for this book is available from the British Library.

Printed and bound in the UK by the MPG Books Group.

St. Jude

Patron saint of the Chicago Police Department

But his sons did not follow his ways. They turned aside after dishonest gain and accepted bribes and perverted justice.

1 Samuel 8:3

For Karla

CHAPTER 1

Chicago Police Department
District 28 Headquarters

Monday, 11:00 a.m. Detective Frank Campello stood in the doorway of the 28th district's second-floor squad room. It was his first day back since the shooting, and everything looked the same. Gun-metal-gray desks stood nose to nose, the walls were still covered in nauseating beige, and the sound of hushed conversations filled the room, punctuated only by the occasional ring of a phone or the squeak of a chair. Everything was the same – except for Rand's riderless desk.

Campello passed his late partner's work station and slid out of his black leather jacket, draping it over the back of the chair. A swarthy man of stocky build with close-cropped black hair and deeply set brown eyes, Campello preferred casual clothing to the department's more generally accepted business attire. On this day, he wore a black long-sleeved shirt that clung to his muscular frame, brown slacks and cordovan loafers. A Sig-Sauer nine-millimeter pistol rode on his right hip.

Taking his CPD mug to the coffee maker at the rear of the room, he met Detective Angelo Silvio.

"Welcome back, Frank." Silvio was stirring non-dairy creamer into his coffee. "I'm sorry about Rand. He was a good cop." He tossed the stir stick into the receptacle and lifted the cup to his lips, pausing to blow before drinking.

"Thanks, Angie." Campello filled his mug and returned the carafe to its nook. "Hard to believe he's gone."

9

Silvio sat on the edge of the table that held the coffee maker. "Things like this are always hard to believe. How can a man like that, so full of life, be here one day and gone the next?" He shook his head. "It doesn't make sense, Frank."

"I'm sorry about Rand," said Shelly Tertwiller as she approached. "I know you two were close." Tertwiller, a recent transferee to the 28th, was a detective with just two years less time on the department than Campello's twenty. Her coffee-colored eyes studied him from beneath a furrowed brow. "You OK?"

"I'm OK."

"I know everyone says this, but if there's anything you need…"

"I appreciate it."

"For what it's worth, the buzz around here says you'll come out fine on the other thing." She was referring to his hearing before the IPRA, the all-civilian review board that replaced the previous Office of Professional Standards. Campello's killing of the suspect who killed Adams had automatically guaranteed him a review by the board. All police-action shootings, regardless of their merit, went before the IPRA.

"I've already been exonerated, Shelly," Campello said.

"Last week, wasn't it?" Silvio asked. "Where've you been, Tertwiller?"

She gave her partner a hard look. "Who's talking to you, dummy?" She patted Campello's hand. "That's good to hear, Frank. We're all here for you. You don't stand alone."

"I know."

"We're family. When one of us goes down, we all go down. It's always been that way and it always will be." She held out her fist and he bumped it with his. "By the way, how's your dad doing?"

"As good as can be expected. He's more forgetful, but he seems to like Marimar and they treat him well."

"You see him?"

"I do. Going this evening, in fact."

She smiled. "Good. Again, let me know if you need anything."

"I will. Thank you."

"I mean it," she said, turning toward him even as she was walking away. "You need help with your case load... paperwork... whatever. Bill and I have your back."

Bill was her husband and a detective with the 31st.

"Got it. Thanks, Shelly."

"Well," Silvio said, "got to get to work." He held his hand out to Campello, who shook it. "We're going to Jeep's tonight. You're coming, right?"

"Absolutely."

Silvio smiled and slapped him on the back. "Excellent. Five o'clock. First round's on you."

Campello grinned and reluctantly went to his desk to begin his first day without Rand; his first day without his partner and friend.

He dropped himself into his chair and undid his tie. His desk, like the others in the room, was nose to nose with his partner's, an arrangement that facilitated communication. Across the great divide, Campello could see Rand, sitting with his feet up and a smirk on his face. *Hey, buddy, how 'bout them Cubs, huh?*

Campello reached across the desk-tops and took Rand's mug in hand. The Cubs emblem was nearly worn off and the white ceramic cup was chipped and stained from years of coffee abuse.

He rolled the cup in his hands before putting it in the left-hand drawer of his desk along with his pistol.

Campello stabbed the computer power button with his forefinger, brooding on old memories until the machine booted up and the CPD emblem emblazoned on the screen. Then he opened a window to Adams' case load; it was significant – weighty, even – and there was little doubt the district commander would re-assign some of them. But Campello wanted to review them so he could have a say in which ones stayed with him and which went elsewhere. The list represented a lot of effort and team work – and he didn't relish the idea of losing control after all the time they had put into them.

He scrolled down the list and began by making note of the ones that were set to go to trial. He ran his finger down the screen as he copied the case numbers in a spiral-bound steno's notebook, silently mouthing them to himself. His hand stopped halfway down the list at an unfamiliar file number. It matched no known classification, suggesting it was a dummy, something Rand had likely been working off the books, anticipating an upgrade to official status in the future.

Campello made a note of it and then circled it. He would research it later.

"You got a minute, Frank?" He looked up to see Julio Lopez, the district commander.

"I was just going over some of Frank's cases."

"You can do that later." He pointed his chin toward his office. "Come on back."

Campello slid the notebook in a drawer of his desk and snatched his CPD mug. He paused at the coffee maker to top off the cup.

"Close the door, will you?" the boss said, settling in the chair behind his desk.

Campello pushed it closed and sat across from Lopez. The office was Plexiglas on three sides, floor to ceiling, and both men knew their meeting was being covertly watched by the entire crew.

"You doing OK?"

"Yeah. I'm fine."

Lopez gave him a non-believing look.

"I'm fine, Julio."

"You have more time coming, Frank. Take it if you need it."

He shook his head.

Lopez's eyes searched him, studied him, before accepting his statement on face value. "OK. I guess you are."

"Anything new on the shooting?" Campello asked.

"You mean, is there any new information?"

"Yep."

"No. The IPRA cleared you. Don't worry about it. You did the only thing you could."

"I wish I'd fired sooner."

"Don't. Rand's time was up. There was nothing you could've done. We all know the risk when we pin on the star."

"Maybe. But that doesn't help much."

"No, I guess not. But it's true. You've got two choices, Frank. You can blame yourself for this, or you can see it for what it is and get on with your life."

"That's what I'm trying to do. That's why I'm back."

"Let it go. Move on."

"I have to move on, Julio. The department is my family. I don't belong anywhere else. There's no one at home so I've got no reason to stay there." He lifted the mug again, and then paused to grin over the top of it. "God knows I haven't done so well in the marriage department."

"Yeah, well, me neither."

Campello lowered the mug and set it on the edge of the commander's desk. "Four times for me."

Lopez winced. "Ouch. OK. You win that one."

Campello crossed his legs. "You didn't call me in here to chit-chat."

"No." He folded his hands, resting them on the desk.

"What, Julio? Just say it."

"We've got a transfer coming in."

"Who?"

"It wasn't my idea. It was arranged before Rand took a hit. But with his passing, I thought you'd be the right guy for—"

"Who?"

Lopez sat back in his chair and ran a hand through his hair. "It's Polanski."

The flush of anger was immediate and Campello fought to control himself. "Polanski?"

"The brass wants him transferred. Since his allegations about the other shooting, the one in the 31st, he's become too hot for them and a danger to himself. The rioting there has escalated and they want him out of the district before he brings them any additional unwanted attention."

"I don't blame them."

"I want him to work with you. At least until I can figure out what to do with him."

"No."

The commander crossed his arms, his expression growing mulish. "I need for you to keep an eye on him, Frank."

"No, Julio."

The commander nodded toward the squad room. "Those people out there respect you. You've got a lot of time and a good record with the department. There isn't an officer in that room that wouldn't walk into hell with you. I need someone who commands that kind of respect to keep an eye on Polanski. So far, we don't have the rioting and unrest going on here that is occurring in the 31st. Your killing of the suspect who gunned down Rand is justified in the mind of the public. But if Polanski stirs up the same concerns here that he did in the 31st, we'll see the same kind of trouble. The brass doesn't want that and neither do I. I don't think you do either."

"I don't want to work with him, Julio."

Lopez sighed. "It isn't up to you, Frank. For what it's worth, it's not up to me either."

"What do you mean? You're the commander." His voice was rising.

"I mean I have bosses too, and they want him here and you're open right now. I can't let him work alone. I don't trust him."

"You've got to be kidding me. You're replacing *Rand* with Polanski?"

Lopez glanced toward the squad room and then leaned forward in his chair. "I'm not replacing Rand with anyone." His gaze locked on Campello, his tone quietly emphatic. "Stuff happens. Rand's gone and I have a new man who happens to be Polanski. So you're going to work with him, and you're going to do it now, or you can take more time off and then work with him when you come back."

"Work with a turncoat? Are you serious?"

Lopez spread his hands.

Campello stared at him in disbelief. "When does this happen?"

Julio slid a note across the desk. "We just got a call. There's a body at Navy Pier."

"What? Now? I haven't even had time to clear the case load and…"

But he no longer had Julio's attention. The commander was staring into the squad room at an immaculately dressed man standing just outside the office door.

CHAPTER 2

Christy Lee didn't have to be in the newsroom until early afternoon, because she was scheduled to cover the mayor's early morning press conference on the riots of the night before.

The violence began after a police-action shooting in the 31st district when a detective alleged that the involved officers had planted evidence on the suspect. So far, no one had been killed or seriously injured in the melee, but the mayor was concerned the situation could change.

City Hall had no new plans for containing the uprising, however, and Christy saw no reason to report on more of the same. For that matter, she didn't see value in press conferences of any kind. They were organized events that purported to be a dialogue with the press, but which were nothing of the kind. Rather, they were one-sided orchestrations designed to put the host in the best possible light while making it nearly impossible to extract any pertinent information. She much preferred going after stories on her own time and uncovering the facts in her own way. Unlike the coiffed TV anchors of the Windy City, Christy viewed herself as a journalist rather than a celebrity, and her job as a profession rather than a path to stardom. She wasn't out to be noticed. She was out for a scoop. That didn't mean she was ignorant of the power of female persuasion, nor did it mean she was unaware of her appearance or the effect she had on men. She was tall, with shoulder-length black hair that cascaded about her shoulders like spun coal, almond eyes inherited from a Chinese mother, and a figure that inspired a second look. She wasn't above using her assets to gain access to men in positions of power, but it was her acumen and her tenacity, supported by sound observation and a hard-won knowledge of the human psyche, that had garnered accolades for her reporting.

The press conference had already begun when she pulled her aging Corolla into line at the Starbucks drive-up window. There were several cars ahead of her so she decided to use the time by contacting one of her sources within the CPD.

It was no secret that the cops were in a tizzy because one of their own had agreed to testify in the recent high-profile shooting and the officer's charges had led to the dismissal of several departmental supervisors as well as indictments against officers Caine and Dorchester. The two men were on administrative leave, pending the trial, and they were viewed by many in the department as scapegoats while the officer who was scheduled to testify against them was considered a turncoat.

But that was always the case, wasn't it? As far as she was concerned, Andy Polanski was a hero. For far too long, too many of the city's uniformed thugs had been virtually ignored when enforcing their own brand of justice and it was time for justifiable retribution. But she held no doubt about Polanski's safety in a department that viewed itself as being above the very laws it was charged with enforcing. The few right-thinking people within the CPD's leadership had also seen the potential for trouble and were intervening by transferring Polanski to another district. Although she had written about the need to protect him, she also knew that a tree of shame grew within the department and its branches reached to the highest levels. The Chicago Police Department was fiercely loyal to its own and viewed anyone who turned on them as the enemy. Polanski was fated to a short and unremarkable career in the CPD. It was unlikely he'd be safe anywhere.

She inched closer to the window as she punched the number into her phone. As soon as the voice came on line she said, "It's Christy. You got anything for me?"

"You looking for something in particular?"

"Polanski."

"He's yesterday's news, Christy. Give it up. There's more to our world than that guy."

"As long as the riots continue, he'll be relevant. There's a story there and I want it."

The voice sighed. "OK. I may have something, but I'm not sure."

She dug through her purse for her notebook and pen while balancing the phone between her shoulder and ear. "Shoot."

"There's been some talk about Polanski being transferred to the 28th."

Christy smiled. The 28th was in the loop, making it close to her home and work. "Is this just talk or do you have something concrete?"

There was a moment's hesitation on the other end. "It's pretty tight. It looks like he's going to be working with Frank Campello."

"Campello? Wasn't he the detective who killed the suspect last week? When his partner was killed?"

"The same."

She pulled to the order station. "Hold on." She placed her order then said into the phone, "That's not going to go down well. Campello a cop's cop and he's going to be working with *Polanski?* There's going to be a firestorm over that."

"It ain't going to be pretty. A lot of the guys at the 28th are pretty upset by Adams' death. He was well liked. Putting Polanski in the mix is like dropping a match in an Iraqi oil field."

"Is he going in soon?"

"Maybe today. They've been trying to keep it hush-hush because of people like you." There was irony in his voice. "The theory is that if no one knows where he's going until he shows up, there will be less time to plan trouble."

"What do you think?"

"Trouble's coming either way. The man is going to meet with resistance."

"Who's the commander of the 28th?"

"A guy named Lopez. Julio Lopez. He's as straight as they come."

"Just so I understand, you're telling me that there's been talk about a transfer and the 28th looks good for it?"

"Yeah. Probably because Rand Adams was killed in a shooting similar to the one that Polanski has involved himself with." He snorted. "Irony. You've got to love it."

"I prefer to think of it as drama. It makes for good news."

"Maybe. But I think when this trial is over most of the drama will be over too. It's all about the cleanup now."

CHAPTER 3

Although Polanski made every effort to break the ice, Campello decided to ignore him and didn't say a word during the short drive from the 28th to the crime scene at Navy Pier. By the time they arrived, a steady drizzle had begun, further adding to the already darkened mood inside the car.

Campello drove to the pier's main entrance, surveying the scene through the rhythmic thumping of the wipers. A cluster of squad cars, some with their blue lights still flashing, was parked at the front entrance along with the crime lab's van. Technicians were milling about behind a cordon of yellow crime-scene tape and a small group of people, who had probably come to the pier for entertainment, were gathered along the barrier and getting more than they had anticipated.

He double-parked the burgundy Crown Victoria alongside a marked squad car.

"Let me do the talking," he said, shifting the transmission into Park.

Polanski said nothing, but slid out of the car. He was tall with a slender build, and wore a tan cashmere overcoat on top of a chocolate suit, white shirt and brown-striped tie. He pulled the collar of his coat around his neck as they approached a uniformed patrolman standing watch behind the tape. The officer, a tall lanky kid who could not have been more than twenty-five or twenty-six, stood with his shoulders hunched against the rain. He stamped his feet in an effort to stay warm.

"Hey, Frank. Sorry about Rand." He raised the tape, allowing the detectives to cross under.

Polanski stuck out a hand. "Andy Polanski."

The patrolman reached to shake hands, but hesitated before withdrawing his hand. Polanski swallowed hard and looked away to the investigators in the distance.

"What've we got, Devon?" Campello asked.

The patrolman nodded over his shoulder toward the Lake Michigan side of the pier. "We've got a young victim in a trash bin. Two kids discovered her and got hold of Brown. He was working the pier." He glared at Polanski.

"Is the coroner here?" Campello asked.

The officer shook his head.

"OK. Thanks." He clamped his star on the collar of his jacket and gave Devon a collegial pat on the back before walking toward the area, leaving Polanski to catch up. At the bin, Campello grabbed the lip of the trash receptacle and pulled himself up. Polanski found a nearby collection of pallets and stacked a couple of them. He stood on the makeshift platform and peered into the container.

The woman was lying on her back, partially covered in a tarp, and largely obscured by garbage and other debris. Her arms were askew and her ashen face was swollen and disfigured. Her neck was bruised, and her eyes were open and fixed.

"She's young," Polanski said.

Campello ignored the man, but noted the same fact. Both of her hands were bruised and her wrists were swollen. He dropped to the ground.

"Any idea when someone from the coroner's office will be here?" he asked a young woman, a lab tech, who was photographing the scene.

She shifted the camera to the other hand. "They're sending Barb. She's on the way."

Until the coroner arrived, there would be no point in climbing into the bin. The medical examiner would collect forensic evidence and make an initial attempt at determining the time of death. She would not want anyone contaminating her crime scene before she had a chance to examine it. But given the rain and the rotting garbage, Campello knew forensics would be questionable.

"When was she found?" He asked.

"An hour ago." The photographer pointed to a tall solidly built man standing nearby in uniform who appeared to be older and more seasoned than Devon. "The officer over there said they got him as soon as they found her." She yelled toward the man. "Officer? These detectives would like to speak to you."

The patrolman came to where Campello and Polanski were standing. His name tag identified him as Brown, the man Devon said was working the pier. The officer looked at the swirling sky and then gestured for them to follow him to an alcove that was behind the collection of dumpsters and out of the wind and rain.

"What time did the kids get you?" Campello asked.

The man took a deep breath and glanced upward, trying to recall. "It must've been an hour ago. No more than an hour and fifteen." He pointed to two boys sitting on a pallet a few feet away in the alcove. "The fat one got into the bin when he heard the cell phone ringing. That's when he discovered the victim. And then the taller one came to get me."

"He climbed into the bin?" Campello asked.

Brown nodded. "Coroner's not going to be happy."

Campello shrugged. "She'll have to work with what she's got. Where were you when the boy got you?"

"I was standing on the south end of the concourse freezing my tail off."

Campello couldn't help but grin. The officer had the weathered look that came with years of walking a beat. He was everything that Devon, the young patrolman at the tape line wasn't, but one day would be. Experienced and knowledgeable. For that matter, the officer was everything that Polanski wasn't. A cop.

Campello glanced over Brown's shoulder in the boys' direction. They were sitting with their knees flexed tightly against their chests. Their arms were wrapped around their legs and they had their eyes focused on their feet. The heavier of the two was gently rocking.

"Where's the phone?" Campello asked.

Brown held out a zip-lock-style bag. It was sealed with tape that had EVIDENCE etched across it in red.

Campello took the bag, aware that Polanski was breathing over his shoulder.

Brown said, "They skipped school to come to the pier. They were dumpster diving when they heard the phone ring. A lot of kids skip school to come down here. Some of them dip into the trash bins looking for things that have been discarded. T-shirts, CDs, trinkets." He shook his head as he looked at the boys. "They'll never forget this day."

Campello opened the phone's recent memory and discovered that a call had come in at around the time the boys heard the ringing.

"Why don't you go talk to the kids," he said to Polanski.

As soon as the detective was out of earshot, Brown said, "Is that who I think it is?"

Campello shot the officer a knowing look.

"I wouldn't want to be within a hundred yards of that guy."

Campello gave Brown a wry grin. "Was the phone ringing when you reached the bin?"

The man shook his head. "No. By the time I got here, the boys had already gotten the phone. The fat kid found it, but tossed it to the other one. He came to get me and handed me the phone."

"You bagged it right away?"

Brown shook his head. "No. The techs did as soon as they arrived."

Campello glanced around. "I don't get it. What was she doing out here?"

Brown shrugged.

"I mean, there's nothing here at night. And it's still early, so it's unlikely she got dumped here this morning. And even with the garbage strike, someone would've found her when they used the bin."

"Maybe not," Brown said. "How often do you look in the trash when you dump your garbage?"

He had a point. But still… Campello pushed several of the buttons on the phone and then said, "It belongs to the girl." He held out the phone for Brown to see. There was a photo of the victim standing in front of the city skyline. Her face was distorted in the photo, suggesting she had taken it herself.

"Anything you can trace?" Brown asked.

"Maybe."

Campello found the recent incoming number again, and then dialed it with his own phone. He disconnected as soon as he had an answer. "The phone call was coming from Silk 'n Boots."

"Isn't that the strip club on Rush?"

"Yep." He punched the voice mail on the victim's phone, before realizing he didn't have her passcode. "I can't access her voice mail so I don't know if there's a message, but we'll have the lab get it. Check her SIM card, too." He punched a button and the phone's memory came into view. "She gets a lot of calls from there."

A sudden gust of wind kicked up, spinning through the alcove and rocking both officers. Brown blew on his cupped hands and then thrust them into the pockets of his jacket.

Campello called to the technician photographing the scene. "How much longer are you going to be?"

She shrugged while continuing to photograph the scene. "Maybe another five minutes. Ten tops."

Polanski had finished his interview of the boys and was approaching.

"OK," Campello said to her. "Send us what you've got when you get it." He turned to Brown, "When you guys get finished interviewing everyone, make sure we get a copy of your report. I'm going to follow this lead before going back to the station."

"OK, but if I was you," the officer said, "I'd sneak out of here on the other side." He gestured toward East Grand Avenue and a familiar Toyota Corolla that was advancing toward the pier.

Campello followed Brown's gaze and groaned. "As if this day hadn't started out bad enough." He turned to Polanski. "I'm going to run a lead. Why don't you get a ride with one of the others back to the office? I'm sure the boys' parents will be there soon and it'd be good if someone was there."

Polanski looked anxiously at Brown as Campello left him, cutting through the concourse building to the other side of the pier.

CHAPTER 4

When she pulled away from the drive-up window, Christy made a second phone call, this time to the 28th, to hear that Campello and Polanski were out of the office, confirming her snitch's suspicions of Polanski's transfer.

A third phone call to the news room at *The Chicago Star* revealed that a reported murder victim had been discovered at Navy Pier and that Campello had been dispatched to the scene. It seemed logical that Polanski would be there too, especially since he wasn't in the office, and wherever Polanski went, she was sure to follow.

She pulled in near the concourse building, taking the spot left by a departing burgundy Crown Victoria that had been double parked. She recognized it as an unmarked squad car, a term that was an oxymoron at best. For all the effort to make them blend in, cop cars stood out like a priest behind bars.

The rain had slowed to a trickle and Christy turned off the wipers as she studied the scene. A crowd had gathered, but most of them appeared to be tourists and there were no indicators that any other journalist had arrived.

She killed the engine, then checked the batteries in her tape recorder. They were good, so she grabbed her things and rolled out of the car. When she reached the crime-scene barrier, she flashed her credentials to the cop standing guard.

"Sorry, ma'am," the officer said. "I can't let you through."

"Officer…" she paused to glance at the name tag over his right shirt pocket, "… Grimes, I am a member of the press and the people have a right to know—"

"Yes, ma'am. I understand. But you will have to wait until a press announcement is made."

"Who is your superior?"

He pointed to a large man in uniform, standing near a dumpster at the rear of the building.

"I want to talk to him."

"At the press conference."

"Now, officer Grimes. Let me talk to him now."

The officer opened his mouth to speak, but then reached for the microphone attached to an epaulet on his jacket. Christy could not hear what was said, but did hear the comeback over the patrolman's radio.

"Yeah, I saw her," the voice said. "Tell her to wait. I'll be right there."

"He says you are to——"

"I heard."

She slung her purse over her shoulder and dropped the tape recorder in the pocket of her trench coat. The damp chilly air was penetrating and she tried to stay warm by pacing the length of the crime-scene tape with her hands thrust in her pockets. The TV news celebs, late as usual, began arriving in panel vans with their antennae raised and the station's call letters emblazoned on the side. By the time the supervisory cop made it to the line, she knew that she would be but one of a gaggle of reporters, all vying for an exclusive or an off-the-record quote from someone in the know. Such information had always been deemed as non-attributable, but her profession had wilted to something less than what it had been and lowered the bar by revealing the identity of off-the-record sources. It pained her, but she held no illusions. News gathering had become a vicious business because news reporting had become a big one.

She moved as close to the restricting tape line as possible, her voice-activated tape recorder in hand as the officer approached. A wall of human flesh pressed against her as the various crews – print and broadcast – gathered around.

"Folks, there is really nothing I can give you now. I suggest you go to the 28th district headquarters and wait for the information officer. He will conduct a press conference shortly and—"

"Tina Marie, *Eye on Chicago*," a young woman standing at the back of the crowd said. "Is the victim the missing girl from—?"

"I know who you are, Tina. And I will not answer any questions here. As I said, there will be a press conference at—"

"But you're not denying it, are you?" she asked.

"I'm not denying a lot of things, Tina. I'm not denying she could be Daisy Duck. All I'm saying is, if you report the story you are apparently determined to report, you do so at your own peril."

A second reporter, Mike Connors, from a competing station, asked if the victim's family had been notified. Since the body had just been discovered, it was obviously too early to notify them and Christy recognized the ploy as a roundabout way of getting to the victim's identity.

"Do I look stupid, Mr. Connors?" the officer asked.

"What can you tell us?" The question came from the back of the crowd.

"What I just did. That there will be a press conference at the headquarters of the 28th sometime this afternoon. The information officer will answer all of your questions then."

Another reporter asked a pointless question, and Christy decided that the give and take would go on for a long time. Glancing to the south end of the pier, she saw the crowd of tourists begin drifting back into the concourse building as they lost interest in the scene. She separated from the cabal of reporters, slipping the still functioning recorder into the pocket of her coat.

As soon as she was in the building, she pushed through the languishing crowd, eastward past the McDonald's to the middle of the building where she was able to pass through to the north side of the pier. Once outside, she was behind the barrier and only yards from the site of the trash bin that contained the murder victim. The deputy coroner had arrived and was beginning her initial investigation, and nearly all official eyes were on her, leaving Christy with open access.

She saw two boys sitting alone under an alcove and figured if they were sitting unchallenged they must have played a role. She approached them.

"Hi, guys."

The taller and thinner of the two looked up. His eyes were red-rimmed. The heavier one ignored her.

"I'm Christy. You guys need anything?"

"We want to go home," the taller one said.

"Have you talked to anyone yet?"

The taller boy pointed to Polanski standing nearby. Christy had not seen him when emerging from the building, but now, in full view, the detective was standing by himself, making notes while the others were engaged around the dumpsters or with the reporters at the rope line.

She excused herself from the boys and approached him.

Polanski looked up from his notepad with a startled expression. "What are you doing here?"

"I'm waiting for your side of the story, detective."

He glanced nervously at the others gathered near the dumpster.

"I can help you," she said. "It isn't often that people see an honest cop standing up for what he believes. Let me tell your story."

"You're wrong. Most of the officers I work with are decent people doing a difficult job."

"You're risking a lot. You need to get your story out. Let me tell the city what really goes on."

He shook his head, glancing again at the cluster of officers and lab techs. "I'm not talking to you."

"Look," she said, under her breath, "I can get the facts out before they're spun into something you wouldn't recognize." She paused for a reaction, but got nothing. "What is it with you, detective? You're getting the blame for the riots. Do you enjoy that?"

"Don't you get it? I'm just a cop who takes his oath seriously."

She snorted. "Then you'd be the first. Maybe the only one."

"I already told you that's not true."

"Then why were you transferred? Can you answer that? Why

aren't you still with the 31st?"

The wind kicked up again, filling the area where they stood. She shivered.

"Leave me alone, Miss Lee." He walked away and she reached into her pocket, switching the tape recorder off.

CHAPTER 5

Campello slowed as soon as he turned onto Rush Street and found an open slot several doors down from Silk 'n Boots, next to an expired meter.

He climbed out of the car and quickly surveyed the area. Rush was a narrow street congested with a mix of tourists, business types, panhandlers and students. It was quiet, for the most part, except for the thumping sound that emanated from the club.

Inside, he saw a young woman writhing on an elevated stage in the center of the dimly lit room. Most of the tables surrounding the platform were vacant, and the canned music he heard on the sidewalk was coming from a panel of equipment at the rear of the room. A DJ sat lethargically in front of it. The man wore a black T-shirt, and a ponytail ran almost the full length of his back. A headband was wrapped tightly around his forehead.

The few customers were ignoring the woman's performance, most of them preferring to drink at the mahogany bar that ran the length of the wall to Campello's right.

Campello showed his star to a balding, middle-aged man in a cage of wire mesh set just inside the doorway. The man looked past the star and directly at Campello before unfolding into a broad smile that illuminated his lined and darkened face.

"Frank, my man."

The bouncer emerged from the cage and Campello did a double-take, scanning the beaming face for a hint of recognition.

"It's me. Jimmy Small."

"Great," he said, still uncertain.

The bouncer continued to grin with his hands on his hips. "You don't remember me? Jimmy too-tall-for-small?"

Campello ran through his data bank until a vague memory surfaced. "Oh, yeah. We ran you in for assault."

"Yeah, that's right."

"'Bout four, five years ago, wasn't it?"

"Seven. You guys came into a place I was working on south State. A little place called Bo Peep's."

The memory was becoming clearer.

"You and Adams were working vice and I had to jump some dude 'cause he was messing with one of the girls. I busted him up pretty good."

The picture sharpened. "Sure. You offered to help us out with a gambling thing we were working, so we were able to get the guy to drop the charges."

"Yeah, 'cept I remember the two of you slapping him around a little yourselves. You said you were helping him come to the right decision." He smiled again. "I knew you'd remember. And I kept my end of the deal. Didn't I?"

"You did."

"I was on parole then. If you guys hadn't stood up for me, I would've gone away for a long time. I never forgot what you did."

"So how long have you been working here?"

"Not long. Like I said, I was bouncin' at the place on State until a few months ago, when Maggie offered me a lot more."

"So you're doing OK, then?"

The man continued to keep his hands on his hips and nodded enthusiastically as he glanced around the room. "Oh, sure. I'm doing great."

The image sharpened further. Campello said, "You married a woman name Maggie, right?"

The bouncer smiled. "Yeah, that's right."

"Then that would be the Maggie that manages this place?"

"Did. I manage it now."

"How is she?"

The smile disappeared. "We got divorced."

"I'm sorry."

"Yeah, well, that happens, you know? We weren't no good anyway. Always fightin', and then her whinin' about my drinkin'." He waved a dismissive hand. "But you know how that goes, right? You been down that road yourself a couple of times."

"Four."

"That last one. What was her name?"

"Kathy."

"Yeah, that's it. Kathy. Man, she was a looker. I saw her once."

"You must be thinking of Carlene. She was the looker. Kathy was a bad choice at a bad time."

Jimmy lowered his voice. "She clean you out?"

"Yep. Wasn't much to clean, though. Jenny beat her to it."

"Who's Jenny?"

"She came after Carlene but before Kathy. If you haven't seen me in seven years you don't know Jenny or Kathy. They were after your time."

Jimmy clicked his mouth. "Man, that's rough." Then a frown creased his face. "I was sorry to hear about Adams."

"Thanks."

"You guys was always up front with me. Always fair." His expression sharpened. "What brings you here?"

Campello showed the cell-phone photo to the bouncer, who squinted at it in the low light.

"Nope. Don't know her."

Campello nodded toward the stage. "Any chance the girl might?"

"I don't know. You'll have to ask her."

"How much longer is she on?"

Jimmy looked at his watch, then at the stage. "Three minutes."

"I want to talk to her," Adams said.

The bouncer shrugged. "It's OK by me if it's OK by her. You want a drink while you're waitin'? On the house?"

"I'm on duty so you'll have to make it a beer. Nothing too hard."

Jimmy ushered him to a table with a smile and a slap on the shoulder.

The club was simply decorated with a minimal amount of chrome, mirrors, lights, or any of the other amenities of the city's finer establishments. Campello sat at the table in the corner of the room with his back to the wall where he could drink the beer and keep an eye on the crowd. For the most part, it was a small cluster of middle-aged men who were more interested in their drinks than the woman on stage. As soon as the music ended, a couple of them gave the girl some desultory applause and Campello watched as Jimmy approached the stage and whispered into her ear. She glanced across to Campello and tipped her head to a door near the bar. He made his way across the floor, leaving the nearly full beer glass, and closed the door behind them, following her down the dingy hallway to a cramped and musty room at the end.

She lifted a worn satin kimono from a hook behind the door and shrugged into it, before pulling off the blonde wig and tossing it onto the clutter of makeup that littered the dressing table. Her natural hair was cut short and dyed a vivid shade of orange. She pulled open a drawer for a packet of cigarettes and shook one into her hand.

"Have a seat." She nodded to a worn sofa along the wall and slipped the smoke between her lips.

Campello clicked open his lighter, leaning forward to offer her its flame. He inhaled deeply on the aroma before closing the lighter and sitting on the sofa.

She tilted her head back and exhaled. "Thanks." She held the pack to him, an eyebrow raised. He shook his head.

"Trying to quit." He dropped the lighter in his pocket and took out the cell phone. "Do you know this woman?" He showed her the phone's photo.

She crossed her legs and began swinging one foot. "No." She held the cigarette between two fingers, her elbow resting on her knee.

"Are you sure?"

"I'm sure."

Her answer was quick, decisive. She wasn't lying.

"What's your name?"

"Why?"

"So I know who I'm talking to."

"Terri Williams."

"You got some ID, Terri?"

She set the cigarette in a notch on an ash tray and pulled her purse from a drawer in the dressing table. When she found her wallet, she pulled the ID from it and handed it to Campello.

"A lot of cops come in here," she said, while he copied the information. "I haven't seen you before."

"I don't work vice anymore."

"What's that got to do with it?" she chuckled.

He smiled. "The woman in the photo was murdered. She received a phone call that came from here sometime after she was killed. It's a lead and I'm following up on it."

The woman accepted the ID from him with a frown.

"You and Jimmy the only ones working today?" He slid the notepad in the pocket of his jacket.

"And the DJ. His name's Bobby Longhorse."

"He been here all day?"

Terri nodded before inhaling deeply. The cigarette's embers glowed.

"That's it?"

The woman tossed her head back and exhaled a plume of smoke into the air, keeping her eyes on him. "Yep."

"What time did the club open?" He punched the button on the phone again to get the call history.

"Eleven."

He scrolled through the phone's memory. The woman had received a call at seven. There had been several over the last several weeks. "Who was here at seven?"

"Me, for one. And Jimmy."

"How about Longhorse?"

She shook her head. "No. In fact, he was late. He… and Rita," she said slowly. "Rita was here."

"Who's Rita?"

"She's supposed to be here tonight, but said she was sick. That means a double for me."

"If she's sick what was she doing—"

"She ain't sick. She's beat up. Again. She came in to pick up her check." The woman took another long drag on the smoke. "I don't care. It's more work for me."

"Beaten up?"

"Her boyfriend. She said he's rich. Going to help her out. Been buying her nice furniture, a car…" She swung her foot.

"What's her full name?" he asked.

"Rita Chavez."

"Where can I find her?"

"Home, probably."

"The address?"

"I don't know, but Jimmy can get it for you. He said you two are friends."

"Is there anything else you can tell me? Anything that might help us catch this girl's killer?"

She shook her head. "Just that I hope you get the guy."

He thanked the woman for her time and left her alone, pausing at the bouncer's cage to ask for Rita's address. Jimmy went back to the office and came out a few minutes later with a slip of paper.

"Thanks, Jimmy."

"Stay in touch, Frank."

He left the darkened club and walked into the brisk chill of an overcast day. A parking ticket peeked out from the wiper of his car. He tore it up and threw it to the wind.

CHAPTER 6

Campello pulled into the flow of Rush Street traffic and drove to the twenty-four hundred block of South State Street. He drew up in front of a hardware store across from the building in which Rita lived. The three-story brick structure housed a liquor store on one end and a mini-mart at the other. A street-level doorway between the two shops led to a staircase and a series of apartments on the upper two floors. According to Jimmy, Rita lived on the third floor.

Campello contacted the dispatcher at the Castle to give him his location before leaving the car and jogging across the street to take the stairs. The sound of blaring TVs, driving music and crying babies wafted from the apartments on either side, but the place was clean and seemed well cared for. He knocked on 301, then stood well to the side of the door with his hand poised over the pistol on his right hip. An attractive young woman opened and peered at him past the security chain. Her lips were swollen and her face was bruised. He showed her his star.

Campello sat on the couch under the window that gave him a view of State Street. The couch looked new and the apartment was well furnished in contemporary style. Cream-colored walls and pale-cream carpeting gave the apartment a warm, cozy feel and the tasteful arrangement of several plants told him that Rita had a domestic touch. Photos of an older couple that he guessed to be her parents, along with landscapes, dotted the walls.

The woman was petite but voluptuous. Her chestnut hair was shoulder-length and straight, and her demeanor was soft spoken, even shy. He had expected something brasher – closer to Terri. But Rita's simple blouse appeared freshly pressed and her jeans were creased. She sat on a comfortable-looking chair with her feet tucked under, as gentle and demure as he could recall his mother being. He showed the photo to her and she shook her head.

"No. Sorry, detective. I don't know her." She spoke with a Hispanic accent. She shrugged. "I'm sorry."

"How long have you been employed with Silk 'n Boots?"

She drummed her fingers on the arm rest as she paused to think. "Three years? Four? That's right. Four next month."

"Where were you employed before that?"

"Why, detective? I already told you that I don't know this woman. Why am I suddenly the interest of your investigation?"

He wanted to tell her he didn't believe her; that his instincts, developed by years of police work, told him she was lying. But there would be more truth to mine, and he wouldn't get it by alienating her at the start.

"You're not the subject of my investigation, Ms. Chavez. But you are peripheral to it. The victim received a phone call this morning and that phone number traces back to Silk 'n Boots. In fact, she has received numerous phone calls from the club. Since you work there and were there when the call came in, I'm interested in you."

"There are others working there too, detective."

"And I'll speak with them. But right now, you're next on the list."

The woman was poised for her age, and clearly unflappable. She paused to consider his remarks, undoubtedly weighing the cost of answering him against the costs to her personal interests.

"I was employed as an office assistant at Green Enterprises."

"The distribution center?"

She nodded and he made a note of the information, shifting slightly on the couch to relieve the pressure created by the butt of his pistol.

"How long were you there?"

She shrugged again. "I don't know. Two years, maybe three."

"There's a big difference from working in an office to dancing. What happened?"

"I felt stifled at the company. Plus, I wanted to perform and I have the talent and body to do it." She smiled and looked at him beneath long lashes. "Don't you think?"

Her flirtatious teasing rang false. That meant she had something to hide and was using the sudden come-on as a way to deflect his question.

"Yes, but a lot of women have the same talent. To be honest, it isn't that hard to find. Why a place like Silk 'n Boots?"

"Why not?"

She had changed her approach. Her answer deflected his question much more effectively than her previous party-girl come-on.

He made sure that his next question would be more difficult to avoid. He focused on her bruises. "What happened?"

She sighed. "My life is not perfect, detective."

She deflected him again, this time with a generic observation.

"Show me one that is. I was told your boyfriend did it. That true?"

She hesitated, and then said, "I had a disagreement with him. It happens."

"A lot?"

"No."

"It must've been some disagreement."

She said nothing, continuing to drum her fingers on the arm rests.

"It'll happen again, you know. It always does."

"Not to me. I can forgive once, but never twice."

"Who's your boyfriend?"

"That's none of your business. I just told you, it's forgiven."

"I'm not going to arrest him, Ms. Chavez."

"Then you don't need his name."

"I can find out. It won't be that difficult."

She stood. "His name is Peter Green. Now I believe I've answered all the questions I'm going to."

He didn't need more answers from her. He had gotten enough. For now.

CHAPTER 7

Another wave of rioting had broken out the night before on the Southwest Side in the corridor of the 31st.

Teams of officers from nearby districts were sent to aid in quelling the uprising. Looting was severe and overshadowed what had originally begun as citizen outrage. The vandalism and violence nearly always began in the late afternoon, frequently running into the late evening or early morning. Dozens of arrests had been made with both citizens and officers injured in the fallout.

Even though no one had been killed, City Hall was concerned it would eventually happen. Violence would then spread to other sections of the city.

Officers throughout the department were convinced that most of the violence was not triggered by the shooting, but by Polanski's declaration that Caine and Dorchester had killed the suspect then planted evidence to cover their crime. The media coverage that ensued made a minor celebrity of Polanski, Campello fumed to himself, *and* the department brass acquiesced to his charges in order to save face and restore calm. Two good men had been offered on the altar of political expediency and Polanski became the department's golden boy.

The situation was unfair. By the time Campello returned to the 28th his anger was kindled.

He stormed into the squad room, intent on approaching Lopez, but was immediately jarred by seeing Polanski sitting at Rand's desk as comfortable and confident as if he had a right to be there. Glancing past Polanski, Campello saw Tertwiller and Silvio huddled over Silvio's desk; Bob Carter, Jerry Hughbanks and Jason Chin were engaged in hushed conversations on the phones. Lopez was in his office, working at his computer. Given that he was management, it was unlikely he was working any leads. Instead, it was far more probable that he was entering the district's stats for the month, making him the Castle's premiere bookkeeper and resident statistician. No way for a cop to end up.

Campello took a deep breath and draped his jacket over his chair before grabbing his mug. Filling it, he eased in behind his desk just as Polanski was ending the call.

"The girl was not sexually assaulted," he said to Campello.

"Anything else?" He sipped the coffee.

"Her name is Trina Martinez. She's an illegal and she and her family were deported two years ago."

"Where's she from?"

"A place called Metlatonoc. It's in southwestern Mexico. Dirt poor."

Campello leaned back in his chair, which creaked. "Is her family here?"

"We don't know. I have an address for her. I also learned that she waitressed at Dillback's. I called them and her boss said she was a hard worker, but hadn't been there long."

"Where's the address?"

Polanski passed a slip of paper across the desks to Campello. She lived at an apartment complex on the near West Side.

"Anything final on the cause of death?" Campello asked.

"Cerebral hemorrhage. She was beaten and strangled, but no ligature was used. That fits with what we saw at the scene."

"Doesn't it, though?" Campello could not restrain himself and shook his head in open disgust. He could see that Tertwiller and Silvio were glancing in his direction, more interested in his conversation with Polanski than they were their own.

"Where've you been?" Polanski asked.

Campello did not like talking to him, did not even want to look at him. But a case needed to be worked and that required a sharing of information. He told Polanski about his interviews with Terri and Rita and about Peter's assault of Rita.

"Sounds like a nice guy. You think he's involved?"

"Don't you?" He nodded at the slip of paper with Trina's address. "You sure you have the right place?"

"Positive."

"Check it out. Talk to the neighbors and see what you can find on this kid."

"I was just about to do that."

"Then do it." He bolted out of the chair and went to Lopez's office. He rapped on the open door.

The commander looked up from the monitor. "Come in, Frank."

Campello sat in the same chair he had sat in earlier that day. "How many guys did you have available to help the 31st?"

Lopez spun his chair around so that he could face Campello and clasped his hands behind his head as he paused to think. "Fifty, I think. I asked Rogers to get whoever he could. Why?"

"Because a lot of good men are risking life and limb to subdue a riot that the weasel out there triggered." He thumbed toward the squad room.

Lopez sighed. "Frank, didn't we have this conversation this morning?"

"And we'll have it again. This case is getting into some deep water. I am concerned that his reputation, to say nothing of his character, is going to get in the way."

Lopez held up a hand. "Back up a minute. What do you mean, 'deep water'?"

"Peter Green is popping up. He owns Silk 'n Boots and the club figures in the investigation. He's also the boyfriend of one of the dancers there, but apparently it's an open secret. And then there's the fact that he likes to beat the snot out of his girlfriend."

"Is she pressing charges?" There was noticeable concern in Lopez's voice.

"Nope. She's forgiven him."

Lopez let out an audible sigh. "Don't they all?" He rose from the desk and closed the door, before sitting next to Campello. "Peter's father, Aaron, is a good friend to this department."

"I know."

Lopez stroked his chin in thought.

"If you want me to drop this, I will," Campello said. "The department has enough enemies, some of them from within." He looked at Polanski who was still sitting at Rand's desk, talking on the phone, blissfully unaware of the violence erupting around his name.

Lopez slowly shook his head. "No, we can't drop a murder investigation. But I would tread lightly here, Frank."

"How lightly?"

Lopez shrugged. "I'm not saying don't do your job. But I am saying, be careful whose toes you step on."

Campello relayed the information about the girl and the facts surrounding her illegal status. "I told him to check out her apartment. I want to see if she had any connection to Peter Green."

Lopez shook his head. "What's he up to?"

"Green?"

"Yeah. What's his angle?"

Campello shrugged. "If he's involved? Who knows? But knowing that family, I'd suspect there's money at stake."

"You can bet on that. There isn't an altruistic bone in his body." Lopez paused, thinking. "The old man has been an Alderman for years so there's no doubt he's up to his eyes in something, but he's always supported us, so we've always looked the other way and—"

Polanski knocked on the door and Lopez motioned for him to enter.

"I've arranged for a uniformed squad to meet me at the girl's apartment."

"Then what're you waiting for?" Campello asked.

Polanski nodded and closed the door. Campello and Lopez watched in silence as Polanski retrieved his pistol from the locked desk drawer and slipped it into the holster on his belt.

"Keep an eye on him, Frank. That's why I assigned him to you.

Don't let him screw this up. Politically speaking, he's tone deaf. He could cause some real pain for this department."

Campello watched as the man left the squad room. "He already has, boss."

CHAPTER 8

The librarian was helpful, escorting Christy to a large room on the upper floor of the Harold Washington Library that held a scanned collection of old newspapers, some dating back as far as the nineteenth century.

The library was named after the city's first African-American mayor, who had died in office. The room in which she sat was cavernous and there was a smattering of people engaged in their own fact-finding missions, but it was quiet and conducive to the research she wanted to do.

Christy sat at a monitor and broke out her pad and pen. She began by reviewing her paper's competitors, starting with the largest. Its report on Polanski and the allegations he made against Caine and Dorchester held no new revelations.

She changed to another competitor and read the ensuing articles. Except for a mention that Polanski was born and raised in Charlotte, North Carolina, they had nothing she didn't already know. She had not picked up on an accent during her brief talk with him and had assumed he hailed from the Windy City. She made a note of his birthplace and the college where he had graduated – the University of Chicago. It was one of the finer schools in the country and his having graduated from there could explain his connection to the city and his ultimate employment with the PD. Like the location of his birth, the fact that he attended U of C was not particularly germane to her objective, but background like this could nearly always shed light on her subjects. But it was the third and final paper she reviewed – a northern Indiana feature that had received most of its feed from

United Press International (UPI) – that caught her eye. The article mentioned Polanski's father, a police officer in his own right, who had died when his son was only ten years old. She wrote down Janek's name for a later Google search.

Her suspicion of the police drove her skepticism, particularly when their actions seemed so clearly to serve their own ends. The official line of moving Polanski to another district because of expressed concerns over his safety and effectiveness as an officer, did not wash with her. It was understandable he had undermined himself with his colleagues at the 31st, but it didn't make sense that moving him to another district would lessen the strain. The transfer wouldn't quell resistance to him – it would only change the location of it. He wasn't safe anywhere, so why move him?

She turned her attention to Campello. There'd be a reason for the CPD's leadership to put him to work with Polanski and she wanted to know what it was.

She read a report on the shooting that had occurred two weeks ago, just days after the one involving Caine and Dorchester. Campello and his partner, Rand Adams, were attempting to serve an arrest warrant for the murder of a young Hispanic woman. The suspect, a local gangbanger known as Hoppity T, lived on the far South Side, but was sharing a part-time living arrangement with his girlfriend, Juanita Delaney, who lived in the vicinity of the 28th. Adams and Campello had staked out the place on an anonymous tip and approached the suspect's vehicle as Hoppity and Juanita arrived at her apartment. According to Campello and the girlfriend, Hoppity went for his gun the second he was out of the car and fired on Adams. The detective went down without drawing his weapon and then Campello fired, instantly killing Hoppity. The final review by the IPRA determined that the shooting was clearly justified, particularly in light of the downing of detective Adams and the corroboration of Campello's statement by Juanita.

Campello was exonerated and the FOP attorney declared it a travesty that Campello had been hauled before the board in the first place, even though it was standard procedure in police-action shootings. The incident did not spark the clamorous outcry that the Caine and Dorchester fiasco had.

Christy frowned. Still this was nothing new, nothing she hadn't reported herself.

She searched another paper. Again, the article covered the surface facts of the shooting, but there was little else.

She tried a third paper before starting an internet search. Opening a Google window, she typed in Janek Polanski in quotation marks and then + Police Officer and + North Carolina. A list of references appeared, most of them Polish in origin, and it was five pages down before she found an article referencing Polish Americans and their contributions to American law enforcement.

Next, she searched for Campello, and there was a list of articles, mostly from the Chicago area, which she had already been through before.

She searched for Rand Adams and found a list of articles extolling the man's heroism and bravery in the face of fire, but offering no new information. But there was a photo of him, taken in his earlier days on the department while he was still a patrolman, alongside a small grouping of the police brass and some local politicians. The caption below the photo credited Adams with leading an initiative to clean up inner-city crime and showed a plaque he had received from a younger Alderman Aaron Green.

Green had his arm around Adams and was smiling broadly for the camera.

CHAPTER 9

Polanski met the uniforms outside the apartment. He had a court order to search the place, but wanted the others there in case he met resistance. The officers seemed to know him and opted to remain in the car, telling him to call them if he needed help. Their reluctance to assist him was obvious, and he told them to drive on.

Trina lived on the near South Side in a high rise that was not far from the 28th's headquarters. The building was nestled among several others, within a short jump of the El tracks, and it shook as a train passed.

Polanski had no resistance in obtaining Trina's key from the manager. He rode the elevator to the fourth floor and stepped into the hallway, where he was immediately struck by the musty smell of marijuana. The hallway was surprisingly well lit, and he found Trina's apartment at the end, near the fire-escape door.

He inserted the key and entered the apartment.

It was an efficiency, and the place was cool and dark. He flicked on a light switch, clicking the door closed behind him. The window shades were pulled tightly across the only window, blocking out whatever light might have seeped through. Pulling the shades open, he could see why Trina would have preferred to keep them closed. The passing trains offered little of interest, and then only through dingy yellow glass that was tarnished more from age than neglect. He closed the shade and began to survey the room.

The furniture had seen better days and the carpeting, though clean, was as dry and stiff as a wafer. The bed folded into the wall and a thin tattered curtain partially covered the cabinets and stove that served as Trina's kitchen. And this was better than home?

He opened the closet. She had few clothes, mostly jeans, along with a couple of blouses and a single pair of battered tennis shoes. Given those on her feet when she was found, it meant she had two pairs, both in dire need of replacement. He held her blouses to his nose and sniffed. There were no tell-tale odors of marijuana or alcohol or other aromatic chemicals, but that did not mean that Trina was free of their influence. The tox screen had not yet come back from the lab.

She kept several T-shirts folded on a shelf, along with underclothes, but there was no dresser or chest-of-drawers.

He searched through the pockets of her jeans, but found only a single stick of gum, still in the foil.

An inexpensive-looking suitcase stood on the floor next to the sofa. It was empty.

In the kitchen he began going from drawer to drawer. The utensils, pots, pans and other kitchenware were shop-worn, but still functional. Her refrigerator held a partially full half-gallon container of milk, a packet of sliced American cheese, two cans of Pepsi, a bottle of mustard, a bottle of ketchup and a half-empty carton of eggs. The pantry revealed a box of crackers, a package of pasta, two boxes of cornflakes, both full, several cans of soup, plus vegetables and fruit.

He pulled the bed down from the wall. It landed with a thud. The bed clothing, like everything else in the apartment, was inexpensive and well worn, but clean. Trina had taken pride in her home and had done the best she could with what she had.

He ran his hand under the pillow and found a neatly folded pair of cotton PJs. They were a pink floral print and appeared relatively new.

He flipped the mattress but found nothing beyond the box spring.

The small desk that stood along one wall was next. There was no phone, not unusual given that Trina was likely relying on her cell. On top, he found a framed photo of Trina standing between an older man and woman who he assumed were her parents. A birthday card sat near the photo. It was signed and there was a hand-drawn heart inside. The postmarking on the envelope indicated the card came from Mexico, likely from her parents.

He opened the drawers and found they were empty except for the top left-hand drawer. Inside, he found several check stubs from Dillback's restaurant, a receipt for some of the can goods, and a bill for her cell phone. He pocketed the bill for later review.

The drawer also held a number of catalogues from varying universities in the Chicago area. They were tied together by a rubber band along with a brochure on a career in nursing. Like anyone, Trina had dreams. And all of them had been snuffed in a single moment. There were no utility bills, since her rent covered all expenses. There was no television, probably because she could not afford the cable bill which was not included in the rent.

He sat at the desk and studied the framed photo. Trina wasn't the corpse he had seen at the pier. She was a person with a family that loved her. But someone decided she was expendable, tossing her into the trash like common refuse.

The lives of the people in the photo were forever changed, even if they didn't know it yet. He would see to it that whoever did this would recognize they had altered their own as well.

CHAPTER 10

ampello received copies of the crime-scene photos from the lab, along with Brown's report, and laid them across his desk. Tapes from the security cameras that rimmed the pier had already been requested. The victim's phone had been examined along with the SIM card, and the voice mail had been opened. There were no messages, which meant that Trina had deleted them as soon as she listened to them. By itself, that wasn't unusual. But the number of calls that were received from a strip club that did not employ her seemed odd.

Neither the phone nor the SIM card revealed anything useful.

The phone was still in the evidence bag and he held it in one hand while he looked through the numbers stored on the call list. In some cases, the calls had been placed less than three minutes apart. None of them were listed as missed calls, meaning that the conversations had been frequent and exceedingly short. Most of the calls between Trina and the club were one way – from the club to her. Some of the other numbers were to Dillback's, where she waitressed. But there were four calls from Rita, which supported his belief that she was lying. There were ten additional calls to a number in her home town. Her parents, maybe? A boyfriend?

He arranged the photos on his desk, studying them from different angles by standing and moving around them. He had learned long ago that perspective was often the key to good police work. None of them revealed anything that immediately stood out and he slumped back in his chair, frustrated.

The remainder of the afternoon dragged by.

The deputy coroner's initial report indicated Trina died of cerebral hemorrhage, but that she had endured a beating that would likely have killed her anyway if left untreated. The autopsy revealed that her spleen had been ruptured and a kidney damaged heavily enough that it would have needed to be removed. Massive internal bleeding had occurred and she had suffered several broken ribs and a broken finger on her right hand.

Forensics was limited and tainted, given the boys' intrusion into the dumpster, the rain, and rotting refuse. There was no DNA under her fingernails and no isolated strands of foreign hair and no prints. Additionally, the tarp in which she had been wrapped was not unique and therefore untraceable. Polanski had not returned to the office yet, so any evidence that might have turned up from the victim's apartment would have to wait until tomorrow.

Campello opened the desk drawer to retrieve his pistol and was immediately struck by the sight of Rand's cup. The day ended on the same sour note on which it had begun.

Dropping his pistol into his holster, he slid the drawer closed and locked it.

He took the stairs to the first floor and nodded a goodbye at the officer working the public desk on his way out of the district office. The northeast wind that had whipped across the pier earlier that day had not subsided and he pulled the collar of his jacket against his neck.

He went to the segregated lot that was surrounded by a one-story chain-link fence. Part of the lot was allocated to the personal vehicles of the officers and staff who worked the 28th. His '65 Corvette, Rally Red with black leather interior, was his passion and the only thing he had managed to salvage from four failed marriages. He had rebuilt the car with his father during the last summer of the previous century, prior to the old man's retirement and subsequent decline, and they had taken great pains in adhering to the original specifications. In addition to their careers with the CPD and their poor choice in women, they shared a passion for Corvettes. The '65 stood as the best in class as far as they were concerned, and Campello babied it with the loving care a concert violinist might show for his Stradivarius. Both were fine instruments, requiring a delicate touch if they were to reach peak performance.

Clearing the entrance to the lot, he saw a late-model Ford Taurus leaning to one side. The left front tire had been slashed and the knife was still protruding, a certain tipoff that the car belonged to Polanski. Though Campello did not like the man, he also did not care for the tactics that would inevitably be used against him. They were childish at best and often played into the hands of the brass who saw value in someone who would turn on others.

He climbed into the Vette and fired the engine. It hummed to life without missing a beat and he savored the moment.

Pulling out of the lot, he exited onto LaSalle Street and began working his way through the rush-hour traffic to the North Side. Tertwiller, Silvio, Hughbanks and the others had already left and were likely on their second round at Jeep's. The bar was a favorite haunt of the cops who worked the loop, primarily because Mickey Rattner owned it.

Michael "Mickey" Rattner had been a cop's cop and worked the 28th in the days when the first Dailey was mayor. He'd been involved in the riots of the '68 Democratic convention, when the 28th earned the name "the Castle", and was forced to crack a few heads in order to restore order to a city that was crumbling as fast as the counter-culture movement could take it apart. His efforts won him a ten-day leave without pay and a bust in rank. After that, his work on behalf of the good people of Chicago waned, and he started to drink. His drinking led him to a place called The Lucky Dog, the favorite watering hole of the local cops at the time, and his life became a free-fall of booze and barflies. Two failed marriages followed, and he eventually retired from the department and bought The Lucky Dog, changing the name to Jeep's – homage to his favorite vehicle (Jeep was his nickname).

Peanuts were free, and drinks were half price to working cops. He tolerated no bull, and often cracked as many heads on a busy

Friday night as he had during the rioting of the convention over forty years ago. The place had retained its former glory and served as the favorite gathering place to a whole new generation of cops.

Campello rolled into the lot and strode into the bar. It was shotgun in design with a row of booths to the right, opposite the bar that ran the entire length of the wall to his left. There was a mirror behind the bar, reflecting the joy or misery of whoever sat in front of it. Music came from a jukebox, one of the few holdovers from The Lucky Dog, and on this night it was belting out Bob Seger's "Old Time Rock and Roll". The song was upbeat and did not fit Campello's mood.

"Hey, Frank!" A standing Hughbanks yelled above the din, motioning Campello to the rear of the bar.

He shouldered his way past a thicker-than-usual crowd and dropped into the chair that his crew had saved for him. Tertwiller, Silvio and Hughbanks were ensconced around a circular table where the line of booths ended.

"What're you having, my man?" Hughbanks asked. His eyes were already glassy.

Campello nodded at the beer that Tertwiller was nursing. "One of those."

"Excellent choice. I'll be right back." He rose from the table and shuffled through the crowd to the bar.

"Where's your partner?" Shelly yelled over the music.

Campello shrugged. "He was supposed to be looking at the vic's apartment, but I haven't seen him." He grabbed a handful of nuts from the bowl on the table. "And I don't care to."

She grinned and raised her bottle in a mock toast before taking a long, hard swig.

"I don't understand guys like that," Silvio said. "He's supposed to be on our side, not theirs. And even if he wasn't, even if he doesn't like us or thinks that one of us has done something we shouldn't, he should work through it. Take it through the proper channels, you know? You don't turn on family." He picked a couple of nuts from the bowl. "Criminals don't. They stick together."

Tertwiller agreed. "That's why they call them crime *families*."

Hughes returned with a bottle that he dropped on the table, before giving Campello a collegial slap on the back. The beer was cold and smooth.

"I asked Lopez to get rid of him," Campello said, setting the bottle on the table and reaching for another handful of nuts.

"He won't," Tertwiller said. "The brass is on his back."

"This Polanski has got everyone on each other's back," Silvio said. "He's got the whole department disrupted."

"So what do you want us to do, Frank?" Tertwiller said. "Tell us what you want and we'll see it gets done."

Campello shook his head. "There's nothing you can do, Shelly. He's here to stay, at least for now, and that's all there is to it."

Hughbanks shook his head. "Something can always be done, Frank." His speech was starting to slur.

"Guys like him usually do it to themselves, Jerry," Campello said.

"Every day he sits here is too many," Silvio countered.

"Bill said that if Caine and Dorchester come out of this, they're going to sue Polanski," Tertwiller said.

"Really?" Hughbanks asked.

She lifted her bottle and paused to nod.

Hughbanks said, "They'd have a case. Their reputations are ruined, their careers are in the tank… he shouldn't be able to walk away from a thing like that." He shook his head. "Does he think he joined the choir? We're cops. We're not Boy Scouts. We're dealing with killers, thieves… rapists. Sometimes you got to fight fire with fire. Everyone knows that."

Campello shrugged and drank the beer. The others all nodded their agreement with Hughbanks.

"We're in a war for our very survival," Silvio said. "The bad guys have everything in their favor and we've got nothing in ours. Maybe we should strike like everyone else. Let the bad guys take control. What do you think would happen then? Huh?" He drank his beer and nodded. "That's right. They'd be begging us to come

back. They'd give us all the help we need and guys like Polanski…
they'd be right where they belong. Out on their tail." He thumbed
over his shoulder.

"I don't like working with him," Campello said, finishing his
drink and glancing at his watch. "But there isn't anything I can do
about it." He stood.

"Hey, what's this?" Silvio said.

"Where you going, Frank?" Tertwiller asked.

"To see my dad."

"Good for you," she said.

"He was a good cop, Frank," Silvio added as Hughbanks left to
get another beer, giving Campello a friendly pat on the back. "Maybe
we can swap him for Polanski."

CHAPTER 11

Marimar had not been his first choice when looking for a place for his father, but the facility was close to home and it was clean and safe and the food was relatively good. But the best care at any facility went to the residents whose family members dropped in unannounced, so Campello made a habit of swinging by at varying times.

The Vette hummed as he began to break free of the heavier loop traffic and by the time he had reached the far North Side, all thoughts of Polanski and dead girls, and cops – good or bad – were left far behind. He stopped at O'Reilly's grocery to pick up a bag of chocolate-covered raisins, his father's favorite treat, and then finished the drive to Marimar.

"How're you doing, Dad?"

The old man's gaze wavered before settling on his son, foggy and unfocused. The sound of beeping alarms wafted into the room from the nursing station at the far end of the hall.

"Who are you?"

"I'm Frank, Dad. I'm your son."

"Frank?"

Campello sat on the edge of the bed, within arm's reach of the old man and his chair. A game show played on the TV. "Yeah, Dad. Don't you remember?" He handed the bag to the old man. "I brought you some raisins."

His father took the bag from him with a bony hand and gingerly opened it. He peered inside suspiciously before reaching in for the treat. He was frail now. He wore a red and black plaid bathrobe over powder-blue pajamas and his thinning white hair was unkempt.

Campello stood and put an arm around his shoulders, only to have it shrugged off.

"Don't do that. I don't like that."

"OK, Dad. Sorry."

The old man slipped a raisin into his mouth.

Campello glanced around the private room. It was clean, small and sparsely furnished. An untouched dinner tray rested on a bedside table and worn curtains framed the room's single window. He scanned the fading photos that lined the walls. Most of them were black and white. There was a picture of the old man in uniform during his early days with the department alongside a family photo of Campello as a boy with a fishing rod in one hand. A photo of his mother hung on the opposite wall, alongside photos of his father's two other wives.

"Dad, I've got a new partner. His name is Polanski. He's a traitor. A real back-stabber."

The old man cursed as he fished another raisin from the bag. "Don't work with no back-stabbers. They'll stab you in the back."

Campello grinned. "He came over from the 31st, Dad. Your old district."

"The 31st," the old man said. "Now that was a good place to work." He sucked the chocolate covering off another raisin. Campello stood and looked at the photo of his father in uniform.

"Dad, do you remember Charlie Donovan?"

The old man nodded. "Old Donovan. Now there was a cop's cop. A real man. A good partner. Did I ever tell you about the time we caught those burglars over on Cicero Avenue?"

He had. Many times.

"No, Dad."

The old man recounted the story in vivid detail, embellishing it as he had for years. "Them was the days."

"It's different now."

The old man waved him off. "You guys today don't know *nothing*

about police work. We used to pound a beat. Walk off shoe leather."
He slipped another raisin into his mouth and then focused on a scene
that was in a place far removed from the walls of his room. "Standing
in the rain, the sleet, shivering at all hours of the day and night." He
sucked on the raisin. "Stamping my feet to stay warm, looking for a
place to buy coffee." He chewed the raisin and reached into the bag
for another. "I want some coffee."

Campello lifted the stainless lid off the dinner tray. The beef
Manhattan was untouched, as were the mashed potatoes, green
beans and chocolate pudding. The coffee, a favorite dinner beverage
of the old man's, remained covered. Campello removed the lid and
tasted. It was cold.

"You aren't eating, Dad."

The old man looked at him with anger in his eyes. "I ain't hungry.
If you're hungry, why don't you eat?"

"You have to eat."

"It ain't your mom's cooking."

Campello's mother had died while he was still young and a series
of tarts and bimbos had drifted in and out of his life and the old
man's bed in the ensuing years. The latest one, Caroline, had taken
off as soon as he became ill. Campello could not remember much
about his mother, but he could remember her cooking.

He was replacing the lid on the coffee when an aide, a young girl
in blue scrubs, came into the room looking sheepishly at Campello.

"He hasn't eaten," he said.

She feigned embarrassment. "Mister Campello. How come you
didn't eat?"

He fished another raisin from the bag. "What're you talking
about? I ate."

She was hesitant to remove the tray. "Do you want me to leave
it?"

"He hasn't eaten. What do you think?"

She nodded nervously and turned to leave the room.

"Here," he said, handing her the coffee cup. "Bring him a cup
of hot coffee."

She took the mug and left. He cut the beef into small sections and pierced one with a fork. "Here, Dad. Try this. It looks good."

The old man took the meat off the fork and chewed methodically while holding fast to the bag of candy.

Campello scooped some of the mashed potatoes and passed them to his father. He missed the mark and a spattering of potatoes dribbled down the old man's chin. "Sorry, Dad." He dabbed it with a napkin before trying again. He was more successful the second time.

Outside the room, across the hall, a woman cried out for her mother. Two doors down, a television suddenly blared before going silent.

"You like it here, Dad?" He stirred the gravy over the beef and cut another small slice.

The old man glanced around the room. "Yeah. Don't you?"

"Sure. It's nice."

"How is Rand?"

The old man's awareness came and went like a fading radio station. He wasn't aware of the shooting and Campello had felt no need to tell him.

"He's fine."

"You take care of that family of his."

He paused to look at the old man, taken aback by the statement.

"I am, Dad. I saw his wife this morning."

"Cops have got to stick together, son."

Campello smiled.

"And watch that partner of yours. Watch him close."

"Thanks, Dad." He passed another bit to the old man. The aide came in with a fresh cup of coffee and handed it to him. He passed the cup to his father.

"Cops ain't choirboys," the old man said, taking the cup from him and echoing the bar conversation of an hour before. "Just watch your back."

CHAPTER 12

Polanski returned after completing his search of Trina's apartment and was not surprised to find that his tire had been slashed. Similar incidents had occurred when he was still at the 31st, ranging from busted windshields and damaged tires to the more mundane, like a drawer full of shaving cream.

He had planned to take the Taurus to check out a lead and then head directly home. But Peter Green would likely be leaving the warehouse soon and Polanski wanted to question the man without the dampening effect of Campello's sarcastic presence. Rather than use up valuable time in changing the tire, he took the unmarked squad car.

He headed to Green's warehouse on the near West Side. The warehouse was actually a series of buildings located on a large lot surrounded by a chain-link fence with a retractable gate at the front entrance. When he reached the facility, he noted that other perimeter gates were still open. A couple of trucks remained at the loading dock as workers drove forklifts or pushed trolleys laden with merchandise.

He drove through the main gate and followed the signs to the office, a two-story brick building that appeared much older than the others. He parked in a stall labeled VISITOR and went into the building.

The reception area was stark, but pleasant and functional. A plain but sweeping staircase ascended off to his left, augmented by a bank of three elevators positioned along the wall behind the receptionist's desk. The floor was tiled in gray slate and a flat-screen

TV was anchored to the wall just above the elevators. No art hung on the walls; the room was void of plants.

The receptionist, an attractive and professional-looking woman, greeted him. "What can I do for you?"

He showed her his star and asked to speak with Peter Green. The woman lifted her phone's hand-piece and punched in a number. After speaking in hushed tones, she told Polanski to have a seat and that Mr. Green would be down shortly. Polanski thanked her and sat on an orange vinyl chair opposite the elevators. His vantage point gave him a panoramic view of the lobby.

He crossed his legs and began thumbing through a magazine, while keeping an eye on the comings and goings of the people drifting in and out. A salesman stopped by the receptionist's desk to confirm a date he had scheduled with a buyer, and several of the dock workers left manifests with her on their way home. Nothing disconcerting until a tall, swarthy-looking man in his mid thirties came into the office. His physical bearing suggested he was used to getting his way. His demeanor was confident, and he appeared agile and solid despite most of his physique being obscured by a three-quarter-length black leather coat. His thick black hair was lacquered straight back, leaving a single comma to dangle over his forehead.

He lit a cigarette in cupped hands while waiting for the elevator, ignoring the NO SMOKING sign anchored prominently on the wall in front of him. Just as the elevator door opened, another man, younger and much less solidly built, stepped out, pausing to say something to the swarthy man in whispered tones. The bigger man nodded and said something in return, before glancing at Polanski and stepping onto the elevator. The younger man approached and stuck out his hand.

"Detective, I'm Peter Green."

Green was every bit the casual CEO. His dirty-blond hair was spiked, and his ocean-blue floral print shirt would've been more appropriate for a bar in the Caribbean than a functioning business in the Windy City. Thin legs protruded from khaki shorts and sockless feet were adorned in sandals.

Polanski put the magazine down and rose to his feet. But as he shook Green's hand, he could not help but notice the swarthy man watching him even as the elevator door was closing.

CHAPTER 13

Green's office followed the same functional design as the lobby. A battered roll top desk stood against one wall under a framed dime-store poster of the Chicago skyline and opposite a worn sofa. A computer sat on the desk and a small television rested on a credenza.

Green sat at the desk with his chair facing Polanski, his hands folded in his lap and his legs protruding outward.

"What can I do for you, detective?"

Polanski had his notebook in hand. "What can you tell me about Rita Chavez?"

Green was no poker player. His countenance fell. "What do you mean?"

"She's been beaten and, according to my partner, she says you did it."

He slowly shook his head. "No, I've never laid a hand on her. Not once. Not ever. Your partner is mistaken."

Polanski shrugged. "Maybe. But she seems pretty adamant."

"Then *she's* mistaken."

"About who beat her?" He emphasized his incredulity.

Green spread his hands and shrugged. "She says toMAYto, I say toMAAHto." He grinned.

"How does Trina Martinez say it?"

He shrugged. "I don't know Trina Martinez."

"Rita does."

"Good for her."

Polanski looked around the room. "You work here full time?"

"Yep."

"What do you do here, Mr. Green?"

"We warehouse and ship for businesses too small to do it for themselves."

"Do you ship across the country?"

Green smiled. "We ship across the world."

Polanski smiled. "I always wanted a career in business."

Green grinned.

"Your father started this, didn't he?"

"Yep."

"And you went to business school?"

"I went to Harvard."

Polanski feigned that he was suitably impressed and made a note. "Has Rita ever worked here?"

"For a brief while."

"Doing what?"

"She worked in the office." He furrowed his brow. "Why the interest in Rita, detective? She's my girlfriend, but I'm not her keeper."

"Rita was attacked. She's banged up pretty good. And as I've already mentioned, she says you did it. Of course, you deny it, but don't seem all that concerned about the incident." He paused for a reaction, but seeing none, he continued. "And then I have a murder victim who was also banged up pretty good and she was connected to the club, just like Rita. A club that you own. So when Rita says you're the one who attacked her, I put two and two together and I get Green."

"You think I killed this girl?"

"I don't know. I ask questions, get answers, and then put it all together with the evidence. If you didn't do it, I'd just as soon clear you off my list so I can get on with it."

Green was silent again. His hands remained calmly folded in his lap.

"Did you, Mr. Green? Did you kill the girl?"

"No."

"Where were you between midnight and eight in the morning last night?"

"I was here."

"Here? Burning the midnight oil?"

"Running a business requires commitment, detective. There are no set hours."

"Of course. I'm a cop. I understand irregular hours."

Green turned in his chair and punched a number on his phone. A voice came over the speaker.

"Yes?"

"Tony, could you come in here for a moment?" He punched the button again and the line went silent.

Polanski positioned himself on the chair to allow rapid access to his weapon, just as the swarthy man came into the room.

"Tony, would you please tell the detective where I was between midnight last night and eight this morning?"

The man said, "He was here most of that time with me. He went home about six."

"And who are you?"

"Tony Delgado. I'm head of shipping."

Polanski made a note. "And what time did you leave, Mr. Delgado?"

"I left around seven."

"That's a long day. Have a big shipment coming in?"

Delgado's eyes narrowed, but remained focused on him. Peter stood from his chair. "I think we're through, detective. If you have any further questions you can direct them to my attorney."

CHAPTER 14

Polanski returned to the district headquarters, and changed the tire. It was damaged beyond repair so he tossed it into the trunk for later disposal.

He arrived home at half past seven. Jenny was holding dinner for him and he kissed her as he entered the kitchen through the breezeway that led from the garage. He removed his coat and jacket and locked his department-issued Sig-Sauer in the lockbox he kept on the top shelf of the hall closet. Jenny waited until he filled his plate with meatloaf, whole-kernel corn and roasted potatoes before serving herself.

The kitchen was small, but yellow walls and white cabinetry reflected the light, giving the room a larger feel. They sat at a circular dining-table, crowded against the wall, positioned between a window and the patio door.

"How was your day?" she asked.

He shrugged. "It's about what I expected. I'm glad to be home." He could feel her eyes on him.

"Who's your new partner?"

"A guy named Frank Campello."

"Did you know him before?"

He stirred the corn around his plate. "No, but I know of him. He was involved in the shooting two weeks ago."

She set her fork down. "Is that the one where the detective was killed?"

He didn't like talking about the job with her. And especially didn't like talking about the downside of it. She worried enough as it was and he didn't want to raise the specter of the inherent risks of police work. She knew them, of course, and had accepted them when he pinned on the star. But it was an unwritten rule between them that she wouldn't ask and he wouldn't tell.

"Yes."

He toyed with the food on his plate, aware that she had stopped eating. "How're the kids?"

"They've already eaten. They're doing their homework. Carrie got an A on her spelling test. She's pretty proud of that."

"That's good."

"We had another phone call today," she said, bluntly.

He continued moving the food around on his plate.

"Do you want to know what they said?"

"Jenny, don't."

"This one wanted to know if I was interested in a real man. It was a different voice. I hung up, but he called back."

"I'm sorry."

"Then I got another call. I thought it was the same man so I laid into him. But it was the deputy prosecutor and he said he wanted to go over your deposition again before the trial. He didn't even ask why I tore into him. He knows we're getting threats and he doesn't even care enough to ask. All they care about is that you testify against those two cops. That's all, Andy. That's all they care about."

His throat was tightening. "It'll be OK. Just a final go-over before the trial."

"The trial doesn't start for months." Her hand trembled, resting on the table beside her plate.

"He's just being thorough."

"You don't have to do this, Andy."

He swallowed hard.

"Is it really worth it?"

He sighed and began massaging his temples. "Yes, Jenny. It's worth it."

"You don't have anything to prove."

He stood and took his plate to the sink, scraping the bulk of his dinner down the garbage disposal. He rinsed his dish and put it in the strainer.

"It's putting added stress on you, me… the kids."

"The kids? What happened to the kids?"

"Josh came home today and said the other kids were talking about the crooked cops. They said his dad was one of them."

"I'm not one of them. That's the point. I don't want to be one of them. I'm trying to make a difference, Jenny."

She stood and put her arms around him. "I know you are. But isn't there another way?"

"How? Do I just stand up in court and say, 'Oh, wait. It's all one big mistake'?"

"Would that be so bad?"

He pulled away from her. "You too?"

"No, Andy. It's not 'me too'. But what's it all for? What's the point?"

"For right and wrong, Jenny. Crooked cops undermine the system. Who can we trust if we can't trust the police?"

He could feel the anger rising and he did not want to fight with her. She had understood, was even supportive of his decision to expose Caine and Dorchester. But time and pressure had taken their toll.

"You can't fight the system, Andy. It's too much for anyone."

He leaned against the counter. "It's not the system I'm fighting. It's two rogue police officers. The prosecutor is backing me. If they didn't think there was merit to this they would have ignored the whole thing and left me to twist in the wind."

"But the others, Andy. Where are they? Where is their support?"

He didn't have an answer for her.

"This isn't about your dad. You can't make up for—"

"Leave my dad out of this." He could feel heat rising in his face.

"I can't leave him out of this." She put her arms around his neck. "You aren't him. You have to be you." She kissed him.

"Then let me."

Her eyes searched his. "You're a good man, Andy. Don't let them use you."

"No one's using me." He pulled her arms from around his neck.

"Ever since that kid was shot there's been unrest and the department is letting you take the fall for it."

He leaned against the counter and crossed his arms. It was a defensive posture, a position he was getting used to taking.

"I know what I'm doing."

"Andy," she said, her eyes searching his, "they moved you to the 28th to make themselves look good. They're politicians, Andy. They're politicians first and police officers second."

"But I'm not a politician, Jenny. I'm a cop. And a good one."

A wistful look crossed her face. "I know you are," she said in a subdued voice. "But the good ones either leave or get changed. They don't last."

CHAPTER 15

Tuesday
8:00 a.m.

Alderman Aaron Green maintained a rented office in the Chicago Board of Trade building, separate from the ones he kept at City Hall and at the warehouse and distribution complex. Those offices were for show. The real work was done in the Chicago Board of Trade building where he could meet with associates and conduct his political affairs away from the demands of his public profile.

He arrived at the office at precisely eight o'clock, after stopping at Starbuck's to pick up his daily latte. He balanced the cup and his attaché case in one hand while he fished his keys from his pocket with the other. He inserted the key into the lock but quickly discovered it had already been opened. When he turned the knob, he saw Tony Delgado sitting behind the desk. The man had a look of urgency on his face.

Delgado's comments about Peter rattled him, but were not wholly unexpected. The boy had never matured and was living an unsustainable life that periodically led to trouble.

"What was his name?" Green crossed his legs and thrust an arm across the back of the leather sofa. His conveyed posture of relaxed confidence was a charade.

"Polanski. He drives a burgundy-colored Crown Victoria. Know him?"

Aaron shook his head. "Not personally. He's the cop that's

testifying against those two in the 31st. He was just transferred because a lot of the cops there don't care for him. They blame him for the rioting."

A flash of acknowledgment lightened Delgado's face. "The media bills him as a super cop."

"That's him." Green flicked a piece of imaginary lint from his leg. "Why did he want to talk with Peter?"

Delgado put his feet on the Alderman's desk, crossing them at the ankle. "Polanski was questioning him about a murder victim who was found at Navy Pier."

Green sighed. "My God."

"He's out of hand, Aaron," Delgado said. "Rita called me this morning. He attacked her and she was interviewed by the police. She's threatening to hand him over if he doesn't back off." He slid his feet to the floor and leaned forward, resting his folded hands on the desk. "He's not focused and we have to run interference for him more often than we should."

"Did he kill the girl?"

Delgado shrugged. "I don't know. I covered for him. Told Polanski that he was with me at the warehouse during the time in question, but truth is, he was in the boat. So yeah, I can put him at Navy Pier. Whether he killed the girl or not…" He shrugged again.

Aaron unfurled his arm from the sofa and leaned forward. "What's his damage?"

"If this cop ties him to the girl I'd say it's going to be extensive."

The Alderman scratched his head. "Can you fix it?"

"Yeah," Delgado said with confidence that bordered on bravado. "I can fix it. But it won't stop here, Aaron. Something's got to be done about Peter."

"He's my son."

"Understood. But the fact remains, we have a lot riding on you and we can't let him destroy everything we've worked for. He's a playboy, Aaron. He's not taking care of business. He's more focused on that club than the warehouse."

The Alderman sighed deeply. "I've raised him on my own. I haven't always done right by him."

Delgado frowned wearily.

"I was able to get him in Harvard but he flunked out. And then Princeton, but the same result." He worked his hands. "I had hopes he could run the warehouse. That maybe with you looking over his shoulder he could make a go of it. Do something constructive with his life."

"He's a big boy now, Aaron. You're not responsible for him. Not anymore. And neither am I."

"What about the girlfriend?"

"She's already been dealt with. The main thing is to keep Peter on a tight leash. We can't afford any more hits."

Green said, "Does Paulie know?"

"Of course."

Aaron shook his head and glanced nervously toward the window and the skyline beyond. "I can't believe this."

"I don't have to remind you there is a lot at stake. Nothing must interfere with that." He tapped the top of the desk with an index finger to emphasize his point. "Nothing."

Green nodded slowly while kneading his hands. "I love my son."

"Of course."

"I thought he could handle the warehouse."

"He can't."

Green nodded. "I know." There was resignation in his voice.

"Listen, Aaron, I'll deal with it. I will clean this mess up and get Polanski off our backs. But you need to talk with Peter. We'll do our part, but you've got to stay focused and do yours." He stood.

Green said, "Polanski is a cop. How're you going to keep him from this? If anything happens to him it'll bring more scrutiny down on the department and that's no good for anyone."

"We'll get him to back off."

"And if he doesn't? Then what? This guy isn't going to cave that easily. He's taking a lot of heat from other cops right now and from everything I've heard, he isn't backing down."

Delgado smiled. "You underestimate us, Aaron. Like I said, you just concentrate on business and talk to Peter. Leave everything else to me."

CHAPTER 16

A small crowd had gathered at the foot of the staircase and was spilling onto the sidewalk. Campello muscled his way past them and up the stairs to the third-floor apartment. The door was open and the squawk of police radios emanated from the residence. He had been to many such scenes in his career and as a result, he knew all of the men and women who worked the 28th and nearly all the officers who worked adjacent districts. Nevertheless, protocol required him to pin his star on the collar of his jacket. The first officer he encountered grinned.

"Frank. How are you?" He stuck out a hand.

"I'm good, Stevie. What've we got?"

The officer was a tall kid with a solid muscular build. He pointed toward the rear of the apartment as his hand swallowed Campello's. "The victim is Rita Chavez. She—"

"Yeah. I know her. Interviewed her yesterday about a case I'm working."

Steve nodded. "Then this might be related. The deputy coroner is already here. She was on her way to the office when she got the call. That's two in two days."

Campello brushed past the officer and into the narrow hallway leading back through the apartment. He shouldered past a tight grouping of officers congregating in the hall and entered the bedroom. Rita lay under the covers on her right side with her back to the door and Campello. He walked to the other side of the bed, past the same technician who had photographed the scene at Navy Pier, and paused to acknowledge the deputy coroner.

"How come you always get the exciting ones, Frank?" she asked.

He knelt at eye level to study the victim's face.

Her eyes were partially open and fixed in the same vacant stare as Trina's had been. The blankets were pulled down to her waist and her hands were tucked prayer-fashion under her pillow as if to support her head while sleeping. She was lying in a partial fetal position and was wearing a sheer pale-blue gown. A bracelet encircled her partially exposed left wrist. He gently pushed the overlapping edge of the pillow aside. The inscription on the jewelry read: *To Rita from mom and dad. We love you.*

"What's the time of death?" Campello asked.

The deputy coroner was standing over him, holding a pad and pen in hands that were gloved in latex. "I would say six to ten hours ago. Give or take."

"Any signs of a struggle?"

"Other than the bruises on her face? No. Those are old, though."

He stood to full height, but did not take his eyes off the victim. "I know. I interviewed her yesterday morning. Almost twenty-four hours ago."

"She tell you who did that?"

"Her boyfriend."

"It always is, isn't it? It seems the pretty girls like this one usually hook up with losers." She stepped around him to the bed and knelt. She motioned him closer. "Let me show you something."

He knelt beside her and she pushed the pillow back to reveal the girl's arms and a small puncture wound with surrounding bruises. "I would say this girl died of an overdose of something and it was probably an injectable. But she wasn't a junkie. There aren't any other wounds or needle tracks. If she injected herself it's a first-time thing. More likely, it was done for her."

"Then she would have had to be subdued. Any other injuries?"

She pushed the pillow farther back to reveal deep discoloration on the girl's right wrist and forearm. "Given the degree of bruising here, I'd say it took considerable force to subdue her. They're fresh and some of them are defensive." She gently pulled Rita's hands free of the pillow to reveal lacerations on the heels of her palms. Then she stood and handed him a medicine bottle that was capped with a rubber stopper.

"Take a look at this."

Campello took the bottle. It was empty. "What is it?"

"Insulin." She nodded to Rita. "This little thing was a Type I diabetic."

The label was in Rita's name and indicated the availability of multiple refills. "It's finished." He counted back to the date of the prescription. "But, it shouldn't be."

"My guess is that she was injected with the entire bottle."

"Would she die quickly from that?"

The deputy coroner shook her head. "Eventually, but not immediately. She was likely subdued until the drug took effect and then the scene was staged."

He stood and glanced about the room. The plush cream carpet matched the living room and flowed seamlessly with the peach color of the walls. Heavy draperies hung over the room's only window and the open closets were full. Shelves lining the walls were crammed with stuffed animals of all kinds. Rita may have been a working girl, but in many ways she was still a child; still innocent. "I didn't get this far into the apartment yesterday."

"I'm going to move her to the morgue after we get a few more pictures. Do you need to look around?"

He spotted a computer on a nearby desk. "Yeah, just for a few minutes." He hesitated.

"Something bothering you, Frank?"

"This girl was a dancer at Silk 'n Boots. But... this place. It's nice. *Way* too nice for the income she'd make."

The deputy coroner agreed. "Dancers can make a nice buck, but not in a place like that. It's not particularly upscale."

He feigned surprise. "Oh? And how would you know?"

She grinned. "Don't give me that. You wouldn't catch me dead in a place like that." The remark, given the situation, was not lost on him.

"Sorry, Frank. I wasn't thinking. That place caters to a rougher crowd. A lot of the girls there are taking some heavy stuff to help them overcome their fears and work up the bravado to go on stage. Most of them come from bad homes. Some of them are shy. Nearly all of them have a need to be recognized. To be noticed. Sometimes they choose that line of work to fill those needs and sometimes to make a quick buck. It's hard to generalize, but I've seen my share of overdoses coming from places like that. But this little girl didn't do that. It was done for her." She looked at Rita. "Of course, I won't know for sure until I complete the autopsy."

He patted her on the shoulder. "Thanks, Barb."

He moved past her and the other officers in the room to the computer. A technician had the machine booted up and was scrolling through the address book. Campello stood behind the woman but off to one side to avoid annoying her.

"Can you print the list?"

"Sure." She checked the printer for adequate paper and then turned on the machine. It kicked on and then hummed and buzzed before spitting a couple of pages of addresses into the tray. The technician handed them to Campello.

He scanned the list. Trina's name and cell number featured, along with several others. But when he was halfway down the page he suddenly felt a rush.

CHAPTER 17

Christy's morning began like any other, hurried against the clock. She was not an early riser; never had been. But her job required access to the people who were, and she needed to get to the office ahead of them. Her deadline for a series of articles on the riots was fast approaching and she needed an interview with Aaron Green.

She was heading south on LaSalle when she received a call. She maneuvered the phone from the outside pocket of her purse and punched the key. "Yeah?"

"Christy, it's Tracy from Orlando. I have something for you."

Christy had contacted *The Orlando Daily News* for background on Janek Polanski after additional research had uncovered the man's connection there. She had put in a call to Tracy, a friend from her college days.

"Shoot."

"Janek Polanski was a police officer with the Orlando PD. He served as an army sniper, then joined the department after his military discharge. After ten years on the road, he was promoted to detective and assigned to vice. I went as far as back as twenty years researching the newspapers down here. I've also interviewed a couple of grizzly old cops who knew him back when and who are still on the force. By all I've been able to find, he was a good cop. The old cops said he was diligent and got along well with everyone. But somewhere along the line, things went sour. He was investigating a high-level dealer when the dealer was gunned down under questionable circumstances. The cops never got the guy who did it. But Polanski was caught with the dealer's supply stash in the trunk of his car. According to the police, he was trying to make a deal with an undercover officer from another department, on loan to the Orlando PD."

"So he took the guy's drugs?"

"Looks like it. The police tried to make a connection by tying him to the murder of the dealer, but there was no evidence. No ballistics, no witnesses, no forensics, nothing."

"But he was a cop. He had the knowledge to cover his trail."

"Exactly. That's what the two guys I talked with said. At any rate, he was arrested and tried. The jury came back hung and the prosecutor declined to retry the case. The family moved to Charlotte and the old man became an alcoholic. The two guys I talked with are still burned by it. They said he cast a cloud on an otherwise good department."

"Anything on the son?" Traffic slowed as she neared the city.

"He's a graduate of the University of Chicago with a major in business. He was recognized by the University for a ground-breaking thesis he wrote on corporate finance. By all accounts, he did quite well and was recognized as someone who could think outside the box. He was heavily recruited, but after college he enlisted in the army. He became a sniper and apparently, was quite good. But when his term was up he got out. It seemed like an abrupt deviation in his career plan. There were articles about him in all the Charlotte papers. You know, hometown boy makes good? And everyone was expecting great things from him when he moved back to Chicago. He was hired by Lockstar as a division head and oversaw the financing of their weapons control systems. But then, for some unknown reason, he left Lockstar just a couple of years later and joined the CPD."

The morning traffic was becoming increasingly congested.

"I'm willing to bet he joined the PD because of his father," said Christy. "That's probably why he joined the army too. Anything on him since he joined the department?"

"Nothing you don't already have. His testifying on the two cops…"

"Caine and Dorchester."

"Right. That made some national news as those kinds of things always do, but in this case Polanski attracted a bit more in the way of media attention. I figured that's probably because of the riots."

"I think those are being laid at his doorstep."

"Undoubtedly."

She steered around a slow-moving truck. "Do you have a feel for this guy?"

There was a moment of hesitation, followed by a sigh. "He's an enigma. He has a head for business, does well in a great school, but then joins the army, which is about as far from the business world as you can get. Then, after he gets out of the army, he moves back to Chicago, not Charlotte or Orlando, mind you, and hires on with one of the biggest defense contractors in the country. He has a good position there, does well, and then, just like before, he leaves to become a cop."

"Just like his old man."

"That's what I'm saying."

"It's almost like he's paying penance."

"Exactly."

"That could explain why he did what he did."

"Definitely."

"He's a man of principle who can't live with the shame of his father."

"That all sounds logical, Christy. But I'd be careful with this guy."

"Careful? What do you mean?"

She hesitated, then said, "He may be principled, but he's also not someone to mess with. He trained as a sniper. In my opinion, he has the heart of a cold-blooded assassin."

CHAPTER 18

Campello sped through the morning traffic in the Vette, aware that he did not have the benefit of a squad car's emergency lights. He called Lopez on his cell, phoning directly to the man's desk.

"Julio, I've got something and I don't think we can sit on this any longer."

"Shoot."

"The deputy coroner is pretty certain that we've got another homicide and that it was made to look like a suicide. I ran the girl's computer and our other victim, Trina, turned up."

"Could be coincidence."

"She denied knowing the victim, Julio. And I have phone calls on Trina's phone coming from the club."

He swerved around a truck, passing it on the right side. "There's more."

"Why don't you just spill it, Frank?" There was agitation in Lopez's voice.

"Rita's last phone call was to Silk 'n Boots. She placed the call a few minutes after I left the apartment."

"She works there, Frank. It'd be natural for her to call the club."

"Maybe," he said, conceding the point. "But my sixth sense tells me that her call was about me. I had just talked to her, after all. But there's something else. I also found Hoppity T's girlfriend, Juanita, in the address book." He passed a string of slowing traffic by moving around it. There was a long pause on the other end of the phone.

"OK," Lopez said. "That's too much of a coincidence."

"That's what I was thinking."

"How do you want to play it?"

"I'm going to interview Juanita, if I can find her."

"Just be careful, Frank. Remember, you killed her boyfriend. She backed you once, but... we don't want any allegations of harassment."

"And that's a second problem. Why did she back me?"

"Everyone doesn't hate the police, Frank. There are people who will tell the truth."

"Maybe. But I killed her boyfriend. Doesn't that color it just a bit?"

There was another pause as Campello worked toward the center of the loop.

"Who do you think killed the girl?" Lopez asked.

"Rita? If I had to guess, I'd say it was Peter Green."

Lopez sighed. "I was afraid you'd say that."

"Come on, Julio. This guy's involved in this one way or another and you know it. He owns the club and there's too many connections to it to be coincidental. Juanita, Trina, and now Rita. And some of them are denying even knowing the others. Plus, when you consider that Peter attacked Rita, that tells me he has a tendency toward violence, certainly toward women. Add that Trina was beaten to death, and something's going on at that club and it's tied into both murders."

"Polanski's here and he just showed me the security camera tapes taken from the shops at the pier. Two of them are on the north end of the pier and three on the south end. All but one of them catches a man moving across the pier. Whoever was there is not identifiable on the tape. He's wearing a Chicago Bulls hoodie and the hood is pulled over his face. The sleeve is torn so it shouldn't be too hard to ID the sweater. If we find it, we'll also find the man on the tape and I'm betting he's the killer. But whoever it is, he was at the pier at around the time the girl was dumped and that makes him interesting."

Campello passed another slow-moving truck, honking and cursing as he did.

"What was that, Frank?"

"Nothing."

"Keep me posted on the interview."

"I will."

"And be careful, Frank," he admonished again. "You may not be well received by our girl."

"Four marriages, Julio. I'm used to it."

Campello reached the girl's apartment and parked curbside. The area had suffered urban blight and he was aware that the classic car stood out like a flawless diamond in a convention of jewel thieves. And worse, because it was a classic, the Vette had no alarm or other protective device.

He got out of the Vette and locked the car, glancing around for possible predators. He was determined to keep the interview to fifteen minutes or less.

He entered the lobby and ran a finger down a series of names stenciled next to a row of mailboxes. Though the shooting had occurred at this address, it had happened outside the building. He had never been in the girl's apartment.

For the third time in two days, he climbed the steps to an apartment and rapped on the door. Just as he had on his first visit to Rita's, he stepped to one side and kept his hand poised to draw his weapon. The door opened and Juanita recognized him immediately.

"Detective?"

"Can I come in?"

She was hesitant, glancing briefly over her shoulder as she stood at the partially opened door. "Is this about the shooting?"

He shook his head. "No. I may have some bad news."

She hesitated as though she were weighing the decision, before opening the door and allowing him to enter.

The apartment was much smaller than Rita's and not as nicely furnished. A play-pen was sitting in one corner of the living area, near a radiator that was hissing and filling the tiny space with moist heat. An alcove that was probably meant to serve as a dining-room held a collection of stuffed animals and other toys. Juanita had a child and revealed that Hoppity was not the father during a post-shooting interview.

"How's the baby?"

The girl folded her arms across her chest in a posture that was more self-hugging than defiant. "She's fine."

"She asleep?"

The girl nodded.

She was tall – he guessed her height at five nine or ten – and trim with shoulder-length brown hair that was pulled in a ponytail. Her sky-blue eyes were light, but penetrating. She was dressed in a long-sleeve shirt and jeans.

He maintained a respectful distance to avoid any hint of crowding or intimidating her.

"Juanita, I'm no threat to you. I have some information I think you should know and I figure you may know something that could help me. I have no legal interest in you. I just need to talk."

She nodded.

"Did you know Trina Martinez?"

The girl glanced at the floor and shook her head.

"How about Rita Chavez?"

She pursed her lips and tightened her arms around herself.

"Juanita?"

"Yes."

"How did you know Rita?"

She redirected her gaze to him. "Did? What do you mean?"

"Rita's dead."

Her eyes reddened.

He continued. "Rita and Trina knew each other, Juanita, and now they're both dead. Trina's name and phone number were in Rita's address book, along with several other girls, including yours."

He showed her the printout. "Do you know any of them?"

Her eyes quickly swept over the list and then she turned her head away. "No."

"Some of these girls have connection to a place called Silk 'n Boots. Have you heard of it?"

She continued to clutch herself. "Yes."

"Do you have any connection with it?"

She bit her lip and shook her head.

He gestured to the couch. "Could I sit?"

She nodded and he sat on the couch. She remained standing.

"How do you know Rita?" he asked.

"She was just a friend."

"How long have you known her?"

"Not long." She was lying, being evasive, but she was also an important link to the deaths of Rita and Trina. Calling her out would run the risk of closing her down completely, particularly given his history with her and her apparent nervous reaction at having him in her home.

"How have you been? Since the shooting, I mean."

"It's not been easy. I know Germaine was a hot-head and we certainly had our problems, but…"

Germaine Thomas was Hoppity's real name.

"I'm sorry things had to go down the way they did."

"How did Rita die?"

"We think she was murdered." He pulled his billfold from his back pocket and handed her his card. "If you remember anything, hear anything, I'd appreciate a call. Day or night."

She took the card and he couldn't help but notice that her hand was trembling.

CHAPTER 19

The car had not been touched, although it had attracted a small crowd of admirers. He returned to the Castle, parking next to Polanski's Ford Taurus. The tire had been changed.

He got out of the car and ran into Shelly and Hughbanks who were on their way out of the building.

"Our snitch ran into a bit of car trouble last night," she said.

"I heard."

Jerry said, "Came as a surprise to all of us."

"Uh huh. I'll bet."

Shelly grinned. "Actually, it did. Some of the guys from the 31st came over to discuss strategy for the riots. On their way out, they took a little recreational time and vented on our boy."

"Speaking of which," Campello said, "where is he?"

Shelly glanced at Hughbanks and he shrugged. "Don't know. We overheard Lopez say he was out on an interview, but that was a while ago."

He glanced around the lot. The Crown Vic was missing. "Did he take the car home last night?"

Shelly shrugged. "Yeah. He was on his way home last night, but came back to get the keys from the cabinet."

Jerry laughed. "Funniest thing. He got the keys, never said a word, and drove off, leaving the car with the flat. It was like he was trying to punish us."

"*Us*, Frank," Shelly said. "The turncoat was trying to punish *us*."

He snorted. "Where're you guys going?"

"We've got some interviewing to do," Shelly said. "Then we're going over to the 31st to talk to some of the guys about our boy. Bob has told me what he knows, but I want to see what I can find out first hand."

"And we want to check up on Caine and Dorchester," Hughbanks said. "This has got to be hard on them."

"No doubt."

"We're going to get this guy out of here, Frank," Shelly said. "I don't know how, but we're going to get it done."

They exchanged fist bumps and the two detectives climbed into Tertwiller's unmarked squad. Campello watched as they drove off before going into the station and taking the stairs to the second floor. The squad room was busy and he went directly to his desk, pulling the folded list he had gotten from Rita's computer from inside his pocket, before draping his jacket over the chair. After booting up the computer, he filled his coffee cup and sat down.

Each of the seven names on the list, including Trina's and Juanita's, had a cell phone attached to it.

He picked up the phone and began dialing the numbers, one at a time. The first one rang and then ended abruptly. He called it again and the ringing ended on the second ring. He frowned and punched in the next number on the list. The number had been disconnected. He dialed a third and discovered it had been disconnected too. The remaining phone numbers were no longer operational. Only the first number he called, attached to someone named Gloria Perez, seemed to still be working.

He picked up his desk phone and punched an in-house number. "This is Campello. I'm going to give you a cell number. Could you find out who the number is billed to and get an address for me?" The voice on the other end of the line took down the number and he ended the call just as Polanski was sitting down at Rand's desk.

"I heard about Rita," he said, settling himself where he did not belong. "Peter Green's our man. He killed both girls."

"Maybe," Campello said. "He's definitely involved."

Polanski shook his head. "Huh uh. He did it."

"You can't make unfounded allegations," he said, deliberately nudging the man about his charges against Caine and Dorchester. "You've got to prove it." He shook his head, with a lopsided grin that was calculated to demean and annoy.

Polanski gave him a hardened stare. "I will."

"What did you find out at Trina's apartment?"

"I talked to her parents. And her sister."

Campello frowned. "I thought she was an illegal."

"She was. And so is her family. They're afraid. That's why they didn't come forward."

"You talked to them last night?"

"Yes. I found them in Mexico."

"Where've you been this morning?"

"Silk 'n Boots."

"How does your wife feel about that?" He couldn't stop himself from chiding the man.

Polanski continued, ignoring the dig. "I talked to one of the bartenders. He said Peter Green is in once in a while and he hangs with the DJ. Some guy named Longhorse. Longhorse used to work for him at the warehouse. I talked to him too, even leaned on him a little, but got nothing."

Campello leaned back in his chair. "Did Green see you?"

"He wasn't there. Not that it matters. I interviewed him at the warehouse last night."

Campello could feel his abs tighten. He could ignore talking to Trina's parents. After all, that had come from Campello's suggestion that he investigate the girl's apartment. But interviewing Green without consulting him, particularly given the politically sensitive nature of the family's standing with the department, was unbearable. "Without talking with me?"

"Without talking with you."

The man was brazen. Challenging him. "Did you discuss it with Lopez?"

"This morning. I didn't have time last night. He was already gone and I wanted to catch Peter before he left for home. I wanted to see him at work. To let him know we were watching."

Campello could feel his anger rising. Polanski was the proverbial bull in a china shop. Always eager to point out the shortcomings of others, real or imagined, but incapable of avoiding the same errors himself.

"While I was there," Polanski said, "I—"

A sudden burst of noise arose from downstairs. Silvio and Chin were coming into the squad room, grinning, each of them carrying several bags of white powder. Chin also had a box that contained a scale, a strainer, and other drug paraphernalia.

"We got 'em. Got 'em with the stuff right there in the open," he said.

"These guys thought they were being creative. Thought hiding it out in the open was better than the old way," Silvio said.

"But we got 'em," Chin said again. "And we got 'em good."

"What's going on downstairs?" Campello asked.

"They're being booked and they don't like it," Silvio said. His grin stretched to a full smile. "It stifles their creativity."

Campello grinned but it was cut short when Polanski said, "Anyway, to make a long story short, when I was at the warehouse I saw a guy I thought I recognized. Then today, while I was at the club, I saw him again. He's Anthony Delgado. He's an enforcer for Pauli Vincent. I checked on the guy and he's been in trouble with the law since he was in diapers. He started out with vandalism, then petty theft, and progressed to strong arming and—"

"I know who he is," Campello said.

"Then what's he doing with Peter Green?"

Campello shrugged. "It probably means Vincent has an interest in him."

Polanski frowned. "Then what does it mean?"

"It means Peter is hanging with a bad dude. It doesn't mean that he's the killer."

"Come on," Polanski said, clearly angered.

Campello set the mug on the desk and leaned forward in his chair. He lowered his voice and spoke directly to Polanski. "Look, I think Green is involved in this too. But just because he's involved doesn't mean he killed the girl." He filled Polanski in on the interview he had with Juanita. He told him about Juanita's connection to Hoppity T, and the connection between her and Rita, and Rita's connection to Trina, even though she denied knowing the girl.

"Something's happening at the club," Polanski said.

"Wow," Campello said, emphasizing the word, making his intolerance for Polanski clear, "you really are bright, despite what people say about you."

Polanski shot out of the chair and came around the desks. Campello rose to his feet, fists drawn. "Go ahead," he said. "Give me a reason."

Polanski stood less than a foot away, glaring at Campello. His anger was clear and restraining himself was requiring all he had.

"Do it," Campello chided. "Take a shot. You know you want to."

"Hey, you two!" It was Lopez. "Cool it. Now!"

Polanski looked over Campello's shoulder to Lopez's office. He gritted his teeth and unclenched his fists. He turned to leave the room, grabbing his coat from the rack on his way out.

"Campello," Lopez said, "in my office. Now."

Campello slowly turned toward Lopez. His fists were still clenched as he followed the commander into the office. Lopez slammed the door.

"What was that out there?"

"Nothing."

"Don't snow me, Frank."

"Nothing, Julio." Although his fists were unclenched now, his breathing was heavy and his heart continued to pound from adrenalin overflow.

"When he comes back, settle it. You two are going to work together so you might as well get used to it. Let him go cool off. But when you see him, tell him I have a lead I want him to follow." He slid a note across the desk.

"A lead?"

"On the murder. I just got that," he pointed to the note, "but it seems your contact, Juanita, called this in early this morning. She asked to speak with Polanski."

Campello frowned. "Why Polanski?"

"I don't know and it doesn't matter. If she feels more comfortable talking to him than to you, then she'll talk to him. Just make sure he gets the message."

"I don't know where he went. The jerk stormed out of here."

"Then check with dispatch and see if they can raise him," Lopez said, raising his voice.

Campello stood and opened the office door.

"And Frank? Be sure he gets the information. Don't play games."

He left the office, aware that everyone in the room had their eyes focused on him and that nearly everyone was telegraphing their desire to see him beat Polanski into the ground.

CHAPTER 20

Andy Polanski paced the headquarters parking lot. His hands shook with rage and his breathing was labored. His struggle, he reminded himself, was not against Campello or Tertwiller or Silvio or even Caine and Dorchester. But the persistent slurs, the innuendos, the middle-of-the-night phone calls to his family and the provocative vandalism had hit their mark. It had required all the discipline he could muster to refrain from knocking Campello out. But if he had, his witness would have been destroyed.

He slipped a stick of gum into his mouth and continued to pace the lot, aware that the officers coming and going were watching him; some of them with suspicion and some with detachment, and others with glee, glad that someone had finally pushed the right button.

He didn't care. But he also didn't want a confrontation, and he knew that one would occur if he let them get to him again; if he lost control.

Polanski needed to get away before one of the officers in the lot lit the final fuse with a condescending remark or an outright challenge. A drive around the block, a cup of coffee or even a brief walk along the lake could calm him, could help him clear his head and regain perspective. His anger was kindled and he knew he would regret his actions if he allowed it to flourish.

He was still pacing when he saw one of the detectives who worked vice pulling into the lot. Polanski approached the man as soon as he was out of the car.

"Keys."

"What?"

"Give me the keys." The unsuspecting detective could see Polanski's rage and tossed the keys to him.

He slid behind the wheel and started the engine just as he saw Campello pulling out of the lot in the Crown Vic, clearly in a hurry.

The man was up to something and Polanski was no longer willing to allow him unfettered access to the case. He decided to follow.

He allowed Campello a bit of leeway, then pulled out of the lot, maintaining the recommended six car lengths behind him.

They drove south on Wabash to Randolph Street where Campello's turn signal indicated a turn west. Polanski followed while keeping the discreet distance, drumming his fingers on the steering wheel.

He continued following the Crown Victoria when it turned left, heading south. The traffic light prevented him from making the turn with Campello, but he kept his eye on the unmarked squad which stopped at the next traffic light one block south. That gave Polanski time to turn south and reach a spot that was four car lengths behind Campello. From this position, he could see his partner's arm thrown across the top of the front passenger's seat, seemingly carefree, but his fingers drummed on the headrest, betraying a sense of urgency.

Polanski waited for the light to turn as the events of the past week paraded through his mind. Although he was different from Campello, he had always considered himself a team player. That was especially true when it was for the good of all concerned. In fact, it was his loyalty to the team, to the CPD, that had been the strongest motivator when he discovered that Caine and Dorchester had manufactured evidence.

He had taken their actions to the district commander with confidence that the man would address his concerns. The men would be disciplined according to CPD policy, and the critically important reputation of the department would be maintained. The department's effectiveness was only as good as the respect of the citizenry, after all, and to ignore the obvious would be to sacrifice the bond of civic trust. But it was apparent within days that he wasn't part of the team and that Caine and Dorchester were. And his career had stalled.

He held no illusions about his transfer from the 31st. He knew that the gossip mill would swing into full fury as soon as he set foot in the Castle, and there would be a faction that would see him as a personal threat. But in his persistent optimism he assumed the attacks would be merely acts like vandalism or snubbing, confined to the personal but not the professional; that his detractors would put the job above personal animosity. But he had been wrong. His new partner was proceeding on the case without him, giving him trivial tasks to make it appear as though he was in charge and Polanski answered to him. Yet Campello had the gall to become hostile when the shoe was on the other foot. Following Campello was the only way Polanski knew to decipher the man's next action and put an end to the harassment, to send the signal that he would be a player in the district for as long as the CPD kept him there.

The sudden blaring of a horn behind him brought him out of his reverie. The light had turned green, and the line of traffic had begun moving. Somewhere up ahead, Campello must have turned. The burgundy Crown Vic was no longer in view.

CHAPTER 21

Campello did not appreciate the fact that he had just interviewed Juanita but that she had said nothing about approaching Polanski. Prior to leaving the district headquarters, he talked with the dispatcher who had taken the call and forwarded the message to Lopez. He learned the call had come in shortly before he had arrived at her apartment and that she was offering the very information he had tried to extract from her. Whether she would talk to him if he showed in Polanski's place was debatable, but he wanted answers and he wanted to keep Polanski from involving himself in the case more than he already had. As he drove to the isolated location, he tried to decipher her reasons for not being open to him when he was at the apartment, but could not come up with any other than possible resentment over the shooting of Hoppity T.

And who was threatening her? The message indicated she had left her apartment with the baby because she did not feel safe there. She would be staying with a friend and promised to tell Polanski everything she knew if he could guarantee her safety.

He turned west on Van Buren and cursed. The media had made a hero of Polanski. He would get calls from all over the city, now. From legitimate sources, to be sure, but also from every law-breaker in Chicago who had a beef against the police. It was inevitable that Polanski would eventually end up in Internal Affairs and then he would have his revenge against the honest cops who had done their job.

He cursed again.

Being a cop was difficult enough, but in Chicago, a city that thrived on its politics, being on the job could be downright painful. But it was the job stress that engendered the camaraderie that existed between the men and women of the CPD. There was no better adhesive than a common enemy, and nearly every cop, given enough time in uniform, began to define the enemy as anyone who didn't stand with them. The CPD, like any law enforcement agency, was a band of brothers – a family, as Tertwiller had said. So when men like Polanski turned on one of his own, transforming himself from cop to "one of them", it threatened the stability of the family. And no one did that. No one.

He was in the area now, past the Kennedy, and he slowed to look for the address.

Polanski scanned as far ahead as he could see. The Crown Vic was not in sight and since Campello didn't have enough time to have gotten that far ahead, it was apparent he was not continuing south, but had probably turned west.

Polanski turned west too, and began a methodical street-by-street search. Again, he could not see the unmarked squad. That left the possibility that Campello had either taken another street when he turned west, which meant that he had gotten a full block ahead while Polanski was reminiscing at the stop light, or he had turned into one of the industrial businesses that predominated in this part of town. At any rate, he could not have gotten so far ahead as to be out of sight. He had to be nearby.

Traffic was reasonably light, so Polanski slowed while scanning the parking areas of the businesses on each side of the street for the Burgundy squad car.

Campello found the address, a small apartment complex with a gravel-lined lot at the far end of the industrial area. He contacted dispatch and gave his location as he turned into the lot.

Polanski did not see the Crown Vic so he retraced his steps to the stoplight at which he had last seen the car and drove one block farther south before turning west again. As he had previously done, he began to work his way along the street, scanning each side for the squad car. There was a smattering of industrial businesses, a concrete manufacturer, a small trucking firm, a warehouse, but no signs of the squad car. If he did not find Campello soon, he would have to accept that the man had gotten away, leaving him in the cold again.

Campello parked nose first into the lot, facing the apartment building, and killed the engine. The complex was small, four units in a single building, all of them opening directly to the parking lot. A ten-foot-high earthen hill ran along the perceived property line to his right, serving as a barrier between the residential dwelling and a defunct concrete company on the other side. A second hill ran along the back of the apartment building and was probably designed to shield the residents from the noise and debris that had once been generated by the salvage yard that lay behind.

His eyes scanned the units in the structure. All of them had curtains in the windows and two of them had screen doors in place although the screens were missing. There were no other cars in the lot, and no dumpsters or other trash receptacles to suggest anyone lived there. A sinking feeling gnawed at his gut and he started the car to drive away, when he came under sudden fire.

CHAPTER 22

Polanski heard the sound of automatic rifle fire and immediately identified it as coming from a Ruger mini 14. He rolled down the window in an attempt to localize it, but the echo created by the building-formed canyon made the effort impossible. He floored the accelerator and pulled into the vacant lot that was straight ahead so that he could be out of traffic and contact dispatch. He asked for Campello's last known location, hoping the man had taken the time to contact them.

The initial blast blew out the windshield, spraying Campello with shards of glass, and was quickly followed by several blasts to the radiator and then the tires, immediately shredding them, sinking the car to the ground. The shooter did not want him to escape and was taking pains to immobilize the vehicle.

The shots were coming from Campello's right, so he opened the door and dropped to the gravel lot, immediately sliding to a position behind the left front fender. The engine block would provide a higher level of protection from the incoming rounds that the car's body could not. The rifle rounds were powerful enough to penetrate the door of the car, making it a convenient tomb for its driver.

Another blast struck the passenger's side of the car, rocking it. He kept his head down, but raised his weapon over the hood of the car, firing rapidly at the hill from where the shots came. He was immediately answered with a hail of lead and he balled himself behind the engine block. The slide of his weapon was locked in place, indicating that in his panic, he had expelled all fifteen rounds of his magazine. He ejected it and slammed the other one into place.

With Campello's location, Polanski called for backup, indicating that shots were being exchanged, and then floored the accelerator. He had lost Campello at the light and the man had gotten farther away than he had thought possible. They were a mile apart.

The gunfire ceased and Campello slid along the gravel, careful to remain as close behind the engine block as possible, while looking under the car and toward the hill. He couldn't see signs of movement, or any other tell-tale indicators of the shooter, and that concerned him. If the man moved under cover of the hill to the rear of the complex, that would put the shooter to his left, leaving him open to the man's fire. The ambush had been well planned.

He pivoted to the left and began scanning along the ridge of the hill, just as the shooter popped into view with the rifle raised in firing position.

Polanski pulled into the lot of the complex that had been Campello's last known location and immediately saw the man crouching behind the doghouse of the car. He was looking to the left, and Polanski followed his eye-line to the hill behind the apartment building. Over the ridge, he could see the shooter poised with a rifle in firing position.

He pulled his pistol from the holster and fired through the open window, forcing the attacker to take cover.

Campello was relieved when he saw the blue unmarked squad enter the lot from his left and skid to a halt, nose to nose with his car. The passenger's door opened and Polanski tumbled out, landing on the hardened gravel just as a shower of lead penetrated the car, passing through the cockpit from which he had just come. He took position behind the right front tire of his car, which put him behind the vehicle's doghouse and engine block, nose to nose with the position Campello had taken. The two of them were behind a makeshift fortress.

"What are you doing here?" Campello asked.

"The same thing you are."

Campello nodded to the ridge that ran along the back and the side of the complex.

"He's moved along that hill to gain a better position."

"I've got backup coming, but—"

The shooter fired again, striking both cars with fury and showering both men with bits of steel, lead, and glass. Polanski could see that Campello was bleeding along his forehead and both sides of his face.

"You hit?"

Campello shook his head. "Cut."

Polanski peered around the front of his car. "He's still behind the building." He continued to crouch and slid past Campello to the rear of the Crown Vic.

"What're you doing?"

"I'm going to take him out."

"You've got backup coming, right? Wait until they—"

Another blast of fire struck the driver's side of Polanski's squad car, rocking it violently.

"We could be dead by the time they get here. He won't see me reach the hill because his view is blocked by the building." Polanski prepared to run for the northern edge of the lot and to the hill. "Cover me."

He took off and Campello fired rapidly at the shooter's position behind the hill at the rear of the complex. He held his fire as Polanski dove over the northern half of the ridge, out of sight.

The shooter fired again, striking both cars. Campello tried to return fire, but the slide of his pistol was again locked in place. This time, he was out of ammunition.

He peered beneath the cars toward the hillside. The shooter was nowhere in sight. From the distance, the sound of approaching sirens grew louder.

He peered from beneath the angle formed by the cars. He couldn't see anything.

Then, from his left, the sound of crunching gravel. He turned and saw Bobby Longhorse standing over him with the rifle barrel raised and a confused look on his face.

Campello inhaled sharply. His weapon was empty and there was nowhere to hide. Longhorse had charged forward over the hill and toward the cars when Polanski had run to the north.

"Drop it!" It was Polanski's voice.

Longhorse hesitated, keeping the rifle trained on Campello and his finger in the trigger guard.

Polanski came into Campello's view with the pistol pointed at Longhorse's head. "Drop it now or I will drop you."

Longhorse lowered the rifle to the ground and raised his hands.

Campello exhaled slowly.

Five squad cars were parked in the lot along with an ambulance. The deputy coroner was standing next to Campello, who was leaning against the fender of a marked squad car while paramedics examined him. Polanski stood alongside another squad ten feet from Campello, talking calmly with a shooting team. Longhorse sat in the back of the car, his hands cuffed behind him.

Campello's hand was shaking.

"You OK, Frank?" the deputy coroner asked.

He was looking at Polanski and didn't answer.

She followed Campello's gaze. "That was a pretty gutsy thing he did."

Campello sighed. His hand continued to shake. "Twenty years on the department, Barb. Twenty years and no problems. And then I'm involved in two shootings in a month."

She looked at his hand. "You're ignoring my question. Are you OK?"

The paramedic said, "He's fine. Some cuts from the windshield, and he's a bit shaken up, but no other injuries. It'd be a good idea, though, to take a ride to the hospital. Let them check you out a bit." He tried to roll a bandage on Campello's head, but gave up when the detective ducked his efforts.

"I'm not going anywhere. You said it yourself. I'm fine."

"OK, then," the paramedic said. "I can't make you go to the hospital, so unless something's changed, I'm out of here."

He packed his gear and walked back to the ambulance. When he was out of earshot Campello said, "Have you got a cigarette?"

She frowned. "Aren't you trying to quit?"

"Last week. Not today."

She hesitated before pulling a crumpled package of cigarettes from her pocket. She handed them to him and he shook one free. He tried to light it, but his shaking prevented him from striking the wheel of the lighter with sufficient force. She took it from him, and lit the cigarette. He inhaled deeply and handed the packet back to her.

She shook her head. "You keep them. You need them more than I do."

He inhaled deeply on the cigarette again. "What are you doing here, Barb?"

"I heard the shooting on the radio. I figured I'd be needed, but when I got here you were still kicking." She smiled.

"Sorry to disappoint you," Campello said, noting an approaching officer who had the shooter's rifle in hand.

"Mini fourteen. This thing is dangerous. Chewed those cars up like they were pancakes."

Campello struggled to suppress the nausea that rose in his throat. "Take it away."

The officer furrowed his brow.

"Get it out of here, officer," he said, more deliberately this time. "I've seen all of that I care to."

The cop shrugged and walked away.

"What're you involved with here, Frank?" Barb asked. "First that little girl, Rita, turns up dead, and now you're getting ambushed…"

"I wish I knew," he said, watching Polanski as he talked with the shooting team.

CHAPTER 23

Because the attack had occurred during daylight hours in a city which had already seen two shootings in as many weeks, word spread quickly, reaching Alderman Aaron Green through a variety of sources and interrupting another boring interview. It was apparent that an open attack had been carried out against Polanski after the man had been lured to an isolated location. When this reached the public discourse, it would appear like an assassination attempt and outcries of a police cover-up would ensue. He had asked Delgado to be discreet, but the enforcer had ignored his wishes and acted like the animal he was.

Green contacted the man by pager and left a pre-arranged code. The four-digit number was an indicator that an urgent confidential meeting was requested. Such a meeting, by its nature, required face-to-face contact rather than a discussion over an insecure cell phone. Wherever Delgado was, he would immediately make arrangements to arrive at the Board of Trade office or he would call and leave a cryptic message indicating he was currently indisposed, but making arrangements to arrive in short order.

After Aaron Green left the message, he poured himself a drink from the bar he kept at one end of the room and dropped himself into the chair behind his desk. Below him, the traffic on LaSalle Street flowed smoothly, but silently. The leaded windows of his office not only filtered the sun's rays, but the city's noise as well.

He sipped the scotch and water with one foot resting on an open drawer. He was lost in thought a half hour later when he heard a rap on the door just before Delgado entered. As usual, he was dressed in black from head to toe, including his iconic black leather coat. Aware that Delgado represented the man who employed both of them, Aaron gestured toward the bar in an act of hospitality. Delgado shook his head and took a seat in front of the desk.

"It's getting colder," he said, pulling off his gloves, one finger at a time.

"What happened?"

He set the gloves on the edge of the desk. "It didn't come from us."

"What do you mean, it didn't come from you? Who else has the moxie to pull off something like this? Who else has the clout?"

Delgado paused, nonplussed as usual, and said, "Think, Aaron."

Green swirled the drink, then said, "Peter? My Peter?"

"Who else stands to lose if the cops keep digging?"

"You, for one."

He nodded. "Yes, and you too. But hitting Polanski is the last thing I want to do. You said it yourself. He's the media's big star. If anything happens to him, it will bring unwanted media attention and that brings unneeded stress. There are other ways of relieving ourselves of him. We don't need to kill him."

Green sipped the scotch and studied the man in front of him. After a lifetime of kissing babies and sucking up when sucking up was called for, he had developed a feel for people and the lies they told. Delgado lived on the razor's edge. He was dangerous, unpredictable, and nearly emotionless. And because he was so reserved he was not easily read. Adding to the frustration, he was also not a man who spoke linearly, preferring to speak with hints or innuendos, dancing around the truth rather than speaking directly to it. That made him difficult to assess, even for a politician. The only way to find out what Delgado was thinking was to ask him directly and evaluate the answer he gave in the light of his personality.

"How will you deal with Polanski?"

"Effectively."

Aaron's rising anger was fueled as much by the scotch as the flippant response. Still, he had to tread carefully. Paulie Vincent did not take rebellion lightly and it was Delgado who enforced Vincent's decisions.

"And how would you do that, Tony?"

"That's up to me. Your concern is to—"

"Tony…" His hand clutched the scotch glass with such force, he was afraid it would break. He set it on the desk.

"Leave it to me, Aaron. We have no desire to bring attention to ourselves. Our only desire is to run an effective business and to maintain the relationship with you that we've enjoyed over the years. I assume it remains satisfactory for you?"

"Yes. Of course." Paulie Vincent had been a major contributor ever since he first ran for Alderman. Each election cycle had brought Paulie's continued support, which amounted to a certain win. Aaron knew that his rise to head of finance had also been engineered by Paulie, and with an effectiveness that equaled his support during the campaigns. But there had been a downside to the relationship, too. And while it remained satisfactory, the costs were escalating.

"Good. That's what Paulie will want to hear. He values your friendship, Aaron, and he wants nothing to stand in the way of that."

"Of course." Resignation replaced indignation. The will to fight fled him, leaving him with the same useless and empty feeling he had endured for over thirty years.

"Excellent." Delgado reached for his gloves. "Do speak to Peter, will you? We simply cannot tolerate any more of his antics."

"I'll speak to him."

Delgado rose and slipped his hands into the gloves. "Remember, Aaron. We cannot let anyone interfere with our mutual business interests. Not even a cop."

"I understand."

"Not even Peter."

CHAPTER 24

After their return to the 28th, Frank Campello was separated from Andy Polanski and interviewed by the shooting team. His interview lasted well over two hours and was conducted in the presence of his FOP attorney. The Fraternal Order of Police had long ago learned that police officers often need lawyers as much as the people they arrest and had developed a system of support that provided them with a high level of legal security to ensure they would not be condemned for performing their duties.

Most of the questioning concentrated on why Campello was at the location in the first place, since the tip had been phoned in for Polanski. The team also expressed concern regarding his ill-advised interview of Juanita, who the team regarded as peripheral, at best, to the investigation of Trina's murder. The grilling had been intense and he left the room angry, noticing that the door to Polanski's interrogation room was still closed. Polanski had captured Longhorse, so it was inevitable that the team would take a greater interest in him.

Campello trudged upstairs to the squad room. His weapon, along with Polanski's, had been surrendered to the interviewers at the scene. It would be compared for ballistics against the bullets that were found at the scene for reasons of the department's potential liability, and to be presented to the IPRA later. The weapons would be returned by the end of the day.

On entering the squad room he was immediately surrounded by the others who were still there and not out running down leads or conducting interviews of their own. He accepted their handshakes and pats on the back before collapsing into his chair.

"You OK, Frank?" Tertwiller asked, sitting on the edge of his desk.

He reached for the coffee mug and his hand trembled noticeably. Silvio took the cup from him.

"Here, Frank. Let me get that for you." He left to go fill the cup.

"I'm OK, Shelly."

She glanced at his hand.

"Second time in less than a month," Hughbanks said. "You a glutton for punishment?"

A wry smile was the best he could do in response to Hughbanks' attempts at humor. "Seems like it, Jerry."

He was tense and he was aware of it; his breathing was erratic, he was sighing frequently, continually shifting positions in the chair.

Silvio returned with a full cup of coffee. He handed it to Campello.

"What was Polanski doing out there?" Tertwiller asked.

Campello crossed his legs and leaned back in his chair. "I don't know. That didn't come up during my questioning, but I'm sure it will."

"You don't think he had anything to do with the shooting, do you?" she asked. "I mean, being a turncoat is one thing, but…"

Campello shook his head, dismissing the idea as soon as Tertwiller raised it.

"How long after the shooting started did Polanski show up?" Tertwiller asked.

Campello paused to think. His mind was clearing, but he still seemed unable to focus on the details. He had a similar experience after the incident in which Rand was killed.

"I don't know, Shelly. It's all a blur. I was following a lead and had a bad feeling as soon as I pulled into the lot. I was beginning to pull out when I came under fire." He shrugged. "I remember Polanski pulling alongside me and—"

"So the question remains," she said. "What was he doing there?"

"I don't know." He raised the mug.

Hughbanks said, "The shooter is a guy named Longhorse. You know him, Frank?"

"Yeah, I know him. He's a DJ at a place called Silk 'n Boots. It's a lead in the case I'm working."

"Did you talk to this guy?" Silvio asked. "Ruffle his feathers or something?"

He shook his head. "No. I asked him a couple of routine questions about one of the dancers there, but nothing accusatory. Nothing penetrating."

"Is that the dancer who's dead?" Tertwiller said.

"Yeah. The kid's name was Rita."

"Is this about the case that came in yesterday? The girl at Navy Pier?" Silvio asked.

"Yeah," he said. He was aware that his eyes were fixated on a distant point and that his mind was clearing, allowing him to begin a replay of the case and the shooting.

"You've got hold of something here," Silvio said, glancing at the others. "You must be pushing some buttons pretty hard to have someone take a shot at you like this."

His mind shifted from neutral to full drive. It replayed the call from Juanita; replayed the ID of the shooter and the vandalized tire on the Taurus. Replayed the confused look on Longhorse's face. "Someone's pushing some buttons, Angie, but it isn't me."

CHAPTER 25

It was the first shooting in which Polanski had been involved, and it could not have come at a worse time. The shooting team's interview had been grueling and most of their questions centered on the last few seconds of his encounter with the shooter. Although he had briefly interviewed Longhorse, he could not explain why the man would want to kill him. Other questions, of course, focused on his conflict with Campello, including the confrontation that occurred less than an hour before the shooting. The questioning then turned to the allegations involving Caine and Dorchester, but his FOP attorney objected and the interviewers dropped the line of questioning. He was told the shooting would go before the IPRA, but should be a formality in the face of the evidence. They offered him the option of taking administrative leave, but he decided to go home for the day, declining any additional time off. He suspected that Campello would do the same thing.

He left the room determined to drive home, but given the potential for immediate post-traumatic stress, the team charged a uniformed officer with driving him in a marked squad car. The officer recognized him immediately, but said nothing in protest. The ride was quiet all the way to Polanski's house, and the officer deposited him as quickly as he could, clearly relieved to have rid himself of the traitor.

Polanski passed through the rear door and went directly to the refrigerator. He found a can of Coke and opened it. His hand did not shake nor was his grip weak, but his throat was dry. Jenny came downstairs, curious why he was home so early. He had not called her as the team recommended because he wanted to deliver the news in person. She had experienced enough bad phone calls and he didn't want her to hear the story over the phone.

"I was involved in a shooting."

Her eyes searched him in innocence, and then she furrowed her brow as she stepped back from him. "Shooting?"

He nodded and sipped the Coke. "I was following Campello and I lost him. I heard gunfire and responded to the sound. By the time I arrived, he was pinned down behind the squad and…" It sounded like the narrative he had given the interviewers and he paused to tone down the rhetoric. "Someone was shooting at him and I helped him out."

"Are you OK?"

"Yes."

She embraced him immediately. "Oh, Andy."

He hugged her, still holding the soft drink in one hand while he nuzzled his face into her neck. Her scent was as comforting. "I'm on leave for the day."

She looked into his eyes, holding his face in both hands. "Just for the day?"

"I didn't kill anyone, Jenny. I've trained for it all my life. Trained to do it under cold fire and from a distance. But this…" he shook his head, "this was different. It happened so fast. And up close." He set the can down on the counter and loosened his tie. "I was prepared to kill him, but he just set the rifle down so I cuffed him and… it was over. Just like that."

"Was he after you? Do you think he's the one who's been—"

"No." He shook his head. "He couldn't have been after me. He didn't know I was going to be there." He leaned against the counter with the heel of both hands. "He was out for Campello."

"Why? What's he doing that—" The phone rang. She glanced at it, then to him. He reached for the receiver but she grabbed it first and stepped out of his reach. He knew she was protecting him, but he didn't want her to receive another harassing call. Not today. He watched as she answered and then paused to listen. She put a hand over the mouthpiece and handed the phone to him.

"It's Frank Campello. He wants to know if he can come over."

They sat at the circular breakfast table in the kitchen. Jenny had made a pot of coffee and set a package of cookies in front of them. Campello asked her to stay, telling her that he wanted her to hear everything, if it was OK with Andy.

"Bobby Longhorse wasn't after me," Campello said, sitting opposite Polanski and next to Jenny. "He was after you."

Polanski glanced at his wife. "How? He didn't know I would be there."

Campello lifted the cup. "Yes, he did." He drank the coffee. "It was a setup and you were the target."

"How?" he asked again.

Campello cast a sheepish glance at Jenny. "After you left, you received a phone call from a lead of mine. Except she wasn't asking for me, she was asking for you. I had just interviewed her, and when she left a message for you, offering to tell you everything she wouldn't tell me, I was angry. She told dispatch that she would be waiting for you at the complex."

"Who is it?" he asked.

"Juanita Delaney. She was the girlfriend of Hoppity T."

"Hoppity T?" Jenny asked him.

"It's a long story," Campello said to her, "but he is the man who killed my partner. I killed him and she testified on my behalf."

Jenny said, "Why would she do that? Isn't that a bit unusual?"

Campello drained his cup and then lifted the pot from the table where she had set it. He helped himself to more and reached for a cookie. "Yes. Very unusual."

Polanski was confused. "So why did she call me?"

"Who knows? All I know is that I came under fire almost as soon as I pulled into the lot." He bit into the cookie. "I knew as soon as I arrived that it didn't feel right. In fact, I think I probably knew this was a setup as soon as I got the message. But I let my anger get the better of me. I let my pride get in the way and I almost got killed because of it."

"Where is she now?" Andy asked.

Campello finished the cookie and swept the crumbs off the table and into his lap. "I don't know. I haven't had time to check. After my interview with the shooting team, I began to think. I didn't have time to talk to you because you were tied up with the team a lot longer than me. When I heard you'd left, I called." He reached for another cookie. "You had the squad car the other night when you talked with Peter Green, correct?"

"Yes."

"And you had it again when you went to Silk 'n Boots."

"Right."

"And I had it when I talked with Rita. I suspect that Green ordered a hit on you after you began asking questions at the club. Longhorse noted the car you were driving and he assumed you'd show when Juanita called to entice you to the location. The shooter had only to fire at whoever was in the car. They wanted you and were expecting you, but when I showed up in the Crown Vic, which was the car he was expecting you to be driving, it was a no-brainer for him."

"And since the shooter couldn't see who was driving, they assumed it was me."

"Yep." He drained the coffee. "When Longhorse was standing over me he had a confused look on his face. He had expected to see you, but when he saw me…"

Jenny's face fell. "Does this mean they'll try again?"

Campello shook his head. "I don't think so. They tried and missed. And Peter Green's not a player. He's not street-wise. This whole thing was amateurish on the face of it. He didn't plan it well. He'll retract and that'll give me time find out what's going on."

"*Us.* Time for *us* to find out what's going on," said Polanski.

"Take some time off, Andy," Campello said. "Sort out some things."

"I've wanted to go to my parents' cabin," Jenny said, looking hopefully at her husband. "This would be a good time to do it."

Polanski shook his head. "*Us.*"

"Okay, *us,*" Campello agreed. "I know we haven't gotten off on the right foot, Andy, and I don't agree with your actions against Caine and Dorchester. At best I think it's cowardly and traitorous and self-serving." He turned to Jenny. "I'm sorry. I don't mean to be so blunt but I don't know any other way." Then to Polanski, "But you came to my aid out there today and that says something."

"I'm no different now than I was when I saw those guys in the 31st covering up a crime."

Campello shook his head. "Sorry. I just don't see it that way. Cops stick together. Besides," he finished off the cookie, "I know those guys and I know their reputations."

"I know them too," Polanski said.

"We're not going to see eye to eye on this, Andy. Not ever. But for now, let's try to put our difference aside and go to work."

"I'd like that."

"How'd you get home today? I saw that your car was still in the lot when I left."

"They had a uniform drive me home. Something about post-traumatic stress. I feel fine. A little shaken, but otherwise I'm none the worse for wear."

"I'll pick you up tomorrow morning. We need to find out what's going on and who's involved in this."

Polanski agreed. "I'll be here. I have a few questions of my own."

CHAPTER 26

After the fragile truce had been formed with Polanski, Campello drove straight to Juanita's apartment. He had hopes that his visit with her would be more productive than the one he had earlier that morning, but he also held no illusions. If Juanita had indeed been the one who had called for Polanski, she would be long gone by now. On the other hand, if she had not been the one who telephoned in the message, she could be in serious trouble. Either way, he determined she would be the best link in building a case against Peter Green.

As he had before, he parked the car curbside. This car though, a tan unmarked squad, did not attract the admiring crowd that his personal car had. Instead, it attracted the penetrating stares that often came with driving a cop car, unmarked or otherwise, particularly when it was driven in this part of town. There was an almost inherent mistrust of the police among the residents who lived in the area, and that was especially true of the youths who seemed to have more time on their hands than they knew how to manage.

He left the car and went upstairs. After knocking on the door and receiving no answer, he loudly announced that he was a cop and declared his concern for the child. He knew that she had probably fled the area, but he wanted the neighbors in the adjoining apartments to hear his declaration if he was legally challenged on his forced entry.

He kicked in the door. Neither Juanita nor the baby was there, but that didn't mean they had left of their own free will. He began a search of the apartment. It appeared the baby's clothes had been taken and there was no baby food in the kitchen. Most likely, then, neither the baby nor Juanita had been harmed. But the missing clothing and food didn't help in determining if she was on the run, or in partnership with whoever arranged the setup.

He left the apartment and telephoned Lopez. After telling the district commander his theories on Juanita and that he had entered the apartment, he proceeded to Green's warehouse and distribution complex. Regardless of what Polanski had said to Longhorse, it was unlikely the DJ would have initiated the attack. Given that Polanski had pressed Peter, it made much more sense that it was Green who gave the order. Longhorse may have been the shooter, but he wasn't the shot caller.

Campello arrived at Green's warehouse and flashed his star to the receptionist. She asked him to have a seat and told him she would call up and have Peter come down.

"Actually, I'd prefer to go up. Where is he?"

She hesitated.

"Here or downtown, lady. I only need to talk to him, but I'd be happy to haul both of you in and do it there."

The woman's face hardened, but she relented, pointing to the bank of elevators behind her. "Second floor, third office on the left."

He smiled as endearingly as he could and thanked her, aware that by the time he stepped off the lift she would have already called ahead and notified Peter that he was coming.

He went directly to the office, walking through the door without knocking. Green was on the phone, undoubtedly with the woman downstairs. He hung up as soon as Campello entered.

"What can I do for you?"

Campello took a seat across from Peter without waiting to be asked. "Someone shot at me today."

"And what does that have to do with me?"

"Maybe everything. Maybe nothing." He glanced around the room. It was the office of a juvenile, the office of someone who played; it was not the office of an administrator for a large distribution center. "Rita's dead and you don't seem all that shook up about it."

"Rita was a friend. I am concerned, of course, but I have a business to run." He cocked his head. "Are you here because someone shot at you or because Rita is dead?"

"Where were you this morning?"

"Here."

The man was thin with wiry hair that was unkempt. He had a very slender build and sat with his legs crossed. His bouncing foot betrayed his nervousness.

"What time did you arrive?"

"To the office?"

"Yes." Green was stalling, trying to develop an alibi.

"Around eight. I drove from my condo directly here. You can check with my secretary if you'd like."

"The lady downstairs? The one who warned you I was coming?"

"What do you want from me, detective? You asked where I was this morning and I answered, and I even gave you a corroborating witness to question."

"And I will do that very thing. But first, I'd like to know if you're familiar with Juanita Delaney?"

"Who?"

"Delaney. She's the one who called this morning."

"I don't know her, detective. And if she called Polanski, I'm unaware of it."

Campello stood. He reached behind his back and extracted a pair of handcuffs from his belt. "Stand up. You're under arrest."

Peter recoiled. "Under arrest? For what?"

Campello grabbed the man with one hand and jerked him to his feet, spinning him around and cuffing his hands behind his back.

"You're under arrest for attempted murder."

"Attempted murder? Are you crazy?"

"Maybe. But even crazy cops don't like to be shot at."

CHAPTER 27

After searching Green and reading him his rights, Campello drove to the 28th and delivered the man to the booking officers. He promised to return and complete his portion of the paperwork before bounding upstairs to the squad room. A good portion of the detectives were still in the room, along with approximately fifty uniforms in riot gear. Most of those were congregated around the wall map, presumably planning strategy for that evening's riot control. Lopez was in his office and Campello marched back and sat in front of the commander's desk.

"Look, I know who he is and all, but he did it, Julio."

"You better be able to prove that, Frank."

"He told me he didn't know Juanita and that he had no knowledge of her having called Polanski."

"So?"

"I didn't tell him that she called Polanski. *I* took the lead, remember? How did he know she called Polanski if he didn't set it up?"

Lopez rested his feet on top of his desk and folded his hands behind his head. "Peter thought he was getting Andy, but got you instead."

Campello shot at Lopez with a thumb and forefinger. "Bingo. He didn't get the Cracker Jack prize he was expecting."

"That could explain a lot, Frank. I've been wondering why they would want to kill you. Not that I haven't thought of it myself."

Campello snorted. "Yeah, well, this guy had it in for Polanski because Polanski was knocking too close to home on the murder at

Navy Pier. Why else would Peter go after him?"

"Because he's a concerned citizen and resents Polanski's attack on two good cops?" Lopez grinned.

Campello shook his head at the dour attempt at humor. "No, I don't think so."

"You'll need more than you've got."

"I know. But at least I can hold him and keep him in place while I do some digging. He won't be out and about trying to kill anyone."

"Someone might. If you're right, Peter wasn't acting alone. There are others involved."

"Whatever he's doing, it's got a connection with the club."

"Speaking of which…" Lopez reached into one of the drawers and extracted a printout. He slid it across the desk.

"What's this?"

"It's a run-down on the club's employees and their arrest records. I've found an unusually high number of Hispanics working there."

"Illegals?"

Lopez shot him a knowing look. "Your murder victim was an illegal too, right?"

Campello nodded as he scanned the printout.

"You think this guy is preying on illegals?" Lopez asked.

"It's starting to look like that. What do you think?" He folded the printout and slipped it in the inside pocket of his jacket.

Lopez shook his head. "I don't know what to think. It certainly appears like the club is a racket. The employees there are hiding in the open and that gives Peter leverage over them. They set themselves up for that when they sneak across the border. Their need to make a living while remaining anonymous sets them up for every type of exploitation imaginable."

"I didn't see any prostitution arrests on the sheet. Isn't that a bit unusual?"

"I saw that too," Lopez said. "Not unheard of, but unusual for a place like that. Most of the money the girls make in a place like Silk 'n Boots comes under the table. Selling sex, drugs… it's part of their world."

"Peter is doing something and my first thought was prostitution. Now I'm not so sure."

"Keep the prostitution thing in your mind. He may be running it under the radar, but let's focus on the murder."

Campello had known Lopez for a long time. Both had started on the department as patrolman in the 31st and there was less than a year's difference in their length of service. And although Lopez seemed supportive of his efforts against Green, he was also doing something he'd never done before. Advising one of his men to take it easy.

"I *am* focused on the murder, Julio. And as much as I don't like the guy, so is Polanski. Our efforts almost got us killed. But there are some threads here that extend beyond the girl's murder and I'm following up on them. They could be Peter's motive."

"Follow up on them, but don't make them the focus of your investigation. A girl was murdered. Find the evidence for that and we'll charge Peter if he did it. In the meantime, we'll hold him on suspicion for the attack against Polanski… or you, whatever the case may be."

"He's behind the attack, Julio," Campello said.

"You have a suspicion, Frank, but you don't have the evidence to hold him. Find the evidence that connects him to your suspicion and we'll charge him. But keep Trina's murder foremost."

Lopez's demeanor had changed. The Greens were a powerful family in Chicago and as a result, wielded a great deal of influence. But that had never stopped Lopez from going after someone before.

"You OK, Julio?"

"I'm fine, Frank. Just find me evidence that'll stand up in court and find it quick. I don't have to remind you of who Peter's father is and the effect a false-arrest suit will have on all of us."

Campello rose from the chair and stood in the open doorway. "I don't care about a false-arrest suit, Julio. Peter's good for it and you know it."

CHAPTER 28

Campello went downstairs to the holding area where Longhorse was being processed in preparation for his transfer to the Cook County Jail. Campello's pistol had been returned, so he left it with the officer in charge of the detention area and waited in an interrogation room. As soon as Longhorse was delivered, he was sat at the table while his right hand was shackled to a ring embedded in the concrete-block wall. The delivering officer asked Campello if he needed anything else. Campello shook his head, keeping his eyes focused on Longhorse.

"You want anything, Bobby?" Campello was pleasant, concerned. "Soft drink? Coffee?"

The man rubbed his shackled wrist with the other hand. "Coffee would be nice."

"How do you take it?"

"Crème. Two sugars."

The uniformed officer left the room to get the coffee and Campello stood beside the door opposite the DJ, leaning against the wall with both hands in his pockets.

"You're in a bit of a fix, Bobby."

He snorted with a lopsided grin. "I've been in them before. I'll be in them again."

"This is a little different, Bobby. You tried to kill two police officers. That's going to carry some time with it. And the lab is going over the crime scene. There's enough there to put you away for a very long time."

Longhorse said nothing.

The door opened and the officer brought the coffee into the room. He sat the cup on the table, along with a packet of non-dairy creamer, two packets of sugar, and a stir. As he left, he told Campello to call if he had a problem.

Longhorse stirred the coffee.

"Who sent you after Polanski?"

"Who said anyone did?"

"Come on, Bobby. You didn't just decide to go after him with an automatic rifle for no reason."

Longhorse sipped the coffee. "Maybe I don't like cops."

Campello laughed. "No, I think you were put up to it and now you're going to take the hit for someone else's idea." He moved to the table, resting both hands on its steel top. "Did Peter Green put you up to this?"

Longhorse chuckled.

"Did Green kill the girl at Navy Pier?"

"Ask him."

"I'm asking you."

"I don't know nothing about no girl at Navy Pier."

"How about Rita Chavez?"

He ignored the question.

"I know you knew her. She was Peter's girlfriend and now she's dead. And guess what? All roads lead to Silk 'n Boots. That means all roads lead to you. Did you kill Rita?"

His eyes riveted on Campello. "I didn't kill nobody."

Campello put both hands in his pockets. "Not for lack of trying. You shot at me today. You shot at my partner. You have a killer's heart, Bobby. So it doesn't make any difference if we put you away for one or three, so long as we put you away."

Longhorse brooded over the coffee, ignoring Campello.

"I've read your sheet, Bobby. You've been a bad boy since the get go. Three counts of truancy followed by two counts of vandalism. Then there was the burglary charge. You did time for that one. And then you weren't out two months before you're back in for armed robbery and assault." He paused for a reaction but got none. "That old lady must've put up a fight, huh? I'll bet she held onto the purse like an old skinflint. But you showed her, didn't you? Slashed her with a knife and then beat her to a pulp. But you got the purse, yes sir. You're a real man, Bobby. Nine dollars fourteen cents and a three-dollar disposable watch. You showed her. That old broad laid in intensive care for six months. She won't resist you again. No, sir. She knows you mean business when you're bagging an old lady."

"Shut up!"

"You did time for that one too, didn't you? Of course, going after a man who'll fight back is an entirely different story. You only do that when you can shoot from a distance. Men will fight back. They won't let you take their purse." Campello chuckled. "And then there was the gig at Silk 'n Boots. You were doing OK, but I'll bet the dancers there couldn't stand you." He lowered his voice. "That means they turned you down, Bobby. They don't want a wimp like you. Not those girls. They're used to seeing men come in and out all day. They're not going to be stuck with a washed-up ex-con who beats old ladies senseless for the coins in their purse. So you decided you're going to make an impression. Show these girls you *can* be a man. And now you're up for attempted murder on two police officers, not to mention all kinds of weapons violations. You see, you aren't supposed to have a gun, Bobby. Not being an ex-con and all. And automatic weapons are a special no-no." Campello leaned on the table again, inches from Longhorse's face. "And I think you killed that girl at the pier – Trina."

"You're crazy."

"What happened, Bobby? Did she spurn you like all the other women you approach? Is that what happened? And then you decided to hit on Rita, only she told you no too, and then threatened to tell Peter, so you had to kill her too?"

Longhorse nursed the coffee, keeping his eyes fixated on the tabletop.

"And here's the thing, Bobby. Whether you own up to it or not, you won't be safe anywhere. Not even in jail. You hear me, Bobby? Someone's going to get to you, even in here."

The DJ set the cup on the table. "I want my lawyer, cop."

Campello pulled away from the table. "I'll get you one. But you won't need him for long. You're a dead man, Bobby."

CHAPTER 29

Word of the shooting reached Christy by way of the newsroom while she was across town interviewing Alderman Aaron Green. She had asked the penetrating questions for which she was known, but had received the generic prescriptive answers for which he was known. Green made it clear he was pro-police; made it clear the department would do all that was necessary to protect the citizenry and property of Chicago. Each time he answered, his voice rose and his gestures were pronounced. Like the blowhard bag of wind from which the Windy City had derived its name, the alderman played the concerned politician to perfection. The interview had been a waste of time, so she excused herself as soon as she was told about the shooting. By the time she made it to the location, only a few officers and lab techs remained, none of them willing to provide useful information. She knew there would also be no point in going to the 28th. All she would receive there would be the traditional press release which was even less useful than a press conference.

She called her source within the department, knowing he was becoming increasingly uncomfortable with their arrangement. Like most deep throats, he showed signs of unease with the press. It gave him no joy to see information she'd picked up from him one day appear in print the next. From where he stood, their relationship was a one-way street. Still, if he got nothing else from Christy, she gave him an opportunity to strike at the bureaucracy he hated and a chance to covertly right the wrongs he had seen. But she held no illusions and knew the relationship was doomed to end. They all did, sooner or later.

"What happened today?"

"The shooting?"

"Yes."

"Someone got shot at." He was deliberately being coy.

"I heard Polanski was involved."

The hesitation was protracted and then ended with a long deliberate sigh. "Yes."

"Was someone within the department gunning for him?"

Another hesitation. "I don't think so," he said. "But someone was and they mistakenly went after his partner."

"But who else would want him dead? If it wasn't someone within the 28th, it would almost have to have come from the 31st. Right?"

"Maybe. Or it could be the case he's working."

"Oh, come on. When has that ever happened? You told me yourself that he was working the murder of a transient. Is that enough to kill for?"

This time the hesitation was longer, more deliberate. Christy knew that she would lose him if she pulled too hard. Like reeling in a large fish, she would have to show finesse if she wanted to keep him on the line.

"OK," she said. "I'll figure that part out for myself. Just answer me this. *Could* it have been someone within the department?"

"No."

"How can you be so sure?"

"Because he's still alive."

He was not forthcoming for the remainder of the call and she decided that going directly to Polanski would offer an opportunity for information she couldn't get elsewhere. But it wouldn't be easy. Any attempts at interviewing him in the office, particularly after a police-action shooting, would be a waste of time. There'd be a rigorous interview with the department's shooting team and FOP attorneys would be all over the situation, making any chance of getting a formal statement from him as impossible as getting one from the President. She wanted to know what happened and she had an intuition that there was more to the story than a few simple questions on a television news program could reveal. Finding the facts and unearthing the true story from them was a print journalist's strength, and she intended to exercise it as much as possible.

After a quick dinner at McDonald's, she arrived at the Polanski residence in her battered Corolla. Night was falling and lamplight shone from the windows. The house looked as tranquil as the others on the street, but that was an illusion. Peace could not be found in a house where the family was under as much fire as this one.

Christy hesitated before getting out of the car, uncomfortable about disturbing Polanski at home, yet determined to uncover the detective's story.

She ran across the street and along the sidewalk to the front door. The yard was well maintained, and yellow forsythia bushes bloomed along each side of the door.

She rang the bell and waited. After a few seconds, a young girl with blonde hair and thick glasses opened the door.

"Hi," Christy said, smiling broadly. "Is your daddy at home?"

The glasses had begun to slide down the girl's nose under their own weight and she pushed them into place with the back of her hand. "Do you want to talk to him?"

"Could I?"

The girl nodded enthusiastically. "Sure." She stepped aside, allowing Christy to enter. "I'll be right back."

The house was simply but tastefully decorated in early American décor with a homey feel. When she was a girl, Christy had imagined living in such a house one day. She had grown up in a home where dysfunction *was* function, and often used her imagination as a means of escape.

"Ms. Lee?"

Polanski was standing on the stairs, his hand resting on the balustrade.

"Detective," she said, hearing an apologetic tone in the word, "how are you?"

He descended the stairs one deliberate step at a time. "What are you doing here?"

"I've come to talk to you."

"I thought I made it clear at the pier the other day that I have no interest in talking to you."

She caught herself ringing her hands. For the first time in her professional life, she was nervous. She had invaded the man's home and she was ashamed. But she persisted and stood her ground. "I think you should. It's in your best interest."

"And you can decide that for me, Ms. Lee? You can say what is best for me and my family?"

"I've been doing this a long time, detective. I know the CPD, and I know that like any other police department, they don't hold well to traitors." She winced at the word. "Sorry. I don't mean to sound so judgmental, but that is how you are viewed by the department. I don't think I need to tell you that."

He stepped off the bottom step and was standing less than a foot in front of her. "And that's news?"

"Getting shot at is, don't you think?"

He stood motionless, studying her with that hardened cop-stare she had come to despise. But then, much to her surprise, it softened, and he said, "If I talk to you now, will you leave me and my family alone?"

"If you answer all of my questions and if you—"

"No. This is the one and only time. You agree to this, or I'll toss your butt out of here."

Deciding that one conversation was better than none, she agreed.

She sat at a circular dining-table with Polanski and his wife. He insisted that Jenny be present because she was his wife and very much a part of his life and the decisions he made. He agreed to no ground rules with the exception that the session not be taped. Christy agreed and opened her pad.

"How has this been for you?"

"The trial or the shooting?"

"The trial."

"It's been hard. I'm ostracized, isolated." He put a hand on his wife's. "Jenny is receiving harassing phone calls while I'm away and that's been hard on her."

"And the kids?"

He shook his head. "Some teasing at school, but nothing beyond that. If there were, I'd have to take action. I think they know that. They don't want confrontation. They just want me out."

"They?"

He shrugged. "Whoever in the department is behind this."

"How do you feel about Campello?"

Polanski sighed, looking off into the distance. "He's a good cop. I don't agree with his stance on this thing with Caine and Dorchester, but I think beneath all the…" he hesitated as though searching for the right word, "*stuff*, he's a decent man."

"Why don't you just leave?"

"My reasons are my own."

She was aware of his father and the stigma he had forced on his son, but she decided not to raise that issue and risk alienating him while he was being congenial.

"Do you think someone was gunning for you today?"

"It's possible."

"My sources within the department thinks it's likely," she lied.

"Who is your source?"

She shook her head. "Sorry, but I think you know I can't divulge that. You're in danger, detective."

"Yes."

"Doesn't that frighten you? At the very least, concern you?"

"I took an oath, Ms. Lee. I swore to uphold the law, regardless of the consequences to me or anyone else."

"Is the law more important to you than anything?" His wife had been silent throughout the interview and Christy glanced at her in a very broad and deliberate manner.

"No, there are things that outweigh my devotion to the law. My devotion to Christ, for example."

His answer caught Christy by surprise, causing her to shift

uncomfortably in her chair.

"The law comes from God and applies to all of us. It helps give us a sense of order. Without it, everyone can go his own way, and where would that leave us?"

His question was not rhetorical. She had no answer to give.

"If the police won't stand for what is right, who will? And you're wrong in your view of the department, Ms. Lee. There are a lot of good men and women who will stand up and be counted. Unfortunately, they're overshadowed in the media by the ones who won't."

"The media didn't create this controversy, detective."

"Maybe, maybe not. But the media will spin things for ratings, and then everyone pays."

"So you're going forward with your testimony against Caine and Dorchester."

He nodded. "I am."

"Alone? Are you prepared for that?"

"If I have to. But I think when the facts come out, I will not stand alone. I have faith in my brothers and sisters in blue, Ms. Lee."

CHAPTER 30

Campello smiled, glad to see the television set off in his father's room. Even with his advanced dementia, he might recognize events on the news, particularly if they involved his son, and would be needlessly upset by the callousness of a media whose only concern was getting one notch ahead of the competition. Nevertheless, the TV couldn't remain off indefinitely. Campello would have to tell him. His father may not remember it, of course, but it would lessen the chance of the surprise and shock that would come with a news report.

He sat on the edge of the bed, next to his father who sat in his Gerry chair, and handed the old man another bag of chocolate-covered raisins. He took the bag without comment and immediately opened it.

"Oh, good. It's been a long time since I had any of these." He fished one of the treats from the bag and popped it into his mouth.

"You want to take a walk, Dad?"

The old man nodded and Campello helped him to stand. Still clutching the bag of candy, the old man held tightly to his son as they left the room.

He had not wanted to place his father in a long-term care facility, but as his dementia became increasingly problematic, Campello was left with no other viable choice. Fortunately, this facility, so conveniently close to home and work, gave care as good as any within his budget.

The old man shuffled along the hallway, taking pains with each step. Several residents already in the room reclined in chairs with their feet elevated, while others sat around the various tables assembling puzzles, playing games, or idly staring into space. The television had not been turned on in this room either, but that wasn't particularly unusual. Most of the residents preferred to sleep, talk with the others, or pursue quieter activities.

"Here, Dad, let's have a seat." He led the old man to a row of chairs that stood under a print of Warner Sallman's *Christ at Heart's Door*. The old man sat, lowering himself into the seat, gripping onto his son with both hands. He clutched the bag of raisins.

Campello watched the old man slide another raisin into his mouth. The chocolate coating ran along his chin.

"Here, Dad. Let me get that." He dabbed at the old man's chin with a handkerchief.

His father neither protested nor acknowledged the gesture. Instead, he reached for another raisin.

"Dad, I've got something to tell you."

The old man looked at him with eyes that were veiled; windows to the soul no longer. "Is it about your mother?"

He shook his head. "No, it's about me."

"Who are you?"

This would be a good day for telling him about the shooting. It would not be a good day tomorrow if he couldn't recall and heard it for the first time.

"I'm Frank, Dad. I'm your son."

The old man gently reared back from him. "My son?"

"Yes, Dad."

"Oh."

"Dad, I was in a shooting today, but I'm alright."

"OK." He slipped another raisin into his mouth.

"I just wanted you to know."

The old man sucked noisily on the raisin.

"My partner backed me up." He could hear the surprise in his voice.

"He's supposed to. That's what partners are for."

Lucidity, a valuable commodity for families afflicted by dementia, even if it didn't come as easily as it went.

"We got the guy."

"Good."

"It was an ambush, Dad."

The old man shook his head as he fished for another raisin. "That's not good."

Campello was unable to suppress a grin. "No. It's not." He shifted in the chair, leaning slightly forward, and began working his hands between his knees. "I was afraid, Dad."

"Good cops don't get scared."

"Maybe I'm not a good cop. I was scared."

The old man closed the bag of raisins and set them on his lap. He said nothing, but sat quietly as if waiting for his son to drop the other shoe.

"It's the second time in a month. The first time happened so fast, it was over in a minute. But this one," he shook his head, "this one seemed to go on forever."

"Where was your partner?" The old man grew more lucid.

"He came just in time." He looked at his father. "And you know what, Dad? He wasn't afraid. It was like he didn't care if he lived or died. He just… pitched right in and subdued the shooter."

"That's what partners are for."

"He's a turncoat, a traitor, and yet he saved my life."

"He's a good traitor."

Campello grinned and looked at the old man. "I didn't think there was any such thing."

"There isn't." He waggled his finger. "But this time, he was good." He glanced nervously about the room. "We better get home. Your mother is going to be mad if we're late for dinner again."

The old man had been swimming above the water, but was beginning to slip beneath the surface again.

"It was good to see you, Dad."

CHAPTER 31

Christy arrived back at the newsroom late. The cleanup crew was busy emptying trash cans and mopping the tiled floor. Ted Flynn was still at his desk, typing furiously. He glanced up as she entered, a look of dismay on his face.

"Demille wants you," he said.

"Is he happy?" she asked, dropping her purse on the desk.

He leaned back in his chair and looked her up and down. "You look rough, kid, and that's saying something. You never look rough."

She glanced toward the editor's office where Clarence Demille sat with his sleeves rolled up, talking on the phone and glaring at her through the open door.

"Who's he talking to?" she asked.

Flynn glanced over his shoulder to the editor's office. "Now how am I supposed to know that? Listen, I wouldn't go in there. That piece on the riots was due an hour ago. He had me write it up and that ain't kosher. He's mad. If I was you, I'd go on home and deal with it——"

She marched toward Demille's office, ignoring her desk-mate's advice.

"Hey, you listening to me?" Flynn called.

"Always."

She knocked on the open door-frame out of a sense of propriety. Demille pointed to a chair beside his desk.

"Yeah, I know," he said into the phone, watching as she sat. "And I don't care. This thing is a shame on the city and this is a town that's had more than its share of that." He rolled his eyes, taking them off her for the first time since she'd returned to the office.

She crossed her legs, hoping they would put the man in a better frame of mind when he tore into her. Missing deadlines wasn't something he took lightly. It was an irresponsible action and required a major shift of manpower.

"Listen," he said in the phone, "one of my do-nothing reporters just came in. I'll get back with you." He paused. "Yeah. I'm going to be here all night, apparently, so I'll call you back." He nodded his head. "Right. Talk to you then." He hung up.

"Listen, Clarence, I—"

"Don't, Christy." He massaged his forehead with the fingers of one hand. "I waited as long as I could. I gave the story to Flynn."

"I know and I'm sorry. But—"

"But what, Christy? Is this where you tell me that your nose for news supersedes your obligation to follow orders? Or that I should give you free rein because I was your professor in journalism school and I know what a free spirit you are?"

She fidgeted with her watch band and gave him a sheepish grin. "I—"

"Or do you tell me that the real story isn't the riots or the millions of dollars in damage? No, wait, let me guess, the true story is the rogue cop who is testifying on two other cops that we reported about several weeks ago and that no other media outlet in this city still considers news. Is that what you were going to say?"

"This guy is an enigma, Clarence. He's either the most honest cop in America or he's as dirty as the rest of them and he's trying to cover his tracks."

He groaned and tossed her a telephone message pad. "Take a look at that."

She pulled it off the desk and read it.

"There were two uprisings in the suburbs last night," he said, pacing the room. "Elk Grove Village. Arlington Heights. A car overturned, businesses looted, a truck driven through a convenience mart."

"Clarence, I—"

He waved her off. "Don't, Christy. Don't even go there." He sighed and lowered his voice, leaning over her, fixing his eyes on her. "I thought you were the best student I ever had. Your ability to see things as they were and then root out the story from the fluff was some of the best natural talent I've ever seen, and I've done this job for forty years. But your prejudices are blinding you. I gave you the city beat over other, more seasoned reporters because I thought… no, I *knew* you could handle it. They had the connections and the clout to ferret out the facts, but you had the nose," he tapped his nose with his index finger, "and that's something I can't buy. I can easily find someone who's connected. But natural talent like yours…" He waved her off in disgust and resumed pacing the room.

"If you think I have this talent, why aren't you supporting me?"

He tapped the message pad that was still in her hand. "Because you're not using it. You're tossing everything to the wind because of your anger with the cops. It distorts everything you do, Christy. You're looking at the world through colored lenses and it's keeping you from seeing the truth."

"Clarence, I interviewed Polanski at his home last night."

"So what?" His voice was loud, shrill. The cleaning crew began looking toward his office. "While you were talking to him, the city burned. You and Nero have something in common."

"That's not fair."

"None of this is fair, darling. It isn't fair that God blessed you with ability and left someone like…" he turned toward the news room, searching for a suitable foil, "like… Ted Flynn with nothing. That guy couldn't report on his own feet and get it right. But he *works*. He takes instruction. He follows through." He leaned across the corner of his desk until he was within inches of her face. "He follows orders."

She massaged the fatigue from her eyes. "OK, Clarence. What do you want me to do?"

He glanced at his watch. "I want you to be on the street tonight, in the middle of the mayhem, getting some solid man-on-the-street stories. Our readers need to *feel*," he clenched his fist, emphasizing his point, "how these riots are affecting the average people."

"And what about Polanski?"

"What about him?"

"Nothing, I guess." She stood. "Anything else?"

"Be safe. You aren't high on the list with the cops. If you get in a jam, you'll be the last person they'll want to save."

CHAPTER 32

Riots erupted again later that evening in the corridor served by the officers of the 31st, with an arson surfacing for the first time. Several buildings were torched, the fire racing through the block. Firefighters were unable to access the nearest hydrants because of illegally parked cars and had to move farther down the street. The delay cost them time which led to significant damage to the businesses in the area and to the local community. Early estimates put the cost in millions of dollars. One citizen was severely burned and another had to be treated for smoke inhalation. Four officers were seriously hurt in the melee, and dozens of arrests were made. The CPD turned out in force, in numbers larger than since the unrest began, but still they could not seem to gain the upper hand. Aaron Green deplored the uprisings in a brief press conference the following morning, saying he would meet with departmental and civic leaders in the afternoon in an attempt to hammer out a solution. That was the public face of it. The private one looked very different.

He arranged an emergency meeting with Bureau of Detectives Chief Roger Hanroty and Deputy Superintendent Franklin Mayron. In his years as an alderman, Aaron Green had been privy to the career rise of many in the department's senior management and had often lent a helpful hand to many of them as well. His long involvement in the CPD had given him a knowledge base that exceeded that of most of the department's leadership. He knew where the skeletons were hidden, along with the interpersonal rivalries and jealousies that often arise when a group of ambitious and highly motivated people are thrown together. It was no secret to anyone, though, that Hanroty and Mayron despised each other and had come to an uneasy truce many years ago. Aaron's awareness of their rivalry gave him power, which is coin in the bank to a politician.

He met with them to discuss tactics on controlling the uprising. They had nothing to offer not already being done, and he feigned interest in their discussion while lauding their efforts. But Peter had been arrested, and Aaron's chief goal in asking for the meeting was to chide the brass on arresting his son and get all charges dropped. An attorney in his own right, the alderman had reviewed the evidence against his son and determined it was virtually non-existent. But his primary impetus in getting the charges dropped had come from Paulie Vincent and Anthony Delgado. Their mutual business interests would not tolerate Peter's persistent screw-ups. Although Aaron was an alderman, the *power* was wielded by Vincent.

During his discussion with Hanroty and Mayron, Aaron learned that the shooter in the attack on Polanski had also attacked Polanski's partner, Frank Campello. The detectives believed the man was hired for the task, and were looking hard at Peter. But when Aaron learned that Longhorse was denying all allegations and was refusing to implicate Peter, the alderman insisted that the departmental chiefs release his son, pending any additional charges. Mayron voiced his view that Peter should remain incarcerated, at least for forty-eight hours, but Hanroty, true to form, went against Mayron's position. Although Mayron outranked Hanroty, he didn't outrank Aaron Green, and the alderman used the division between the two men to secure the release of his son. Since no charges had been filed, none were required to be dropped and Peter was released.

By the time Aaron returned to his office, Peter was waiting.
"Hi, Dad."
Aaron set his briefcase on the desk and then slapped his son with all the force he could muster. Peter recoiled, with his hand to his face

and shock in his eyes.

"You are destroying everything I've managed to build!"

"I'm not doing—"

"Shut up! I'm tired of your excuses. Sick of playing nursemaid to you. When are you going to grow up, Peter?"

He lowered his hand. "I did grow up, Dad. Or haven't you been home two nights in a row often enough to tell?"

Aaron struck Peter again, harder, driving him against the wall. "Everything I've done has been for you! The late-night meetings, the years spent building the business, the times I've gotten into the sewer and played politics… it's all been for you." He seized his son by the lapels and shoved him onto the sofa. "Did you stage an ambush against that cop?"

"No."

"Don't lie to me, boy! I'm fighting a powerful impulse to hand you over to them."

"I'm not lying!"

"What about that girl at the pier?"

"What? I haven't killed anyone! You can ask Tony."

Aaron leaned to within a few inches of his son's face. "I did ask him. And you know what? He thinks you probably did it."

Peter shifted on the sofa to distance himself from Aaron. "I can't help what he thinks, can I?"

"Did you do it, boy? Did you?"

"I've already said no. What else can I say?"

His son's ability to lie with a straight face had always troubled Aaron.

"Why do the police think you did?"

"I don't know. Why don't you ask them?"

The flippant answer angered him and he drew back to strike his son again, but stopped when Peter withdrew into a fetal position with his hands covering his head.

Aaron cursed and withdrew his hand. He bolted off the sofa to fix a scotch and soda. Carrying it back, he dropped himself next to Peter.

"I've got Raoul on it."

"What does he say?"

He lifted the drink. "I haven't talked to him yet." He sipped the scotch and soda. "But I will."

"I didn't do anything."

"The police think you've got something going on at the club."

"I don't."

"They say the girl who was found at the pier had ties to the club. And then there's Rita."

"Dad, Rita was a sick girl. She had a lot of problems. I can't be responsible for anyone other than myself."

"That's the problem, Peter. You've never been responsible for yourself." He swirled the glass and then drank. His initial anger began to subside, disappointment settling in its place.

"I am responsible, Dad. I run the warehouse and it—"

"*Tony* runs the warehouse. *I* run the warehouse. You talk on the phone and occasionally sign things."

"That's not fair."

"Fair's got nothing to do with it." He set the glass down on a table beside the sofa and began using his left hand to count off the fingers of his right. "You flunked out of Harvard. You failed at Princeton. You got thrown out of U of C, and you are incapable of living on your own without an allowance and my help." He sighed and rested his hands on his knees. "You're thirty years old, Peter. When are you going to step up to the plate?"

"Mom—"

"Your mother is gone. It's just you and me, Peter, and I won't live forever. What will you do then? Where will you go?"

"I have the warehouse, the club, my—"

"The warehouse will go to Delgado and Vincent and you know that. And the club. When was the last time it made any money?"

"It makes money."

"How, Peter? Booze and lap dances? Without the money I pump into the place it would be closed already."

"The club makes money, Dad. It always has. I'm a better

manager than you think." He began to cry. "I can do things. I'm not like you say."

Aaron softened, as he always did, and cursed himself for it. He put his arms around his son and held him close.

CHAPTER 33

Wednesday
7:30 a.m.

Campello arrived at Polanski's house in the tan Crown Victoria. He had two large coffees and offered one to Polanski as the detective slid into the passenger's seat.

"I don't know how you take your coffee," he said, "so I got some creamer and sugar. They're in the glove box."

"Black is fine." He buckled the harness and took the coffee from Campello who brought him up to speed on the way to the station about his interrogation of the DJ the previous night.

"He didn't act alone," Polanski said.

"Agreed."

"And I think you're right. I think he was gunning for me."

"Which means you're rattling something somewhere."

"The only person of importance I've approached was Peter. I came right out and asked him if he killed Trina."

"He denied it, of course."

"How'd you guess?" Polanski drank the coffee and watched as the cityscape passed by his window.

"Longhorse has lawyered up, but I thought it'd be a good idea if you took a pass at him. See what you can get," Campello said.

"Absolutely. By the way, just so you know, Christy Lee came by last night."

Campello looked sideway at his partner. "What did she want?"

"She heard about the shooting, but was mostly digging about the trial."

"What did you tell her?"

"Nothing."

"That broad doesn't quit."

Polanski shook his head. "No, she sure doesn't."

They rode in silence for the remainder of the trip and when Campello turned into the Castle's segregated lot, he was aware of his colleagues' scrutiny as he chauffeured Polanski to work.

Campello was stunned. "Peter Green walked? How could you do that?"

"Uh, lack of evidence?" Lopez said.

"He arranged the hit on Polanski, Julio, and you know it. He even said as much. Just one day, and I could have gotten all you needed."

"It doesn't matter, Frank," Lopez said. "The prosecutor declined to pursue charges." They were sitting at a table in the break room, down the hall from the squad room. After opening a packet of sugar, Lopez opened several drawers in search of a coffee stir. Finding none, he found a casing knife in the strainer alongside the sink and used that. He tossed it in the sink when he was done.

Campello said, "I wanted to get him behind bars before he took off or made another attempt." He watched as the commander drank from the cup while keeping his eyes focused on him over the rim.

"Frank, we want the person who killed Trina."

"We had the person who killed Trina and you let him go. As soon as Andy began focusing on Peter the ambush happened. Doesn't that tell you something?"

"*Andy*? Not *Polanski*? Not '*that guy*' or '*the turncoat*'? So you guys are best buds all of a sudden?"

They sat at a table.

"Suppose I get the evidence I need on this guy?" Campello asked, ignoring Lopez's remarks. "Are you going to keep him in house if I arrest him again?"

"First of all, Frank, I'm not the one who let him walk. The prosecutor makes those calls. And, yes. If you get some evidence that we can hold him on, I will keep him if the prosecutor will let me.

That's how it works, buddy."

"OK." He stood to leave.

"Where you going?"

"Andy is interrogating Longhorse. He'll crack, Julio. Give us a little rope and he'll crack."

"I didn't ask where Polanski is. I want to know where you're headed."

"To get the evidence we need."

The blue CPD tag was in place on Juanita's door. She still wasn't home and that concerned Campello.

It would be pointless to tangle with Peter again until something more concrete turned up. Longhorse was the best lead, but if he didn't talk, there was another lead that might.

He drove to the address of the only functioning cell phone found on the list from Rita's computer. The newer squad was in much better condition than the previous one, and skirted through the morning traffic. He was beginning to wonder why he hadn't had the car previously and what that said about his standing with the brass.

He drove north along LaSalle, past his own apartment and toward the uptown area of Chicago. When he reached the apartment, he circled the block a few times, looking for a place to park, before finding one curbside, two blocks away.

Campello got out of the car and glanced around. Brownstones dotted the tree-lined street along with a smattering of older, well-maintained homes. Cars were parked along the curb and a large number of local residents filled the street, carrying grocery bags, retrieving their morning papers or simply engaged in conversation. The neighborhood was entrenched with longtime residents, people who knew each other well. They shopped at the local grocery, sent their kids to the same schools, and worshipped in the same church. It was the kind of place in which everyone should live.

He climbed the steps to the first-floor residence. He knocked and a young Hispanic woman opened the door. She had short hair with a smooth complexion and wore hoop earrings, a tight-fitting orange

T-shirt and jeans.

He showed his star, eliciting a heavy sigh from the woman.

"Are you the one who's been calling me?" she asked.

"I don't know. What number has been calling you?" He flipped the badge-case closed and slid it into the inside pocket of his jacket, glancing over her shoulder into the apartment.

She gave him the district's number and then glanced over her shoulder, tracing his gaze.

"There's no one else here, detective," she said. "And you are the cop who's been calling me, aren't you?"

"I think so. It sure sounds like you have the right number."

"What do you want?"

"I want to talk to you about Trina Martinez."

"Why?"

"Can I come in?"

She hesitated, but then stepped aside, allowing him to enter.

Like Rita's, the apartment was small, clean, and expensively furnished. Off-white walls bounced light around the room and the place had a light, airy feel. She had a collection of oriental dolls along one wall, and photos that Campello assumed were her parents and siblings on another. He recognized some of the artwork as pricey originals and classical music played from a Bose stereo that sat next to a rack holding a large number of CDs.

"Mozart?" he asked, taking a stab.

"Paganini," she said, clearly amused.

"I'm a Beach Boys kind of guy."

"Why are you asking about Trina, detective?"

They were both standing. He by the door, she with her hands on her hips.

"Trina's dead."

"What?"

He told her about the girl's death, the murder, and the subsequent investigation. He did not tell her about the DJ or his suspicion that Peter Green was somehow involved.

"There's more," he said.

"More?"

"Rita Chavez is dead too."

Tears filled the girl's eyes immediately and she dropped onto the couch with her hand to her mouth. He sat next to her.

"You know something, Gloria. You've got to tell me what you know."

"I can't." All pretenses were gone; all bravado had been cast aside.

"Trina and now Rita… something is happening and it's tied to the club."

"When did Rita die?"

He told her the circumstances and how he found her name in Rita's computer, about Juanita's disappearance. "What's going on, Gloria?"

"They're leaving. He's rolling it up."

"Who's rolling what up?"

"Peter. He's closing everything down." She dabbed at her eyes with the tail of her shirt. "What do I do now?"

"What's he rolling up? What's he closing down?"

"The sex shop. He runs a sex shop where the girls are forced to perform in exchange for protection."

"Protection from who?" he asked.

"From you."

CHAPTER 34

Polanski sat with his back to the wall and his chair tilted on its rear legs. His eyes were focused on Longhorse who sat next to his attorney, a court-appointed shyster named Denton Kirkpatrick.

"So how about it, Bobby?"

"I don't know, man. I just don't know."

"You help us and we help you. Your lawyer will tell you it's a pretty good deal."

"My client will want everything in writing." The attorney, a man who looked to be in his late twenties with thinning hair and horn-rimmed glasses, alternated his gaze between Polanski and his client. He had been very quiet, staying out of most of the discussion between the detective and his suspect.

"Sure," Polanski said, uncertain whether Lopez would go along with the offer. "I'll get it in writing. But first, I need to know if your client has anything that's worth my time. And then I need to know if he's willing to come through. Once I leave this room, all negotiations are over and I withdraw the offer." He studied Longhorse for a reaction, but saw none.

"Just a minute, detective," Kirkpatrick said. "I want to speak with my client."

Polanski stood from the chair and slid it toward the table. "I'll be just outside the room. Technically, Bobby, we won't consider that leaving the room. But your time is running out."

He went into the hallway, coffee in hand, watching as others moving about the area worked hard to avoid noticing he was there.

Although the ice had broken with Campello, Polanski held no illusion that it would thaw anywhere else soon. Most still considered him a pariah. Nothing short of a major event was going to change that.

He drained the coffee, tossing the cup into the nearest receptacle. A rap on the inside of the door told him the attorney was ready to discuss terms and Polanski waited while the attending officer inserted the key, allowing him back into the room. He took his previous seat.

"My client will answer your questions in exchange for a reduced sentence and isolation while awaiting trial."

"I can't promise the reduced sentence, counselor, but I can speak to the state's attorney and recommend it. As for the isolation, I can pretty much guarantee his safety."

Kirkpatrick looked at the DJ and nodded.

"OK," Longhorse said. "What do you want to know?"

"Who hired you to attack me?"

"Peter Green."

"Why?"

"He runs an escort service. You were getting too close."

"He was willing to kill me because he runs an escort service? Are you kidding me?"

Longhorse shook his head. "No. Not because of that alone, but because you were closing in on him." He leaned forward and lowered his voice as though he were relating the greatest secret in the world. "He killed that girl, man."

"Trina?"

"Yeah. The one at the pier."

"What about Rita?"

He shook his head. "I don't know nothing about her. Nothing at all."

"Tell me about Trina."

"We was on the boat, *his* boat, and we were all having a nice time. I was spinning and the girls was dancing and everybody was drinking and having a marvelous time. Then Peter starts hitting on this chick."

"Trina?"

He nodded. "Yeah, Trina. He just starts really coming on to her, you know? And she doesn't want it. But he just wouldn't give up. And I don't understand that, 'cause he can have any woman he wants. The guy's loaded. Babes are coming on to him all the time, you know?"

"Absolutely."

"So he's making passes at this Trina chick, and she's saying no and goes out onto the deck. Then he gets mad. Really mad. And he goes after her."

"Did you go out on deck?"

He shook his head. "Naw, man. I stayed below and did my job. I'm paid to spin tunes, not chase down women for him. So I keep doing my thing and after a while, he comes back down and he's wringing wet. His hair's wet, and he's just sweating like a pig. And he says, 'Bobby, you gotta help me. I think I killed her.' And I said, 'Trina?' And he says, 'Yes.' So I take a break and go out on the deck with him and she's dead. She's just dead!"

"You didn't see him do it?"

He shook his head and Polanski looked at Kirkpatrick. "Anything to add, counselor?"

The attorney shrugged. "It's his story, detective."

"Go on," Polanski said to the DJ. "Then what?"

"Our first thought was to throw her overboard, but the party was moving to the upper deck and we didn't have time and we were afraid of the noise, you know. So we rolled her up in a tarp and put her in the storage locker. By then a lot of the people from below deck were coming up and we didn't have any options but to keep her."

"So you tossed her in the trash when the boat docked?"

"Yeah, sort of. Except we didn't dock. It started to rain so we pulled into the pier because some people wanted to get off and take cabs or whatever to their hotels. This was a big shindig, you know? So I carried her off the deck and dumped her in the first place I could find."

"*You* dumped her?"

"Yeah, that's what I just said."

"So if we search your place we'll find a Cubs hoodie with a torn sleeve?"

"Yeah. That's mine, but it ain't there."

"What do you mean?"

"After I ditched her, I had to change clothes. I did that when we got back to Peter's place. My clothes are there, including the hoodie."

"Why did you have to change clothes?"

"'Cause I got soaked, man. The rain started up again."

Polanski breathed slowly, deliberately trying to conceal his glee at the DJ's confession. "And you'll testify to this in court?"

"Sure. If you honor my deal."

"Absolutely."

Longhorse looked at his attorney who put a reassuring hand on his client's arm.

CHAPTER 35

Polanski was in Lopez's office, reporting on Bobby's eyewitness account, when Campello entered.

"I've got some news," Campello said.

"Get in line, Frank."

Campello raised an eyebrow and took a seat on the sofa next to Polanski.

"I interviewed Bobby Longhorse," Polanski said. "He lawyered up, but talked anyway. It seems he was on Peter's boat for a big party. A lot of bigwigs at the thing. Longhorse said Peter was supplying women for the party and he started hitting on one of them."

"Trina?" Campello asked.

"One and the same. Anyway, he pushed her pretty hard and she rebelled. He followed her to the upper deck and killed her. Bobby helped him dispose of the body. It was Bobby we saw on the surveillance video. Apparently, Peter is running an escort service out of the club and caters to the muckety-mucks. Judges, aldermen, some of the mayor's aides... and that's what he was doing at the party. Trina wasn't part of that and Longhorse doesn't know what she was doing on the boat, but things went crazy and she's dead."

"I have something that may add to his testimony," Campello said, adjusting his position on the sofa. "When I was at Rita's apartment one of the lab techs printed the address list from her computer. The list had Trina's name, Juanita's and several others. I've been trying to call the list, but all of the numbers have been disconnected except for Gloria Perez in Uptown. I interviewed her. She was resistant at first, but when I told her about Trina and Rita, she started to talk.

According to her, Peter is not only running an escort service, he's using illegals to do it. He puts them in a position of playing ball or going back home. He likes to prey on women who have small children, but isn't choosy."

"Juanita has a child," Lopez said.

"Exactly," Campello said.

"You think Juanita was coerced into calling me?" Polanski asked.

Campello said, "It's a definite possibility. She was nervous when I was there. I assumed it was because she didn't want to talk with me, for obvious reasons. But now," he shook his head, "I wonder if she hadn't been approached already."

"You think someone could've been in the apartment while you were there?" Lopez asked.

Campello shrugged. "I hope not. But it could explain her demeanor."

"Did she have her baby with her?" The district commander asked.

Campello shook his head. "Not in her arms. Not in the same room. When I asked, she said the baby was sleeping in the other room. The door was closed."

"Someone may have been there with her," Polanski said.

"Longhorse?" Lopez asked.

Campello shrugged. "Maybe. He would've had enough time to get across town, but why not just whack me there?"

"It's like you said," Polanski added. "He didn't want you. He wanted me."

"Where is Juanita?" Lopez asked.

Campello spread his hands. "I don't know. I don't know if she's in danger or part of the setup."

Lopez turned to Polanski. "Andy, is Longhorse willing to testify to what he told you?"

"He wants to deal, but… yeah. He'll do it."

To Campello Lopez said, "Frank, will Gloria testify in court?"

Campello shrugged. "I don't know, Julio. She's scared."

"Talk to her, offer her protection. It sounds like she might need it. Get her to agree to talk. If I'm hearing you guys correctly, she could corroborate Longhorse's story. If we find that hoodie in his apartment, it will be difficult for Longhorse to retract his testimony." He focused on Polanski. "Longhorse can turn on you at the drop of a hat. Don't take anything for granted."

Polanski nodded. "Longhorse changed clothes at Peter's place. It's likely the hoodie is there and now we have a witness willing to testify," Polanski said.

"We have a witness, Julio," Campello said. "The state's attorney can't ignore that."

Lopez sighed. "No, I guess not."

Campello glanced at Polanski. Lopez's reluctance was understandable, given Aaron Green's clout. But it was no longer possible for the commander to ignore the obvious. The two detectives rose to leave.

"Just be sure we keep Longhorse talking," Lopez said. "And Frank?"

"Yeah?"

"Get Gloria to talk."

A phone call to the warehouse revealed that Peter Green was not at work, but at home. Campello and Polanski drove to his residence on Lake Shore Drive.

He occupied the southeastern corner of the thirtieth floor of Quantum Towers, the city's newest – and most elite – residential complex. The building afforded him a panoramic view of the lake and was within easy walking distance of Navy Pier. Campello and Polanski took the elevator to the thirtieth floor in silence, along with two uniformed officers, Rebecca Klein and Tom Jared, who carried the bludgeon that they would use to open Green's door. The device was normally reserved for raids or other instances where a forced entry was met with resistance. Peter's previous arrest had been spontaneous. But Campello was uncertain who would be in the apartment with Peter and so decided to take back-up. Also, he was still chafed from the ambush, convinced that Peter was behind the assault. He felt he owed the trust-fund twerp some shock and awe of his own, courtesy of the CPD.

The uniformed officers were the first to emerge from the elevator when it reached the floor, and they stood to each side as the detectives exited. Scanning the wall directory, Polanski pointed to the right and gestured for the arrest team to follow him. They traversed the hallway to Peter's condo, pausing at the door in silence when Campello held his index finger to his lips and listened at the door. He silently mouthed that the television was playing and then moved Jared into place. They would enter in a diamond formation, with each officer and detective taking their individual positions. It was a standard police tactic and one that ensured the safety of the suspect as well as the arresting officers.

When Campello counted three, Jared swung the bludgeon, striking the door near the lock. Despite the fact that the condo had probably cost upward of a million dollars, many times the combined annual salaries of the officers at the scene, the door flung open easily, and Jared tossed the heavy instrument into the room, pulling his pistol.

They rushed into the condo with Jared on point, Campello keeping his pistol trained on the left side of the room, Polanski on the right and Klein on the rear. Campello yelled that they were police and told Peter to get on the floor. Green was the only one in view, and he was watching television in his underwear. He had a bottle of scotch on a nearby table.

"What is this?" he asked, standing. "You got no right to—"

Polanski reached Peter first and grabbed him by the neck with one hand, while keeping his pistol trained on him with the other. "On the floor." He forced Green forward and down and he complied. Once on the ground, Polanski holstered the gun and knelt over Green with his knee in the man's back. He cuffed Peter's hands behind him.

"Anyone else here?" Polanski asked.

Green cursed him.

Polanski raised his head to check on the others and saw that

Campello had already begun a search of the bedrooms. Jared and Klein were taking the other areas, searching through drawers, closets, even tossing the sofa's cushions.

"I'll have your badge for this, Polanski," Green said.

Polanski kept his knee on the man's back and his eyes trained on the officers searching the condo.

"Bingo," Campello said, coming out of master bedroom with a printout in hand. "He's got the same information on his computer that Rita had on hers."

Polanski took the printout and scanned it. He called to Klein. "Can you take this and his computer to the lab? See what you can find out? More names, connections, that sort of thing?" He turned to Campello. "Maybe she'll be more successful than you were." He grinned, but suddenly became aware that Klein had not moved. He turned to her again. "Officer?"

She ignored him and said to Campello, "What do you want me to do, Frank?"

Campello looked from her to Polanski and then back to her. "Do what my partner says."

CHAPTER 36

Aaron Green received word of Peter's arrest before he was taken to the Castle for booking. Within minutes, the alderman was on the phone to Superintendent Mayron who declined to intervene this time, given the mounting evidence and the fact that he had been instrumental in securing Peter's earlier release.

Not to be stymied, and with resources at his disposal, Aaron Green called his attorney, insisting the man drop everything and rush to protect Peter's interest. Tony Delgado would protect Aaron's.

The alderman paged the enforcer again, passing the same code as before, then drove to the Chicago Board of Trade office. Delgado had not yet arrived, and Aaron fixed a drink before collapsing behind his desk.

He began thinking on how to lay the groundwork for excising his son from the business while also ensuring Peter's future financial security.

Peter was unable to meet the challenges of life. His mother had been the primary parent, and when she died, the responsibility passed to Aaron. Although he knew he had provided well for his son, he understood that he had not been the kind of father the boy needed. Discipline, tempered with love, would have been far more beneficial than luxuries given with an occasional disciplinary hand. His parenting had been intermittent, often manifesting only as intervention when the boy was in trouble, followed by punishment. There had been no parameters, no guidance. He hadn't had time. The demands of the business, his political career and the city had taken precedence. Peter was largely left to raise himself. The alderman felt acutely aware of that as he nursed his drink; knew that he had failed. But he would make it up to Peter. If he failed as a father when Peter was young, he would not fail as a father when Peter was a man. Things would turn out OK. Life had a way of correcting itself.

He finished the drink just as Delgado entered the office, wearing his black leather coat over a blood-red shirt, a black-and-red tie, and black pants. His shoes were shined to a gleaming finish, outdone only by the sheen of his hair.

"What is it, Aaron?"

The alderman raised his glass in offer of a drink. This time, the enforcer agreed and Aaron left the desk to go to the bar. He fixed another scotch and soda for himself and a whiskey sour for Delgado. He handed the drink to the man before settling behind the desk again.

"I need your help."

Delgado sipped the drink, pronounced it good, and then said, "Peter?"

"How'd you know?" he said, allowing a wry grin.

"Isn't it always?"

The remark stung. "This cop, Polanski, has a thing for him."

"Isn't that the cop who was involved in the shooting?"

The alderman nodded. "You didn't know that?"

Delgado gave him a penetrating look. "No, Aaron, I didn't know that. I had nothing to do with it. We don't work that way. There are better and less intrusive ways of dealing with our problems."

"Someone did."

"Peter. Isn't that clear by now? Peter had the DJ at the club attack the cops."

"And you know this to be true?"

"What do you think, Aaron? That I sit around all day waiting for you to call? You have your sources and I have mine. It's why our partnership works so well." He drank the whiskey.

"They have arrested him and are going to charge him with the murder of that little skank at the pier." He drained the scotch, but continued to hold the glass in his pudgy hand.

"You have contacts, Aaron. You practically run the government in this town. Pull in some chits. Make some threats."

"I did some of that yesterday. I spoke with Mayron again today."

"And?"

"He's afraid. He's backing away."

"Then put the heat to him. You can shut off the money flow with a stroke of your Mont Blanc."

Aaron shook his head. "It isn't that simple. I have City Hall to deal with, political pressures and obligations." He set the glass on the desk. "I need your help," he said again.

Delgado sighed. "How?"

"I have my attorney on the way to the 28th. I am confident he can take care of Peter's legal issues, but I'm afraid this cop won't quit."

"It isn't just one, Aaron. There's an entire department. Even if we eliminate Polanski, we would have Campello to deal with and the others who would eventually follow him."

Green shook his head. "Eliminating them in the traditional sense will only raise further suspicions and cause more headaches. You've said it yourself, Tony. The old ways don't work anymore."

"You want Polanski out of the way, but you don't want him dead."

"Yes."

"And how do you propose we do that, Aaron? It's one thing to buy off a witness or lose a piece of evidence, but getting a cop out of the picture is a different matter. And more to the point, what's in it for us?"

"Polanski's reputation is virtually non-existent as far as the rank and file is concerned. He turned on his own and that is something no cop ever does. The men he's preparing to testify against are well-respected, seasoned cops, cited for bravery on many occasions. If Polanski were to be tainted, the men and women in blue would not be upset."

"And those two cops would go free because the charges would be dropped."

Green continued, "And the riots may cease because it would clearly appear that Polanski's allegations are false. Most of the looting stems from the belief that the cops lied and planted evidence on the kid they shot."

Delgado laughed. "Most of the looting stems from greed, Aaron. It has nothing to do with civil unrest."

The alderman acknowledged the veracity of the statement. "At any rate, if Polanski goes, so do his suspicions. The department will be glad to be rid of a rogue cop... and the riots." He paused. "Can you do this for me?"

Delgado nodded thoughtfully. "It'll take some work. But that leads us to the other half of my question. What's in it for us?"

"Besides stabilizing our partnership and securing our mutual interests?"

Delgado's eyes narrowed and homed in on him. "That sounds dangerously close to a threat, Aaron."

Green shook his head. "The threat doesn't come from me. The threat is a mutual one and it comes from one rogue cop."

Delgado studied him. "OK," he finally said, setting the empty glass on the desk and rising from the chair. "I will see what we can do. But this is the last time, Aaron. You see to it that Peter never causes us embarrassment again." He lowered his voice, stressing his point. "Ever."

CHAPTER 37

As part of their new compact, Campello had promised to keep Polanski informed. His personal feelings about Polanski had changed as a result of the ambush, but had not totally abated. He still disliked having to work with him. But the initial hearing before the IPRA was scheduled for later in the day and since both of them would eventually be on the line, it made sense to present a unified presence to the board.

It was unusual to have the hearing scheduled so soon after the shooting, but no one had been hurt and Longhorse admitted to being at the scene. The hearing had also been expedited by a request from the highest levels within the department. Such requests were unusual at best and suspicious at worst, but with Polanski's pending testimony, it was likely the Chief and his cohorts wanted to maintain the impression of character that was above suspicion. It was also likely they wanted to protect themselves from liability. Polanski's charges and willingness to state them publicly at trial had put the department's brass in a quandary. Aaron Green had asked the commissioner to hold off on the firings and investigation, citing the sacrifices the two officers had offered during their long careers and the need for a proper review of the facts surrounding the charges.

Campello called Polanski and outlined a conversation he had with Jimmy Small.

"That guy you saw at the warehouse, the tall dude?" Campello said.

"Delgado?"

"He's been tagging along with Peter Green. Comes into the club."

"I knew that. The question, though, is why?"

"I have the same question. So I'm going to ruffle his feathers a bit. I'm going to go talk to Vincent. If I'm lucky, Delgado will be there. But even if he isn't, word will get to him. We should be hearing from him soon," Campello said.

Polanski's end of the line was quiet.

"Are you ready for the review?" Campello asked, taking a different tack.

"As ready as I'll ever be."

"I want to suggest that you not sweat this, but the fact is, the hearing is important. It can go either way."

"I let God sweat things."

"God?"

"The Creator? His Son is Jesus?"

Campello was speechless.

Polanski continued, unabashed. "I don't think I could face the barrage of criticism, the attacks, without Him."

Polanski's end of the line was quiet again, but Campello was stymied.

"At any rate," Polanski said, finally breaking the silence, "I'm going back downstairs to interview Longhorse again. The state's attorney is willing to cut the deal he wants, but he's going to want more."

"I wouldn't get my hopes up."

"It's his loss," Polanski said. "We might have a problem, though."

"What?" Campello asked.

"Longhorse said you threatened him. Told him he was a dead man."

"Not exactly. I told him if word got back to his cohorts that he'd... oh."

"Yeah. He's taking it as a personal threat from you, but either way, his attorney is requesting segregation for him."

"That shouldn't be a problem," Campello said.

"None. And the state is prepared to sweeten the deal, maybe even get the feds to drop the weapons charges if he gives us what we want."

"He'll go for it. He's a low-level street dealer and he's never done any significant time. It's always been petty stuff. He'll sing if that's what it takes to get out of jail."

"Let's hope so," Polanski said. "If he rolls over, we can wrap this thing up."

"Except for the hearing," Campello said.

"Except for that."

CHAPTER 38

Campello drove to the complex of brownstones on the near North Side. Paulie Vincent occupied a condo housed in one of the buildings on North Dearborn, minutes from the club.

Traffic thickened once Campello crossed Oak Street, a path with which he was familiar, since he lived on North LaSalle, a scant five minutes from the head of Chicago's most notorious crime family. Despite the close proximity and the antagonistic nature of their chosen career paths, Campello had never met Vincent, but knew the man's biography in minute detail.

Paulie Vincent rose to the head of what Capone had once termed "the outfit" by a schizophrenic combination of stealth, candor, blind luck, careful planning, aggression and patience. His criminal career began as most begin, with petty crimes escalating to more significant ones. Despite numerous brushes with the law, he served very little time and his contemptuous disregard of the judicial system grew. He progressed in a steady and focused vector through his increasingly honed talent for organization. His meteoric ascent began when he infiltrated the city's unions. Before long, his crew obtained such a grip on Chicago's labor force that when Vincent said "strike", they struck. CPD's intelligence held strong suspicions that the current workers' strikes in all their various quarters were somehow tied to Vincent, but could not prove it. Nevertheless, the man remained virtually untouchable because of the significant influence he wielded – or purchased – within the city's political structure. Because of his innate power and tremendous influence, particularly in the face of an apathetic public, Vincent was seldom molested by the CPD or by anyone else. But that didn't mean he had no vulnerabilities. Most of those arose from within his ranks. A man in Vincent's position often had to live his life looking over his shoulder, trusting no one, and eliminating those who could expose him. It was a precarious perch on which he sat, and no one knew that better than Vincent.

As the well-known house came into view, Campello began searching for a place to park among the other cars pulled against the curb. The brownstone was well protected, isolated from adjoining structures where the police or feds could set up cameras or eavesdropping equipment, and virtually impenetrable from the street or the alley behind.

Campello saw a delivery vehicle pull away from the curb, directly across the street from the crime lord's palace. He snapped the magnetized emergency light on top of the car and made a broad U-turn, pulling the unmarked squad into the tight fit. Once parked, he removed the beacon and slid it on the floorboard. He contacted dispatch with his location and paused to scout the area.

Traffic had thinned this far north and fewer pedestrians populated the streets. An occasional bus would belch its way along the street and a smattering of cabs made pickups and deliveries. But it was the men outside the house that most intrigued him.

There were two of them. Each of them stood well over six feet, with the broad shoulders, lumbering gaits, and disfigured faces that came from time in the ring. They wore sport coats with tell-tale bulges; in one case, the bulge was under the right armpit; in the case of the other, on the right hip.

The house was a traditional turn-of-the-last-century brownstone, face-lifted sometime during the past ten years. The three-story structure sported a cupola on each side encased in impressive swathes of ivy. A row of well-pruned trees rose behind a chest-high wrought-iron fence that encased the yard. A majestic staircase led from the flagstone sidewalk to the imposing mahogany front entrance.

He suppressed his resentment that a creep like Vincent could live among the decent people of the neighborhood, thriving while so many others struggled to put food on the table and clothes on their children's backs. Crime often does pay, he acknowledged, and it pays well.

He got out of the car, allowing traffic to pass, then jogged across the street and approached the house. Amazingly, the gate was unlocked and he passed through it before one of the men, the larger and younger of the two, immediately confronted him.

"This is private property, sir."

Campello showed the man his badge and his ID. "I'd like to speak with Mr. Vincent."

"Do you have a warrant?"

"To talk to him?"

The two looked at each other for a moment, but apparently decided to kick the decision up the chain. "Stay here," the first man said.

They left him standing on the sidewalk, but inside the compound, while one went inside and the other resumed his post at the bottom of the steps. Within a minute, the first man came out and nodded to the second man. He motioned for Campello to follow him.

The living-room was done in pale yellows and an expensive Persian rug overlaid hardwood floors. Despite the close proximity to Dearborn Street and the steady flow of big-city traffic, the condo was surprisingly quiet. A gentle fire flamed in the gas-log fireplace. Two different guards stood in the room, each of them as imposing as the men on the sidewalk.

Paulie Vincent may not have mellowed since the CPD had begun tracking him, but he had aged and his health had declined. The man sat in a wing-back chair opposite the fireplace, tethered to an oxygen machine by way of a transparent plastic mask that he held over his mouth and nose. The previously robust and jowly face that Campello had seen when perusing the man's file was now thin, angular, and sallow. His hair was considerably grayer and thinner; his eyes dimmer, although just as penetrating.

The guards removed themselves from the room as soon as they

ushered him in, but made it clear they were within earshot if Vincent needed them.

Campello sat as soon as the man gestured for him to do so. "Thank you for meeting with me," he said.

Vincent nodded, but continued to hold the mask to his face.

"This is a quasi-official visit," he lied, "and I've come to pay you the courtesy of informing you of something that is threatening both of us."

Vincent frowned, but said nothing, opting to keep the mask over his face.

"A hit was conducted against a police officer and we believe that hit was sanctioned by one of your people."

Vincent removed the mask. "I don't know what you're talking about," he rasped, immediately replacing the mask.

Campello sighed. "Mr. Vincent, I am a police detective with two decades of experience. Please don't insult me."

Vincent studied him through eyes that had narrowed to slits. He removed the mask long enough to speak. "Who do you think arranged this hit?"

"Anthony Delgado," he said, tossing a wrench in the man's world.

"I don't know him."

Campello snorted. "Well, if you ever meet him, I'd stay away. He's a very dangerous man and exceedingly stupid. He tried to kill an officer yesterday, and that is something we simply won't tolerate. We're going after him and we're not going to stop until we unwind everything in his sordid world and put as many of his friends in jail as we can." He stood. "I was under the mistaken impression that he was employed by you. I apologize."

Vincent removed the mask. "Thank you for your courtesy, detective. I will not forget it."

CHAPTER 39

ampello was visiting Paulie Vincent and Christy's curiosity was piqued. Could the detective paired with the most honest cop in Chicago be in bed with a crook that made Al Capone look like Mister Rogers?

She watched the brownstone from a position one block south, her view partially obscured by a cluster of small trees. There was no mistaking the detective had been ushered directly into Vincent's inner sanctum without resistance or fanfare. By itself, the visit may be nothing unusual and she had no real reason to suspect Campello of wrongdoing. But Polanski had been assigned to work with him and that aroused her interest in him enough to tail him.

She sighed and unbuckled her seatbelt. She was no fan of surveillance and knew she could be in the car for a long time. Having had nothing to eat, she began fishing in her purse. She found a packet of gum and removed the foil before popping a stick into her mouth. Twenty minutes later, Campello came out of the house, shaking hands with the two men who had given him access. Her hunger and her curiosity had intensified.

"What are you up to, detective?"

She continued watching Campello as he waited until traffic cleared before bolting across the street to his car. He started it and pulled away from the curb, heading in Christy's direction. She scrunched behind the steering-wheel, making herself as invisible as possible, while watching the detective's passing car in the driver's-door mirror. When she was confident that Campello was a discreet distance away, she started her Corolla, reconnected her seatbelt, and drove away from the curb in a traffic-jarring U-turn to begin her pursuit of him.

They traveled south, winding their way through traffic and working their way onto State Street. Campello drove at a leisurely pace, which made following him at a steady and discreet distance much easier. If he was aware of her, he had given no indication.

They passed through the north end of the loop and as soon as they had crossed the river the unmarked squad car moved to the turning lane. She followed suit and they were soon heading to the industrial area of the city. Within minutes Campello stopped just short of the entrance gate to Green's Warehouse with his turn signal flashing. She sped past him and drove on for two blocks, before circling back and parking across the street in the vacant lot of a former trucking firm.

She killed the engine and clocked the time that Campello had entered the warehouse complex, writing it down in her notebook. The detective had visited Paulie Vincent at home, followed by a call to a business owned by the city's most powerful alderman, and he had done it all within an hour.

"What are you up to, detective?" she asked for the second time.

She glanced at her watch, prepared for a long wait, when a tap on her driver's-side window jolted her upright. It was Frank Campello and he was not happy.

CHAPTER 40

S he rolled down the window.

"Why are you following me?" he asked.

Deciding it was fruitless to feign ignorance, she countered with, "Why are you in bed with Vincent?" She knew her assumption may not have been true, but the question was provocative and would get her out of a defensive position.

"I'm not in bed with anyone, Ms. Lee. But I am a cop and you are coming dangerously close to interfering with a police investigation."

She had been threatened with arrest before and it held little sway over her. But she was not the favorite journalist of the embattled police department and she knew there were some within the CPD who were just itching for a chance to make an example of her. If she was going to gain ground with Campello, an offense was the best defense.

"I'm doing a job too, detective. The people have a right to know."

His composure relaxed and he smiled. It was off-putting.

"What do they want to know about, Ms. Lee?"

"The real reason an honest cop like Polanski was transferred and then assigned to you. How come you're visiting Paulie Vincent and then a business owned by Aaron Green? And I personally would like to know why you were ambushed in place of your partner."

Campello glanced over the top of her car toward Green's Warehouse, drumming his fingers on the passenger's-side door-frame. "Open the door, Ms. Lee."

"I don't think I—"

"If you want answers to your questions, open the door."

She reached across the front seat and unlocked the front passenger's door.

"Get in, detective."

He marched around the rear of the vehicle and climbed inside.

"Drive," he said.

"Where to?"

He looked over his shoulder toward the office complex. "I don't care. Just away from here."

She started the engine and pulled out of the lot, heading east. She turned south onto Wabash but caught the light at the El tracks. The rumble of the overhead train eliminated any chance at a normal conversation, so as soon as the light turned, she drove east and maneuvered around the block and onto Clark Street, where she began heading north.

Campello turned to glance back. Satisfied they had not been followed, he said, "I don't like the press. Especially now. So anything I say to you is off the record."

"Now wait a minute. I—"

"Off the record, Ms. Lee."

It was important to find out what Campello was made of, if she was to ferret out the facts behind Polanski's transfer. She didn't want to agree to his request, but decided that a conversation with Polanski's new partner, even if not acknowledgeable, was better than none.

"OK. Off the record."

He shifted in his seat. "What did Polanski have to say?"

"He said he thought you were a good cop. And beneath all the bravado, probably a decent man."

He snorted. "Did he say that about me?"

His question caught her by surprise and she glanced at him. He was a big man, not unattractive, and the cop-like air she had noticed earlier had given way to a boy-like charm.

"Yes."

He nodded, then shook his head in disbelief, and sighed as he idly watched the passing cityscape.

"Does that upset you?" she asked, priming the well.

"Upset me?" He chuckled. "I get disappointed from time to time, angered, maybe agitated, but I never get upset. Not anymore. That would imply that I care, and I stopped caring a long time ago, Ms. Lee. I take life a day at a time and don't put my trust in anyone other than the department."

She could not stifle the laugh. "How could you put your faith in the department?"

He turned toward her. "You just did."

He was right and his answer deflated her. She had, in fact, allowed a total stranger into her car just because he carried a star made from fifteen dollars of steel in a twenty-dollar vinyl case.

"That badge means something, Ms. Lee," he said, as though he had just crawled out of her head. "I take it seriously. And I trust the men and women who carry it."

"So I should trust everyone who carries a badge?"

"Yes."

"Are you insane? Can you honestly tell me that everyone who carries a badge is a good guy?" She passed a bus that had stopped.

He turned toward her again. "No. I said you should trust everyone who carries a badge. I didn't say everyone who carries one is moral or good or even trustworthy." He turned further in his seat until he fully faced her. "That badge is a symbol, Ms. Lee. My partner died upholding the principles that badge represents. And that's why you should trust the police. Without that kind of commitment, you don't have structure and without structure you don't have anything. That doesn't mean you won't get disappointed from time to time or that some wayward cop won't let you down. But if you don't trust the police you don't respect the police, and that means you won't obey the law."

"You do care."

"What?"

"You said you don't care, but you do."

"I was speaking generically. Everyone cares. But not everyone cares about everything. The way people view me or their opinions of me don't matter. But I insist they respect the job I do."

"And what about Polanski?"

"What about him?"

"You don't respect him, and he carries the same badge you do."

He groaned. "Because he didn't trust the police to police their own. He took it outside the family rather than to the cops who police the cops because he didn't trust the system. That means he doesn't trust the police, and that, Ms. Lee, puts him in the corral with you. If he doesn't trust us, he doesn't respect the law. He has no business enforcing it."

"Maybe he was wounded by what he saw," she said. "Maybe his faith was violated and he didn't feel like he could trust anyone any longer."

"Join the club. I've been a cop for twenty years. Don't you think my faith has been violated? But I don't give up and I don't turn on my brothers in blue."

The traffic began to thin as they continued moving north and she began to pick up speed. "So you don't trust him? At all?"

"I don't know. He has a candy-eyed view of the world, and in this business that can get you killed."

"It seems to me his view is dead on."

Campello shook his head. "We aren't choirboys, Ms. Lee. Sometimes we have to give to get."

"In other words, you have changing principles. You sell out."

"Do you have a husband, Ms. Lee?"

She was taken aback by the question. "None of your business."

He chuckled. "Relax, lady. I'm not interested. Do you have anyone you're close to? A parent? Sibling?"

"Of course."

"Suppose that person had been kidnapped and was buried alive with only a few hours of oxygen left. And suppose I caught the person who did it, but he wouldn't tell me where your family member was unless I played ball with him. Would you want me to do that or would you want me to take a Polanski-style position and insist he go to jail for the lesser charge, even if that meant your family member would die?"

"How often does that happen, detective?"

"Every day, Ms. Lee. We have to play the hand we're dealt and sometimes that means good cops do bad things."

"The ends justify the means?"

"Sometimes. But you see," he said, "that's just my point. Nothing is black and white in my world."

"But isn't the law black and white? Right or wrong?"

"The law is. But people and their needs are not. Sometimes we have to bend the law to protect the greater good."

"So where do you draw the line, then? What's to keep someone like Caine and Dorchester from planting evidence on anyone they see fit?"

"The man they *allegedly*—" he leaned toward her, "presumption of innocence, Ms. Lee – the man they *allegedly* planted evidence on was wanted for murder and had a list of arrests as long as the Chicago river."

"So what?"

"So they did what the law failed to do. They got him off the streets."

"And replaced one criminal with two."

He chuckled in a condescending way. Their debate was going nowhere.

She decided to change course. "How are you going to testify at Polanski's hearing?"

"Truthfully, Ms. Lee."

CHAPTER 41

Campello returned to the 28th after Christy dropped him off at his car. A mob of press people had gathered, blocking access to the building's front entrance and crowding the lobby. He decided to take the back staircase that entered the second floor by way of the locker room.

The detectives' squad room was alive with activity and he was nearly mobbed when he came into the room. Tertwiller reached him first.

"Where've you been, Frank?" she said. "We've been trying to reach you."

"I was running down a lead. What happened?" he said, deflecting her.

"Polanski's been busted."

"What?"

Silvio said, "Internal Affairs discovered that Polanski contacted some of the dealers that Caine and Dorchester busted. He wanted a piece of their action and agreed to get Caine and Dorchester off their backs."

Campello couldn't hide his disbelief. "Polanski was getting a piece of the dealers' action in exchange for protections?"

"IAD thinks so, Frank," Silvio said. "And they *like* the guy. Crazy, right?"

"No one likes him," Tertwiller corrected, sarcastically. "Even the guys in Internal Affairs are cops first."

Campello looked around the room. "Where is he?"

"Polanski?" Tertwiller asked. "He's gone. They dragged him out of here a few minutes ago."

Campello glanced over his shoulder and toward Lopez's office. He was on the phone and the door was closed. "What does the boss have to say about it?"

Silvio said, "He hasn't. Yet. Some uniforms came in and told Polanski he was under arrest and a guy from IAD went into the office to talk with Lopez. The whole thing was over in minutes."

"He's been on the phone ever since," Silvio said.

Campello said, "Something doesn't feel right about this."

Tertwiller said, "Something didn't feel right about him coming here in the first place, if you ask me."

"Listen, Frank," Silvio said, "we're going for a beer later. You want to come?"

"Sure. Count me in." He kept his eyes on Lopez's office and when he saw him hang up the phone he said, "I'm going to find out what's going on."

Silvio gave him a friendly slap on the back. "You do that, detective. Just remember, Jeep's at five."

"I'll be there."

He did not wait for an invitation from Lopez. He went into the office and closed the door.

"Not now, Frank," Lopez said with his elbows on his desk, massaging his temples.

"What happened?"

"You heard, didn't you?" He nodded toward the squad room. "I saw them pounce on you as soon as you came in."

"What happened, Julio?"

Campello listened as the district commander recounted the events the others had described for him. Lopez seemed genuinely concerned for Polanski's safety.

"He's already been booked and taken to the Cook County jail." Lopez was slumping in his chair.

"There's got to be more than that, Julio. You're leaving something out."

"Do you remember that coke bust that went down the other day?"

"Yes."

"Some of it turned up missing that evening." He focused on Campello. "They found it in the trunk of Polanski's car."

"So what? It's a setup and you know it, Julio. Polanski would rat his mother out to the League of Decency if he thought it would make his career. That doesn't mean he's a criminal."

"Correction. He is very much a criminal, now. The state's attorney is filing charges."

"Julio, there's more to this than—"

"We ran his financials. He has over a hundred and fifty thousand sitting in the bank." He ceased massaging his temples and looked directly at Campello. "Tell me, Frank. Where does a cop get that kind of money?"

"Julio, Polanski didn't put that money in the bank. He didn't steal the drugs and he didn't take down two good cops just so he could milk some drug dealers." He gestured over his shoulder to the squad room behind him. "He turned on them. And he's reaping the whirlwind for having done so. But he isn't guilty of dealing drugs and you know it."

"The facts say he is. Polanski looks guilty. And that has greatly upset the state's attorney who is resting his entire case against Dorchester and Caine on Polanski's testimony. He's out for blood, now, and he doesn't care whose it is."

"The prosecutor isn't stupid, Julio. He has to know Polanski is being railroaded."

"By everyone, Frank? If it was just the money and the missing drugs, that'd be one thing. But there are dealers lining up to testify that Polanski has been strong-arming them. How's the state's attorney supposed to ignore that? How's she supposed to believe that there's a conspiracy against Polanski that is so great, it encompasses the CPD and the criminal element of the city?" He folded his hands on his desk. His gaze intensified on Campello. "And there's more, Frank. Longhorse is retracting his agreement to testify against Peter. But he's willing to testify against Polanski, for a deal."

Campello had a sinking feeling. "Where's Peter, Julio?"

"He walked. The sweatshirt you found in Longhorse's apartment and the computer? It *all* walked today. Vanished. We have no evidence, no testimony, no forensics, and no reason to hold Green."

CHAPTER 42

Campello left by way of the building's lobby. Most of the press had vacated except for a smattering of the diehards, primarily the print journalists who had more time to develop their stories and so remained to ferret out facts. Christy Lee was there, too. She saw Campello as soon as he descended the staircase and pounced on him like the proverbial tiger.

"What happened to Polanski?"

He kept moving and she followed him through the lobby door and into the parking lot. The wind remained strong and the day overcast.

"My readers have a right to know what is happening with their police department, detective."

Campello stopped to look at her.

"Well?" she asked, her eyes searching his from beneath a furrowed brow.

"What are you doing here?" he asked.

"Covering a story. What else would I be doing here?"

He pointed to the Castle. "I was in there only a few minutes. How did you get here so quick?"

"What do you think, detective? That I just sit around all day waiting for a phone call? This is my beat. I have my sources too."

He sighed, hands on hips, studying her. "This is off the record."

"No."

"Have a nice day." He started walking again.

"OK, OK," she said, tugging on his arm.

He stopped again and glanced around the parking lot, over her shoulder. There were a few officers coming and going, but no one seemed to be paying them any attention.

"How much do you know?" he asked.

She told him and it was apparent she hadn't gotten very far. She only knew what the Public Information officer was likely to have said. She did not know about the drugs, the money, or the growing list of illicit dealers who were lining up, willing to testify that Polanski was a crooked cop who had been shaking them down for years. She also did not know that Longhorse had retracted his testimony against Green and the little evidence they had against Peter had vanished, and that he had walked again, even as Longhorse remained behind bars. In short, she didn't seem to know a whole lot.

"You don't know much."

"Then tell me."

He was incredulous. "Why? I've already broken my own rule by talking to you once. Why should I tell you anything?"

"The people in this city have a—"

"Stow it, Ms. Lee. We have a Public Information officer for that."

A gust of wind kicked up, ruffling her hair. "You may not believe this, detective, but I care what happens to Polanski. Even if you and the others don't. I care what kind of a police department this city has."

He moved closer, crowding her. She did not back down.

"They why do you magnify every failure and subdue every success?" he asked.

"I—"

"I'll tell you why, Ms. Lee. Because our failures are news. And they're news because they are rare."

He stood motionless, allowing his comments to sink in before turning suddenly and striding away.

"I can help him!" Christy called.

Campello stopped.

"If you think the power of the press can be used against you, then you must know it can be used *for* you, too."

There were risks in talking to her. She was a reporter, after all. But Peter's second release and Polanski's frame-up told him he was facing insurmountable odds if he decided to go it alone. He had always trusted his fellow officers. Now, given recent developments, he was no longer sure who he could trust. He turned to face her.

"I think Polanski is being framed."

She was flabbergasted.

"Why?"

"Off the record."

She acquiesced. "Off the record."

He moved closer to her and told her that two kilos of cocaine from a recent bust were missing from the evidence room and that they were found in Polanski's car. He told her that money had been found in his account and that testimony from some of the city's more prominent drug dealers would be forthcoming. He told her about the list he had found on Rita's computer and how it matched the one in Peter's apartment, and how the officer there had been no more successful than he in finding the people on the list.

He glanced around the lot again. Several uniforms and plain-clothes officers milled about the area, coming and going, but no one seemed to notice his conversation with the reporter. "I don't care for guys like Polanski. I never have. But he didn't do this. He's coming before the IPRA and they will use this against him even though it has nothing to do with the ambush. Unless I'm wrong, he will be exonerated in the shooting, but then be held over for another hearing on the drug charges." He nodded toward the building. "They want him out. It doesn't matter if he goes to jail or gets fired. It'll be enough if he isn't there anymore."

"You think he's innocent, don't you?"

"Yes."

"I do too. I was hoping there was at least one decent cop in this town."

"There are plenty of decent cops, Ms. Lee. You're talking to one of them. Do you want to work with me on this?"

"Yes."

"Then you need to understand you can't go running to your paper for cover when things begin to go south."

She pursed her lips. Her face hardened. "I don't need anyone to protect me, detective."

"Trina and Rita thought so, too."

Her jaw clenched. "I don't need anyone to protect me."

"OK. Because unless I'm missing something here, there will be no one willing to do it." He nodded again toward the building. "We aren't just going against the department, Ms. Lee. We're going up against a group that is powerful enough to kill us, then buy your newspaper while making your readers think it was a good idea. Do you understand what I'm saying?"

"Perfectly." Her face was full of determination, and that meant she didn't have a clue.

CHAPTER 43

Campello and Lee took the tan squad car to Polanski's house. Even though he was the man of the hour and the target of the very media that had hailed him as a hero only days before, the house was quiet, with no gathering of news crews or camera trucks in sight.

"Where is everyone?" Campello asked as they drove up and parked across the street from the house.

"Most likely they're collecting background information," Christy said. "They'll want to interview the department leaders, and then the dealers who are leveling charges, and then they'll want to get a feel for how the two cops at the 31st feel about it. Then, when they have enough, they'll be back like alligators on a wounded poodle."

"My, my, how the mighty have fallen," Campello said, eyeing the house.

"Something like that," she said.

They got out of the car and crossed the street to the house. A late-model Ford that had not been visible from the street was parked in the driveway.

"He has company," Campello said, reluctantly. "Maybe we should—"

"It won't get any better. There will be a team of reporters and news crews here by this time tomorrow night. If we're going to get his side of the story, now is the time to do it. He'll be holed up before long."

"He doesn't have long. The hearing is tomorrow."

They walked to the front entrance and Christy rang the bell. The door swung open immediately.

"Yes?" A tall patrician-looking man stood in the doorway. His blue blazer hung on his frame and an open-necked gray shirt exposed a prominent Adam's apple. A thick thatch of gray hair hung over his forehead, overshadowing ocean-blue eyes.

Campello showed the man his star. "I'm detective Frank Campello. I'm Andy's partner." He nodded toward Christy. "And he knows Christy," he said, not wanting to identify her as a reporter.

The man offered a hand to them. "David Stackhouse. I'm Andy's pastor," he said, stepping aside. "Glad you're here. Andy needs all the friends he can find."

He led them into the living-room where Andy and Jenny Polanski sat. They seemed genuinely glad to see Campello and Christy.

"I guess you've heard by now," Polanski said.

Campello agreed. "I think the whole city's heard. If not, they will soon."

Polanski groaned. His tie was undone and his shirt rumpled. His eyes were red-rimmed and his hand trembled as he fidgeted with the coffee cup in front of him. It was the first time Campello had seen the man in distress. All of the assaults, verbal or otherwise, the petty vandalism, and the shunning he had endured had not seemingly affected him. Even after the gun battle he seemed even keeled, unperturbed. But now he was under the kind of fire that he wasn't equipped to handle and it was clear he was out of his element.

"Mind if we sit?" Christy asked.

Polanski shook his head and the two sat in chairs across the table from his own. The man who answered the door took a seat also.

"Can I get you anything?" Jenny asked. "Coffee? Do you want coffee?"

Campello shook his head and Christy held up a hand. "No thanks," she said.

"For what it's worth," Campello said, "we think you were set up."

A faint smile of nervous tension crossed Polanski's face. "It's worth a lot. I can handle the heat that comes from doing the right thing. But this thing," he massaged his neck with one hand, "I can't fight this."

"Tell us what you know, detective," Christy said. "Tell us what you know and maybe you won't have to fight this alone."

Polanski shook his head. "It doesn't matter anymore, Ms. Lee."

"Of course it does. Your career depends on getting to the—"

"I'm going to resign."

Campello shot a glance at Stackhouse. The pastor's expression made clear he had not counseled Polanski to quit.

"That's it, then?" Campello asked.

"Excuse me?" Polanski said.

"I said, 'That's it, then?'"

"What would you have me do, Frank? I have no one in the department that I can trust. I—"

"You can trust me."

"And me," Christy said.

Polanski's laughter was humorless. "How do I combat the testimony of people who are exposing themselves to charges in order to come after me? Who approached them? Who has that kind of clout?"

"Some of the people you've irritated have that kind of power," Campello said. "People on both sides of the badge. And unless I miss my guess, they're working together."

"Detective," the pastor said to Campello, "what can we do? Where do we go from here?"

Campello gestured to Christy. "We are going to put our heads together and come up with some answers. I think that between the two of us, we can shed some light on who is doing this and why."

"I'm pretty good at my job, detective," Christy said, first to Polanski, and then with a smile to his wife. "I think I can do what detective Campello cannot do and vice versa."

"Your part, Andy," Campello said, "is to hang in there long enough to give us a chance. If you resign, you're admitting to something you didn't do."

"And if I don't, I'm exposing my family to a lifetime of pain."

Jenny squeezed his hand.

"You don't understand, Frank," Polanski said. "The harassment doesn't stop at the office. It follows me home. Jenny is receiving threatening phone calls, our house has been vandalized... our cars. I can fight something I can see, but I can't see these people. And now... now I know there are too many of them."

"They're also afraid," Christy said. "That's why they attack from the sidelines. You exposed some corruption that should have been exposed a long time ago. And I can help you finish it."

"No offense, Ms. Lee, but exactly how are you going to fight a combination of organized crime, corrupt politicians and corrupt cops?"

"With the press. They're afraid of the light."

"So what do you say?" Campello asked.

Polanski looked at his wife. She squeezed his hand and he rose to begin pacing the room. All eyes were on him.

"This is going to get a lot darker before it gets better," he said.

"Undoubtedly," Campello agreed.

Polanski's eyes met his wife's. She nodded.

"OK," he said. "We can hold on a bit longer."

Campello and Christy left the house, promising Polanski they would do their best. As they approached the car, Dave Stackhouse came out of the house and called to them. They stopped, allowing the minister to catch up.

"I appreciate anything you can do, detective."

Campello shrugged. "Just doing my job."

Stackhouse shook his head. "You're going to do a lot more than that. You could restore Andy's purpose in life."

Campello grinned and held out a hand. "Whoa, Father. You think too much of me. I'm not that good. But I do think he's been railroaded and—"

The pastor was shaking his head. "That's not what I mean." He looked back at the house and then crossed his arms. "How much do the two of you know about Andy?"

Christy shrugged. "I know he took a chance when he ratted on those two cops. It was a gutsy thing to do."

"Do you agree with her, detective?"

Campello shook his head. "No, I don't, Father. I think it was a stupid and self-serving thing to do."

The priest grinned. "I think so too, though not in the way that you mean. You see, Andy's father was a police officer too."

Campello glanced at Christy. "I didn't know that," he said.

"And his father was fired from the department for much the same reason as Andy might be if this thing isn't resolved."

"He was framed?" Campello asked.

Stackhouse shook his head. "No, but he was caught with some heroin in the trunk of his squad car and he was selling it out of that car. He lost his job and did time in prison. Andy was a young man at the time, just a teenager, and it affected him. He never reconciled to his father, even after the man was released from prison on medical grounds. When his father died, Andy left business and joined the police department."

"I already knew some of this," Christy said. "He's making up for his father."

Stackhouse nodded. "Yes. And isn't it ironic that Andy is being accused of his father's crime?"

"It takes a lot of swing to pull off something like this," Campello said. "This isn't coming solely from the department. This is organized from outside the department."

The pastor shrugged. "It doesn't matter, detective. A man's reputation and his view of himself will be destroyed."

"It's why he is the way he is, isn't it?" Christy said. "He walks a straight line because he can't escape being his father's son."

The minister shook his head. "No, that's only true in part, Ms. Lee. He walks as he does because he is a Christian and can walk no other. His faith is important to him. He knows he is being watched, not only by God, but by others who share or know of his faith, and this is also important to him." He spread his hands. "Do you know of St. Jude?"

Campello and Christy shook their heads.

"To make a long story short, he is the patron saint of lost causes. And, I might add, the patron saint of the Chicago Police department."

Campello snorted. "Are we a lost cause, pastor?"

Stackhouse shrugged. "Only if you surrender. The police stand between us and chaos. Andy takes his job seriously. He is a true son of Jude."

CHAPTER 44

They drove to a coffee shop after leaving Polanski's and sat at a table near a window that looked out onto Michigan Avenue. Grant Park was only just visible to the south, and the art museum to the north. But for the most part, they had an unhindered view of Lake Shore Drive and the lake beyond. The setting sun cast an orange hue across the wind-rippled water that reflected like a mirage against the darkening sky. Campello sat with one arm cast over the back of a chair as Christy stirred creamer into her coffee.

"I've been dodging you for the better part of two years and now here we are, working to save the career of a man I detested just a few days ago." He shook his head in disbelief.

"Tell me about it. I didn't care for you or your kind, and now I'm supposed to investigate charges against a police officer and help him clear his name." She drank her coffee and wrinkled her nose before adding another sugar. She stirred the mixture and tasted the coffee again, this time without commentary.

"There's more to this than clearing Polanski. Something is wrong and it involves players at a higher level than the department."

"Don't kid yourself, detective. You work in a very dark place."

He frowned. "What's your problem, lady? Why do you hate the police so much?"

She set the cup down and eyed him with suspicion. "I'll make a deal. I'll tell you why I don't trust cops, but you tell me why you do. Deal?"

"Deal. You first."

She cleared her throat, pausing to glance at the people walking along the sidewalk just outside the window. Most of them were bundled against the cold and were heading for cabs or buses. Some were heading to their homes in the city while others were looking for a quick ride to Union Station and the trains waiting to shuttle them home. She was facing south and nodded toward Grant Park.

"My brother was arrested there."

Campello glanced briefly over his shoulder at the park. "Grant Park? So? A lot of people have been arrested and a lot of them in Grant Park." He cocked one eyebrow and studied her sideways. "Were you here in sixty-eight?"

She shook her head. "I wasn't born yet."

"Your brother?"

"No. He was older than me, but he wasn't around then either."

Campello swirled the coffee, glancing into the cup. "What was he arrested for?"

"Ben was a good kid. You understand that, right? Just because he was arrested doesn't mean he was a bad kid or that our parents failed us."

Campello shrugged. "OK."

She stared at the darkening horizon. "Ben was easily led. He was a pleaser. He wanted to be accepted so badly." She diverted her eyes to the table-top in front of her. "He fell in with the wrong crowd, as we used to say. He began doing drugs. Nothing hard. Pot, mostly. And he got caught at a street fair that was being held in the park, and he was arrested."

"That's it? You hold it against the cops because your brother was busted for marijuana?"

"Let me finish, OK. There's more to it."

He held up both hands in surrender. "Sorry."

"He was arrested the same day and at the same location as an Alderman's son. The Alderman's son was released as soon as he was taken to the station. My brother was held over for arraignment and while he was waiting he was attacked." Her eyes reddened. "There were four of them. They attacked him because he wouldn't give up his seat." Her lip quivered. "He was so small. So gentle. He didn't have a chance."

She pulled a napkin from a holder on the table and dabbed at her eyes. "Ben was taken to the hospital. He had a concussion and slid into a coma before we could get to him. He lingered for several days but never regained consciousness." She bit her lower lip, fixing her gaze on the darkening horizon. "When he died, my parents blamed each other. It wasn't their fault, of course. But that didn't stop the pain." She sighed. "My parents divorced and my father killed himself not long afterward." She shrugged. "That's my story."

"I'm sorry," he said.

"Yeah, well. If my brother had been politically connected he would be here now. The law wasn't enforced equally. Someone took care of someone else because they had clout. My brother didn't have anyone like that."

The server approached their table with the coffee pot in hand. She eyed Christy with concern, but refilled both cups and left without a word.

"OK," Christy said, dabbing at her eyes again. "Your turn."

"Nothing quite so dramatic, I'm afraid. My father was a cop and worked two shifts a lot of the time to make ends meet. My mother died when I was nine and I spent a lot of time alone. Occasionally, Dad would come home early or have a night off, but he was usually so tired he didn't have time for me. I was always a bit of a loner." He gave her a sheepish grin. "Being alone now is one of my greatest fears."

"It is for a lot of people," she said.

"It was for my Dad, too. A string of floozies followed after my mother's death, but before long, he remarried. I'd like to tell you that my stepmother and I got along, but I'd be lying. I hated her from the start and she hated me. They divorced in short order." He shrugged. "Anyway, that went on a couple of times and this last one left when Dad got sick."

"Sick?"

"He has Alzheimer's. He's in Marimar."

"Oh."

"But it wasn't all doom and gloom. We did some things together. Not much, maybe, but some. We share a love of classic cars. He helped me restore the '65 Corvette I have."

"That's something," she said.

He grinned. "Yeah, it's something. And I became a cop, like my old man. And the department became my family. My closest friends are on the job. I love what I do and I dread the day I have to retire." He sipped the coffee.

"So…" she hesitated. The mask of self-assurance and bravado had fallen. Campello watched her, intrigued. He was attracted to her vulnerability.

"I guess we understand things a little better now," she said. "Know where each other is coming from."

He nodded slowly, smiling reassuringly. "I think so. We're a lot alike, you and me. This thing we're going to do… it's not going to be easy."

She flashed a small grin. "Nothing good ever is."

CHAPTER 45

Polanski's arrest had the anticipated effect. Rioting continued as it had the previous nights, but the tone was greatly subdued. The level of violence was significantly less, the amount of damage had decreased, and the number of the participants was a fraction of what it had been. The sudden change did not go unnoticed by the department's brass nor by Alderman Aaron Green. He called for a hastily arranged late-morning news conference and stood before the microphones with the Chief of Police on one side and his impeccably dressed son on the other. Peter's arrest had made the news, but had been quickly overshadowed by the charges pending against Polanski, Peter's chief accuser.

The press conference was held at City Hall and Christy was determined to be there. Here was one political announcement she did not want to miss.

The press had jammed into the center of City Hall, behind a line barrier. A microphone and a small podium bearing the seal of the City of Chicago were in place. Despite Christy's best efforts, she arrived later than planned and was standing near the back of the crowd when Aaron Green, Peter, and the Chief of Police emerged from behind the closed door of Green's City Hall office and marched the podium. She spotted an opening to her right and began nudging her way through the pack of journalists. By the time Aaron, Peter and the Chief were in their predetermined positions, she had made it to the second row and a position that would put her eye to eye with the alderman. Somber-faced, he began with an opening statement as he read from prepared notes.

"It is with a heavy heart that I have become aware of the recent charges filed against Chicago Police Department detective Andy Polanski. Detective Polanski appeared to be a rising star with the department when he stood firm in his allegations against two police officers."

He looked across the crowd of reporters that had gathered. "All of you are aware the recent riots have been attributable in no small measure to Mr. Polanksi's allegations. His charges were investigated and appeared to have merit. Unfortunately, the premature leak of the investigation was ill received by a public that thirsts for equal justice under the law. The resultant outburst has led to millions of dollars in property damage, hundreds of arrests, and the tarnishing of Chicago's public face. It would now appear that Mr. Polanski's allegations are questionable, at best, in light of his recent arrest and the developing evidence which would suggest an ulterior motive for his charges against officers Caine and Dorchester.

"I have made it my mission since becoming an Alderman always to support the police and aid them in their quest to keep the peace and protect the citizens of Chicago. The recent charges against one of our city's finest have not deterred me from that mission. But I do think it is fair to point out that my son has been repeatedly harassed by detective Polanski and has suffered arrest on two occasions. In each case, he has been released for lack of evidence when cooler heads prevailed.

"The recent riots, the terrible damage to the reputation of officers Caine and Dorchester and the two arrests of my son are but a few examples of the damage that can occur when a single public servant violates the trust that has been placed in him. Not only has he violated our confidence, but he has persuaded others to do the same. And while I do not believe we can label an entire department guilty of having the same lack of character that detective Polanski is alleged to have, I also must say that this type of behavior cannot be tolerated."

He cleared his throat. The Chief of Police looked solemnly ahead while Peter stood with his hands behind his back, staring at his father with the doe-like look that spouses of politicians often feign while on the campaign trail.

"Detective Polanski will face a review by the IPRA this morning. Pending that, I will launch an independent investigation, recusing myself from any personal participation, given that detective Polanski and his team have pursued my son with abandon."

He glanced at his notes and then folded them, sliding them into the breast pocket of his coat. "On a positive note, the decrease in the violence of last night should serve as an indicator that the participants in the previous nights of unrest were not doing so merely for greed. If that were the case, Mr. Polanski's arrest would not have affected the level of rioting as it has."

He scanned the audience for a reaction, but seeing none, said, "I will take a few questions."

Before anyone could react, Christy said, "Alderman Green, it seems to me that only detective Polanski is being held on charges while an entire department went after your son. How is it possible that one aberrant detective was so persuasive in convincing others to help him in his vendetta?"

Green cleared his throat. "Ms. Lee, I am not suggesting that detective Polanski is on a vendetta. I will wait until all the facts have been presented before I render an opinion. But I am saying that Mr. Polanski is facing some serious charges of his own and this brings into question all of his actions, professional or otherwise. My son has been arrested twice and twice he has been set free. And—"

"Charges were filed the second time, correct?" she asked.

He nodded. "Yes, that is correct, Ms. Lee. But again, he was allowed to walk free and those charges were dismissed."

She was about to follow up when a curvy blonde from one of the network affiliates muscled her way in with a follow-up question:

"Kimberly Crane," the blonde said. "Unless I have misunderstood you, sir, you have said that the riots were due in no small part to Polanski's allegations, and you have hinted that the sudden drop in the violence last night could be attributable to the dispelling of his allegations in light of his arrest. Was Mr. Polanski made the scapegoat in order to achieve control of the violence?"

Christy was astounded. The woman's question was insightful, even if she did look like a mannequin auditioning for a spot on a national news show.

"Young lady—"

"Kimberly," she said. "Kimberly Crane."

He cleared his throat. "Ms. Crane, I resent your implication that Mr. Polanski was in any way framed or otherwise maligned in order to discredit his testimony and use that as leverage to gain control over the rioting. The good men and women of the Chicago Police Department have met the unrest with resistance that has cost them a great deal in manpower, time, and personal injury." A sardonic grin enlivened his face. "If a simple frame job of Mr. Polanski was all it was going to take, I can assure you they would have done it a long time ago."

Laughter rose from the audience as other hands went up and a stew of shouted questions arose. But Christy had all she needed. Now she would wait to hear from Campello.

CHAPTER 46

Frank Campello had spent part of the night tracking down Caine and Dorchester. Though he knew the men, his relationship with them had been confined to the professional, the cross-sharing of leads that inevitably arise between adjacent police districts. But he managed to find them and offered to buy them a beer if they would be willing to talk off the record about their experiences with Polanski. Discovering that Campello was Polanski's new partner, they jumped at the chance, and by the time Campello arrived at Jeep's, both men were sitting in a corner booth along the wall opposite the bar, each of them with an open bottle in front of him. Christopher Caine sat on the side of the booth facing the door. He raised a hand and grinned broadly when Campello entered, gesturing for him to join them. The bar had just opened and the two were the only patrons in the place. Campello walked to their booth, shook hands with both of them, and slid next to Sean Dorchester.

"You guys been here long?"

Caine grabbed a handful of nuts from the bowl on the table.

Dorchester said, "Naw. We just got here. Seems like this is the only place we can go, now. You know? Cops are always welcome at Jeep's."

Campello caught the eye of the bartender, pointing at the bottles on the table. The man acknowledged him, pulling a bottle from beneath the bar and popping open the cap.

"I know," Campello said. "But take some peace from this. Polanski is in hot water himself and that may be a plus for you guys."

"Amen," Caine said, high-fiving Dorchester.

"Listen," Campello said, pausing as the bartender set the bottle on the table, "tell me what you know about Polanski."

"What's there to tell?" Dorchester said. "You ought to know him by now. You're working with him, right?"

Campello shrugged and took a long swallow from the bottle. "I only worked with him a few days and then he got arrested."

"Serves him right," Caine said.

Campello nodded and swiped his mouth with the back of his hand. "Tell me about it. Speaking of which," he grinned broadly, "what *can* you tell me about the weasel that'll help me out?"

The two men gave each other knowing looks.

"He's as straight as they come, Frank. A regular by-the-book kind of guy," Dorchester said.

"Except in his case, that ain't good," Caine said, waving a dismissive hand over the table.

"Absolutely not," Dorchester agreed, lifting his bottle. "We're not talking about straight as in being a stand-up guy. We're talking about straight as in, 'I'll put you on report.'"

Caine laughed. "Yeah. Hey, Frank, did you ever see that movie called…" He looked at Dorchester. "What was the name of that movie? The one where the psyche attendant is mugged and the four crazies that's with him go loose on the town?"

"*The Dream Team.*"

Caine snapped his fingers. "Yeah, that's it, *The Dream Team*. Ever see it, Frank?"

Campello shook his head.

"They got this one crazy in the movie, played by Christopher Lloyd, and he goes around town with a clipboard threatening to put everybody on report." He laughed. "Just like Polanski. Just like Polanski." He laughed again and swigged the beer.

"Except in this case," Campello said, "somebody listened to him."

The two men grew serious.

"Yeah, that's right," Dorchester said. "Somebody paid attention to him and now we're in trouble."

Campello glanced around the room. They were still the only customers in the place and the bartender was occupied with a game show playing on the TV suspended over the bar.

"Maybe not. Level with me. Did you guys plant the weapon?" He spread his hands. "I don't care. I've had to do stuff myself. It's a war out there. But this guy is leveling some serious stuff and if you didn't do it, or even if you did, it don't make no difference to us."

The two men eyed each other, but it was Dorchester who spoke first. "You said it, Frank. It's a war out there."

"Absolutely," Caine said. "It wasn't too long ago that you lost your partner to the other side. What would you have done to protect him?"

Campello scooped a handful of nuts from the bowl. "I killed the guy that killed him."

"Right," Dorchester said. "But what if you couldn't? What if the guy killed your partner, then tossed his weapon and threw his hands up?" He looked toward the still-preoccupied bartender before leaning across the table and lowering his voice. "What would you do then, Frank? Arrest the guy? Read him his rights? Or execute justice?"

Campello tossed his head back and swallowed the nuts. "I'd kill him."

"Just like you did, right?" Caine asked.

Campello nodded, washing the nuts down with a drink of the brew.

"It was like those two guys in California a few years back. Remember?" Dorchester said. "They came out of the bank wearing armor and they had all this firepower and they was gunning at the LAPD. Cops going down all over the place and then, when the bad guys were shot and the cops gained the upper hand, they wanted ambulances and actually thought they should go ahead of the police." He grabbed a fistful of nuts. "Imagine that, Frank. These guys start the trouble and shoot a bunch of cops and civilians, but when the cops give it back, they want the paramedics before the cops they shot." His face was red.

"Like you said," Caine added, "it's a war out there and we got no one we can trust except each other."

Campello spread his hands. "Hey guys, no argument here. If you planted the weapon on that guy, I'm up with it. If you didn't, that's cool too. I figure he fired on you or you wouldn't have fired at him in the first place."

The two looked at each other.

"That's exactly right, Frank. He turned on us so we turned on him," Dorchester said. "We did what we had to do, Frank. We took the guy down and we ain't going down with him. You know?"

"I do," Campello said. "I'm with you."

CHAPTER 47

Campello left the bar and drove back to the 28th. He had turned off his cell phone, not bothering to leave his location with dispatch, since he wanted to keep his meeting with Caine and Dorchester off the record for as long as he could. It was possible, of course, even likely, that the two would contact some of their friends at the 28th to declare what a solid guy he was, and that was fine. But with their implicit admission to having planted the weapon on the kid they killed, his view of them had changed. He could not support their actions.

He reached the Castle shortly after noon and went directly upstairs to the squad room. It should have been quiet and nearly empty when he arrived, since most of the detectives would be at lunch or out chasing leads. Instead, Tertwiller and Silvio were congregated in Lopez's office and a cluster of uniforms were gathered together in the squad room. Tertwiller caught sight of Campello and Silvio looked up, motioning for him to join them. Campello stopped at his desk long enough to hang his jacket over the back of his chair and deposit his weapon in the secured drawer of his desk, alongside the steno pad he had been using on his first day back. Rand's Chicago Cubs cup sat there too.

Lopez sat with his feet propped on his desk and his hands resting on his head. Tertwiller and Silvio occupied the chairs in front of the desk so Campello stood, leaning on the closed office door.

"We're deciding how to proceed now that Polanski is jammed up," Tertwiller said.

Silvio shook his head and snickered. "Seeing him go is almost as bad as seeing him come."

"The important thing for now," Lopez said, "is that everyone in this office cooperates with Internal Affairs. Polanski has been their darling for a while now, and they aren't going to take kindly to his having deceived them."

Campello listened to the exchange, feeling like a man straddling the Mason–Dixon Line. On the one hand, he sympathized with the department and its need to discharge itself of someone like Andy, someone they admittedly would never be able to trust. On the other hand, he had a deeper appreciation for him and the predicament he found himself in. Standing up for Polanski was going to mean alienating friends that had stood by him throughout the length of his career, not to mention four divorces and the decline of his father. They were, as Tertwiller had said, a family. But not acknowledging Andy's position would be wrong as well. Someone had planted those drugs. Campello was sure of that. And it had to be someone within the department.

"Frank?" Lopez said. "Got any thoughts?"

Campello shifted his weight from one foot to the other, crossing his arms. "Not really. I haven't worked with the guy all that much. I say we let IAD do their thing. If they ease up on him, we know what we're dealing with. If they fall on him, he's out. Either way, we will know more than we do now."

Tertwiller nodded. "He's right, Julio. We don't have to be proactive on this. We can let Internal Affairs do that. We can just react to their initiative the same way we would with any other case they'd investigate."

"Except this isn't like any other case they'd investigate, Shelly," Silvio said. "This is a fink they've marked as one of their own. If they find fault with this guy, it's going to be egg on their face. To me, it's pretty much of a no-brainer. They're not going to find anything wrong."

She eyed him with disbelief. "He had drugs in his car. A whole gang of dealers are lining up to testify he's been squeezing them. And Caine and Dorchester were working narcotics when Polanski charged them with evidence tampering."

Lopez sighed. "It stunned me. I thought this guy was on the up and up. Maybe a little too tightly twisted, but a by-the-book kind of guy."

"I don't care if he's by-the-book or not. He's made false allegations and ruined the reputations of some decent cops," Silvio said.

"Bob said that when word reached the 31st, the whole squad room cheered," Tertwiller said.

Silvio spread his hands. "There you go. The guy dug himself a grave and now he's fallen into it."

"Well," Lopez said, "let's just make sure that no one else does. Frankly, I'm glad he's gone. But as the district commander, I'm sorry to find out he's such a putz and that he got caught here. It'd been much better if he got busted at the 31st."

"There's going to be some press over this," Silvio said to Lopez. "You know that, right?"

The commander shrugged. "So? I've got to deal with it either way."

"They've portrayed him as a saint, now they'll portray him as a martyr," Silvio added.

"Maybe not," Tertwiller said, crossing one leg over the other. "They may pick up on his deception and write it up the way it really happened."

Silvio snorted. "That'd be admitting they were wrong about him in the first place. How many people you know can do that?"

"One thing's for sure," Lopez said. "They'll be at the hearing this afternoon." He swung his chair in Campello's direction. "You OK, Frank?"

"Sure. Just taking it all in."

"No, I mean, are you OK for the hearing?"

He shrugged. "I have to be. Nothing I can do about it now. Besides, Longhorse fired on me first."

"Well, be prepared. The board isn't going to take kindly to Polanski and it could spill over on you."

"We'll be behind you, Frank," Tertwiller said. "Like I said the other day, we're family."

CHAPTER 48

Campello made it to the IPRA office on West 35th Street with only minutes to spare. He took his seat at the lead table, opposite the dais at which the review committee would be seated. Since this first hearing was all about Polanski, he was already there, and Jenny was seated at the rear of the room. Tertwiller, Silvio, Hughbanks, and Lopez were present, too, and so was Christy, sitting quietly among the few journalists allowed inside the room.

The administrator of the IPRA, Dimitri Baranova, was a civilian, as all members were, and had been a recent appointment of the mayor's in response to the previous administrator's sudden retirement. He took his seat on the dais, flanked on each side by the other members, and gaveled the meeting to order.

"The facts of the case have been reviewed by me and members of the Authority. We have reviewed the police investigation, and have received and read the coroner's preliminary report, and the witnesses have been sworn." He directed his attention to Campello. "Detective Frank Campello, would you please give us your version of the events, as closely as you can recall."

Version? The spin was slight, but noticeable. Campello inched toward the microphone on the table and began by giving the facts of the events in as much detail as he could remember. He did not tell them that he had decided to pursue the lead on his own or allude to his confrontation with Polanski only minutes before the events transpired. He saw no benefit to giving them more than they had asked for. When he was done, the administrator thanked him and then directed his attention to Polanski.

"Detective Polanski. Would you please give us *your* version of the events?"

Polanski gave a concise description of the events, how he had decided to tail Campello, and how the sound of gunfire aided him in locating his partner. He described how he managed to flank Longhorse before finally overtaking the DJ just as he was about to shoot a disarmed Campello, taking him into custody without firing a shot. His testimony complete, he pushed the microphone away and sat back in his chair.

Baranova was about to speak when he was interrupted by a woman who had entered the hearing-room through a side door. She handed him a note, and whispered in his ear as he held his hand over the microphone. She left the room as quickly as she had entered.

"We will recess this meeting for fifteen minutes in light of some new developments. I will remind everyone to not discuss this meeting with anyone outside this room and that all witnesses remain under oath." He stood and everyone stood with him as he exited the room with the other members in tow.

"What was that all about?" the attorney asked. He turned to Polanski. "Did someone approach you? File a complaint?"

"Nothing. I haven't heard a thing."

Campello had a sinking feeling.

The attorney said, "Well, something's happened. This hearing is only about the relevant facts related to the shooting. It has nothing to do with the recent allegations against you, Andy."

Allegations, Campello thought. It is a very different word than *charges*, which had also been filed.

Campello rose to stretch. From the back of the room, Shelly Tertwiller gave him the thumbs up. Silvio grinned.

Polanski sat with his head lowered and his hands folded on the table.

"You guys want something?" the attorney asked.

Polanski shook his head. Campello asked for a Coke.

As soon as the attorney left, Campello leaned toward Polanski and said, "Bobby Longhorse and Delgado are working together."

"How do you know that?"

"I talked to Terri Williams, a dancer at the club."

Polanski groaned. "That means regardless of what happens to Longhorse, someone could still be gunning for me."

Campello said, "Maybe. Maybe not. I talked with Vincent earlier."

Polanski stared intently. "And?"

"I told him we were after Delgado and that we knew he was behind the attempted hit on you."

"We do?"

Campello shrugged. "Never hurts to stir the water once in a while."

"What'd he say?"

Campello chuckled. "What do you think?"

Polanski paused to think, drumming his fingers on the table. "Deny, deny, deny."

"Yep."

Polanski nodded toward the door that the administrator and the review authority members had gone through when recessing. "What do you think happened?"

Campello didn't want to tell him that Longhorse was likely going to retract his testimony. Besides, he could be wrong. The situation had become dynamic, changing as often as the tide of Chicago politics. He looked over his shoulder and saw the attorney returning with two cans of Coke. "This thing is cut and dried. It should've been a no-brainer."

The attorney took his seat between them and handed one of the cans to Campello and opened the other for himself. The members of the review board returned to the room as Campello pulled the ring tab on his can. He rose with the others in the room as the board took their seats on the dais, then sat and took a long slow swallow of the soft drink.

Baranova began, "Some new testimony has come to our attention that—"

Polanski's attorney jumped to his feet. "I object, sir. I have not been—"

"I understand, counselor," Baranova said, holding up his hand. "But this isn't a court of law. It is a fact-finding body charged with the responsibility of determining the appropriateness of police conduct. All police-action shootings, or any police violence, for that matter, default to this body for review. If new information has developed, we will evaluate it."

The attorney sat, mumbling to himself.

The administrator gestured to an officer standing at the rear of the room.

The door opened and Bobby Longhorse marched in the room with a uniformed officer on each side. His hair had been cut, he had shaved, and he wore a navy-blue, double-breasted blazer over a pale-blue shirt with a blue-and-gold tie, and khaki dockers. This was not the Bobby Longhorse that had been trying to kill them in an ambush, and Campello cast a sideway glance to Polanski.

Longhorse took his seat to the right of the dais and within easy visibility of Campello and Polanski.

"Sir, would you please state your name for the record?" Baranova asked.

"Robert James Longhorse." He spelled it for the court recorder.

"And you are employed by a local establishment known as Silk 'n Boots. Is that correct?" Baranova asked.

He nodded, but was immediately told to answer verbally. He did.

"Mr. Longhorse, would you please tell this board about the facts in your possession?"

He seemed confused by the question. "Sir?"

"Tell us what you know that is relevant to the proceedings, Mr. Longhorse," Baranova said, clarifying his previous question.

The DJ cleared his throat and focused his eyes on the floor. "Detective Polanski came to the club a few days ago. I had just come off the floor and was fixing myself a drink at the bar when he approached me and said he was taking control of the loop territory and that I could work with him or I could leave town."

Polanski shook his head and whispered into the attorney's ear.

"And what do you think he meant by 'the loop territory'?" Baranova asked.

Longhorse sighed. "The loop is the area that is run by me."

"You are dealing in illegal drugs, is that correct, Mr. Longhorse?"

"Yes."

"Have you had contact with Mr. Polanski before?"

Longhorse shifted in his seat, as though the testimony was uncomfortable for him. He kept his eyes on the floor. "Yes, sir."

"Please elaborate on that, Mr. Longhorse."

"Well, sir, I've had difficulties with officers of the 31st on several occasions. Most of the time it—"

"Let the record show," Baranova said, "that Mr. Polanski was formerly of the 31st district. Go ahead, Mr. Longhorse."

"Most of the time my problems came from two vice cops. They would—"

"And who were they?" Baranova asked.

"Caine and Dorchester. I never knew their first names."

"Go on."

Longhorse continued, "They've intercepted several shipments that guys like me depend on. I've had personal run-ins with them, but was always clean at the time and they had no reason to hold me."

"Are you familiar with one Tacquiel Sherman, otherwise known as The Tacker?"

"Yes sir, he worked for me. He was a mule. He shuttled deliveries between me and customers."

"Did he carry a weapon?"

"Yes sir. He was always armed. Most of us are. He had several clashes with the officers from the 31st and told me he would never let them take him. But I told him he didn't need to worry about those guys because another cop at the 31st had approached me about a deal."

"A deal?"

"Yes, sir. The officer said if I would cut him in for twenty-five percent of my total take, he could personally see to it that I would not have to deal with those officers again, so long as I kept my business in the 31st."

"And that was a good deal for you?"

Longhorse nodded. "Yes, sir. I was taking significant losses because of those two guys, Caine and Dorchester, and it seemed like a better deal to eat a regular twenty-five percent."

"And who was the officer that offered you the deal?"

For the first time since entering the room, Bobby Longhorse looked toward the witness table. "He's right there." He pointed directly at Andy Polanski.

CHAPTER 49

Polanski was exonerated of any wrongdoing in the shooting incident and Longhorse was remanded back to the custody of the authorities. Baranova expressed his "abiding concern" that Polanski had more for which to answer and indicated he would forward the information that Longhorse had supplied in his testimony to the department and to Internal Affairs. As soon as the hearing was over, the press rushed forward to get statements from the two officers, but both exited the room by way of a side door into a closed hallway. They left the attorney to handle the PR.

"What was that all about?" Polanski asked, stunned. "He did a complete turn-around in there."

Campello told him about Lopez's suspicion that Longhorse would do exactly that.

"So they got to him, too?"

Campello started to speak when the side door opened and Jenny Polanski, followed by Christy Lee, came into the isolated passageway.

"Not now," Polanski said, looking past his wife and to the reporter.

Christy opened her mouth, but hesitated when she saw the deploring look in Jenny's eyes. Instead, she said, "If you take this hallway through that door," she gestured to a door at the end of the passageway, "it will take you past the lobby and out to the main entrance. I can't promise they won't be waiting on you, but it's the best shot you've got."

Jenny Polanski put an arm around her husband. Turning to

Christy, she mouthed *Thank you*, before walking with him along the exit route the reporter had given them.

"That man perjured himself in there," Christy said, referring to Longhorse, as soon as the Polanskis were out of earshot.

"Andy has irritated some powerful people. And they're not all cops."

"Some of them have to be," she said. "There's no way this could be pulled off without some interference by the cops."

Campello couldn't disagree. "We need to talk about this… devise a plan, maybe. Let's get out of here and grab something to eat. We can talk."

"OK. An early dinner sounds good, actually. Where do you want to go?"

"My place."

She recoiled. "Your place?"

"It's quiet and out of the public eye… and I can cook."

She snorted. "I don't know if I want to be alone with you, detective."

"Lady, trust me. You've got nothing to worry about."

Polanski had left with his wife, so Christy and Campello took the tan squad to his apartment. The ride was largely silent, broken only by light conversation that was occasionally peppered with details from the hearing. Once home, Campello nosed the car into the underground garage, sliding into his reserved slot. They took the elevator to his floor.

"Take a left," he said, pointing the way to his apartment.

The hallway carpeting was thin, but in good repair, and sconces positioned along the wall cast a gentle glow of ambient lighting.

He unlocked his door, pushing it open to allow her to enter first. He followed, flicking on the light.

Christy was surprised and intrigued by Campello's home. It was small, but cozy and well apportioned, not fitting her perception of him at all. The walls were done in a pale yellow, and the off-white carpeting was plush. A flat-screen television rested on an oak credenza, opposite a tasteful arrangement of a sofa and recliners. Several plaques and awards, mementoes of his career, hung on one wall, and a rack of CDs stood to one side. A large ornate bookcase lined the opposite wall, its shelves over-laden with books, some of them stacked two deep. A set of sliding patio doors looked out onto the lake and the city skyline. A small kitchen opened directly onto the living-room; a wine rack rested on the counter.

"Not bad," she said, "for a narrow-minded cop." She smiled at him.

"Thank you." He opened the pantry and began surveying the options for dinner. "Help yourself," he said, pointing to the wine rack.

She pulled a bottle of Pinot Noir and studied the label while he set a pot of water to boil and prepared the pasta. He heated the stove and prepared the sauce.

She cleared her throat to get his attention. "Do you have a glass or would you prefer I drink from the bottle?"

He winced. "Sorry." He got two glasses from an overhead cabinet and set them on the counter. She opened the bottle and poured both glasses half full of the red wine.

"It's going to be a while before dinner is ready." He gestured to the living-room and she followed his lead, pausing to stop at the bookcase. She ran the fingers of her free hand along the spines of his books, tilting her head to the side as she read the titles.

"Poe, Dickens, Twain… *A Tale of Two Cities*, I loved that one."

"Me too," he said, smiling. "A poignant ending."

"Emily Dickinson?" She turned to him. "You read poetry?"

"Sure. I read everything. The classics, poetry… contemporary fiction. I'm a big fan of Koontz, Follett… Michael Connelly."

She smiled. "You are well read, detective."

He sat on the sofa and she joined him. The city skyline beyond the lakeshore was visible through the patio doors, a twinkling horizon in the approaching darkness.

"I sit on the balcony most evenings," he said, "when it's not freezing. The moon, the lake… it's peaceful. A lot different than the world I inhabit during the day." His gaze was fixed on the distant cityscape.

He was not the man Christy had projected him to be. The cop-swagger, the hard stance against Polanski... it was bravado; a protective shell. Campello was sensitive. A lonely man in a lonely profession. And she was drawn to him despite herself.

"We need to come up with a plan," he said, setting his glass on the coffee table and turning his attention to her.

"Who would've ever thought?" She sipped her wine, studying him over the rim.

"Strange bedfellows?" he asked.

His choice of words was not lost on her.

"Before we begin," he said, "I need to know that this won't end up in the papers."

"I'm a reporter."

"That's not what I asked."

She crossed her legs. "Depends."

He turned his gaze to her. "No, it doesn't. Are you interested in doing the right thing or not?"

"Are you?"

He sighed. "We're not going to get very far, Ms. Lee, if we don't set some ground rules. There are some things I'm just not going to tell you if I think you're going to write them up for consumption tomorrow morning."

He was formal, distant, calling her *Ms. Lee*. Did he feel what she felt? "But I am a reporter."

"So how about a compromise? We talk openly with each other and work together on sorting this out. If you feel the need to write anything up, you can use what we find, but you can only use me as an unnamed source. Does that work for you?" He slipped off the sofa to check on dinner.

She sipped the wine and paused to think. When he returned, she said, "OK. But I will reveal anything I think is relevant."

"Except for my identity."

She hesitated.

"Or else this is over before we begin."

She sighed. "OK, it's a deal. But whatever comes of this, I get an exclusive on it. And I won't reveal your identity."

He studied her face in the partial light that came through the glass door from the apartment. "I met with Caine and Dorchester."

"Yeah?" She slid toward him.

"They so much as admitted they planted the weapon."

Her eyes widened. "Then that's it. Polanski is telling the truth."

He held up a hand. "Now hold on. Maybe he is and maybe he isn't. It might have been a righteous shoot and they planted the weapon out of a panic and he saw it. Used it as an effective tool."

"Then their actions would still be wrong. Besides, you don't really believe that, do you?"

He shook his head. "No."

"You think he's being set up?"

He nodded. "I do. But by who?"

She laughed. "Are you for real? The department. Who else?"

"Oh come on, Christy. How can the department pull off something like this by itself?"

"Like planting drugs in his car? Easy."

"I mean like getting Longhorse to recant his confession and compelling high-profile dealers to testify against him even at a cost to themselves. Who in the department has that kind of reach?" He shook his head and picked up his wine glass. "Someone else is pulling the strings."

"Weren't you visiting with Vincent? Don't you think that… you do, don't you? You think Paulie Vincent is behind this."

"It's the only thing that makes sense. Think about it. All of a sudden there are known dealers coming out of the woodwork to testify against a cop? And then Longhorse takes the stand at the hearing to deepen the allegations?"

"That could mean Aaron Green dances at Vincent's command, too. If that's true, Vincent's reach goes a lot higher than anyone thought and that leaves us with two possibilities. Either he is involved indirectly, or he's got a pipeline into the 28th that may go through our favorite alderman. And don't tell me you haven't thought about that."

He had. But he wasn't going to admit it. This trust thing with a reporter was new and untested.

"And that means we don't know who to trust," she said, "which takes us back to where we were an hour ago."

He finished his wine. "Right now, we are going to have to put aside our differences and come up with a plan. That OK with you?" The smell of pasta wafted through the apartment.

"Yeah," she said. "But right now, let's eat. I'm hungry."

CHAPTER 50

They dined and then talked until late in the night, assessing the situation and planning strategy. By the time Campello took Christy to her car and returned to his apartment, he was able to get slightly less than four hours' sleep. The following morning, he checked on his father – a surprise visit that found the old man sleeping comfortably while his breakfast grew cold – and then drove to the Uptown area to meet again with Gloria Perez.

She answered the door on the first knock and he held out two large coffees. "I know you like lattes," he said, grinning.

She cocked her head to one side and took one of the cups from him. "And just how would you know that?"

"I'm a detective. That means I'm a trained observer."

A faint smile creased her face and she stepped aside, allowing him to enter.

The apartment was as spotless as it was last time, and once again, a classical tune played.

"Paganini?" he asked, recalling the name from his previous visit.

She grinned and shook her head. "Vivaldi. *The Four Seasons.*"

"Of course. My mistake."

She gestured to the sofa and he sat. She took a chair opposite him and removed the lid from the cup. She blew gently, tasted suspiciously, and smiled.

"You heard about detective Polanski," he said. It was a statement and not a question. News of Polanski's fall had been the chief topic of the local morning news programs and of the Chicago papers.

True to her word, Christy's name did not appear as a byline on any of them. He knew her restraint was a huge effort for her.

"Yes. Everyone has, detective. When a cop like him falls, it's news." She sipped the coffee.

"I believe it was a setup."

"I have no doubt."

He set the cup on the coffee table. "Why are you still here? Every lead I have that connects to Peter is gone. Rita is dead, Juanita is missing, and all of the other girls on Rita's list are unreachable... why are you still here?"

"Chicago is my home."

He shifted on the sofa and crossed his legs. "That's it?"

"Did you look at the names on Rita's list, detective? I mean, *really* look at them?"

He shrugged. "I called them, but none of them were reachable. At least, not at the numbers I had."

She repositioned herself, tucking one foot under her. "They're all illegals, detective. Every one of them. Including Rita."

"Go on."

"Green, and I'm talking about the old man, is moving illegals through his warehouse. They are smuggled in trucks from a variety of businesses and locations and brought to Chicago. Once they're here, they can go where they want. Most often, though, he has work lined up for them and he gets a finder's fee."

"Aaron Green is working as an employment agency for illegals?"

"Something like that. He collects a fee from groups seeking to import the aliens, and often collects from the aliens themselves. Then he collects a finder's fee from the employers who are looking for help and even collects campaign donations from them for his protection."

"How is this tying into the club?"

"Peter is enticing the youngest and most attractive of the girls into dancing with the promise of a large income, stardom... whatever it takes. Some of the girls are led or forced into prostitution and the ones that rebel are sent home."

"Longhorse told my partner that Trina was killed for refusing Peter's advances."

"I don't doubt it. The old man is bad, but Peter is much worse." She drank the coffee.

"What about the other girls on the list?"

She shrugged. "Who knows?"

"And that takes me back to my original question. Why are you still here?"

"I'm not an illegal, detective. I was born and raised in Chicago. But I did work at Silk 'n Boots for a while."

"Doing what? I don't mean to be indelicate, Gloria, but your name is not on that list for no reason."

"I started out as a dancer. But Peter kept pushing me to do more for the customers. I needed the money at first, so I agreed. After a while I began to have second thoughts and started to complain. He told me if I was willing to manage the other girls, I wouldn't have to spend any more time with the customers. I'd have my hands full managing the business."

"How many girls were involved?"

She shrugged. "Me at first. Just me. But by the time he offered to have me manage the others, I had a pretty good idea that nearly all the girls were involved."

"Not all?"

"I'm sure there are some that aren't, but I'd have no idea who they are."

"Are you working for Peter now?" he asked.

She laughed and shook her head. "You cops. You really are as dumb as they say. Didn't you talk to Rita?"

"Yeah," he said, confused.

"Rita began managing the business after I left."

He glanced around her apartment again. The fine art, the upscale furnishings… "Why was Rita killed?"

She shook her head. "I don't know, but my guess is she got into trouble with Peter."

"You think he would kill her?"

"In a heartbeat." She set the empty coffee cup on the table beside her. "You've got to understand something, detective. Peter is incredibly sensitive when it comes to his old man."

"Sensitive? How do you mean?"

"His father is highly successful and highly motivated. Peter is none of those things. But he is prideful. So when Aaron tells him he's never going to amount to anything, that irritates Peter. He's started this escort business independently of his family. But he's running girls out of the warehouse to do it."

"Does Aaron know this?"

"How could he not? He's connected. He stays on top of things."

"And yet he lets Peter keep on keeping on."

"Of course. There are other players in the scheme."

"Paulie Vincent?"

She gave him a confused look. "I don't know who he is, but I know Tony Delgado and his crew. One of them worked me over pretty good one night."

"What for?"

"I told one of the girls to quit. She was having second thoughts and she wanted out." She shook her head. "That girl could sing. She wanted a chance to make it in the US so I told her to take off. I was managing the operation so I thought I had the right. You know?"

"Yes."

"Anyway, word got back to Peter and he slapped me, so I slapped him back. In front of the others. That night, when I was going to my car, one of Delgado's crew came around." She shivered. "I was in the hospital for two weeks and rehab for two more. That's pretty much the time I decided I was going to leave."

"And Rita?"

"She was seeing Peter and wanted a chance to manage the girls. I was too banged up to work the johns so I was able to get out."

"You were lucky."

"Very. Most of the girls who leave get carried out."

"So your interaction with Delgado was nil?"

"Yeah. I know he keeps an eye on Aaron's warehouse and on Peter, and I know Aaron can only go as far as Tony will allow."

"Was Tony involved with the girls when you were managing?"

She shook her head. "Only to the extent that he wanted to keep Peter happy for Aaron's sake."

"That's probably the reason you're still alive."

"Any reason will do," she said.

CHAPTER 51

Campello checked his BlackBerry for messages after leaving Gloria's apartment. He and Christy agreed the previous evening on a simple code that they could use if either of them needed a quick response from the other. When scanning along his list of messages, he saw one from her that had the red exclamation point. The message had come in shortly after he arrived at Gloria's.

It read: Longhorse dead. Story is going to press soon. Thoughts?

He called her and she answered on the second ring.

"Longhorse is dead?"

"As Christopher Columbus. He was found hanging in his cell this morning."

"How come no one has called me?"

"Did you check your voice mail?"

"There wasn't a record of it on my phone. It would be there if anyone called."

"That's odd, isn't it?"

"Very."

She was silent for a moment. "Can you see what you can find out? My editor wants something on it by this evening's deadline. I want to cover all the bases, but I want to know what I can say that won't compromise us."

He was astounded. The woman of the night before was unwilling to do anything that might suggest a surrender of her journalistic integrity.

"I'll see what I can find out."

He arrived at the 28th, leaving the squad in the segregated lot. Across the top of the car he saw that Tertwiller and Silvio were leaving and were engaged in animated conversation. If they saw him, they gave no indication.

He entered the building through the ground-floor lobby. Although it was still early, the area was alive with activity. To his left, two men were being booked on charges of theft. To his right, a young woman was being booked on suspicion of drug possession, and, on the far side of the room, two middle-aged women who looked as though they should be standing in front of a classroom were, instead, being charged with solicitation by an undercover officer.

Upstairs in the squad room, Hughbanks and Chin were hunched over Chin's desk, preparing to meet with the assistant state's attorney. Their drug-bust case was still yielding results, netting a large swathe of the city's gang hierarchy.

Campello paused at his desk, as he did every morning, to hang his jacket over the back of his chair and take his CPD mug to the coffee maker. He poured a cup from the half-full pot and replaced it on the hotplate.

He paused to glance around the room as he drank the coffee. Except for Hughbanks and Chin it was empty and unusually quiet. He rapped on the open door of Lopez's office.

The commander was on the phone and motioned him into the office. Campello entered, but left the door open. When Lopez hung up, Campello said, "What happened to Longhorse?"

"He died."

"He didn't die, Julio. He hanged himself. There's a big difference."

"Is there, now?" He folded his hands on top his head and rocked gently backward in his chair, studying Campello.

"What's wrong, Julio?"

"You said it yourself, Frank. A suspect is dead."

"I didn't say it. You did. I asked what happened."

"When did you talk to Longhorse last?"

He shrugged. "I don't know. At the club? I haven't talked to him since he tried to kill me. That sort of thing raises all kinds of barriers to good communication."

"You think this is funny?"

"I didn't until now."

Lopez glanced into the squad room, lowered his hands to his desk and slid forward in his chair. "Longhorse didn't hang himself. He was hanged."

"And you think I did it?"

Lopez continued to stare.

"If I wanted him dead I would've done it the day he ambushed me."

"He told his attorney you called him a 'dead man'."

"And he is, isn't he? I told him that his best chance was to cooperate with us. That if he didn't, his associates would assume he squealed."

"Where've you been, by the way? It's after ten."

"I was interviewing Gloria Perez. She gave me some very good background on Peter Green."

Lopez inhaled sharply through his teeth. "You've arrested him twice and each time he's walked. His old man can make a lot of trouble for this department. Focus on the murder, Frank. You're putting me in a difficult position here."

"I am focusing on the murder, Julio. Peter Green did it and I know it and so do you."

Lopez rose from his chair and began jabbing his finger at Campello in staccato bursts, punctuating each word. "You-don't-have-any-forensic-evidence-at-all."

Campello set his mug on the desk. "So what? How many times do we ever have enough forensic evidence? This guy did it, Bobby Longhorse said he did and we had gathered enough evidence to issue a warrant, but then it disappeared."

"Watch it, Frank. You're coming dangerously close to—"

"To what, Julio? Insubordination?" He rose from the chair and stood, meeting the district commander eye to eye. "Let me repeat this, in the event there is a misunderstanding. Peter Green killed Trina Martinez and likely killed Rita Chavez and I'm going to put him in jail for it if it's the last thing I do."

CHAPTER 52

Peter was off the hook again, at least for now, and that allowed Aaron time to plan for the future. The repeated harassment of the CPD was not entirely unjustified, of course, and he knew that sooner or later his son was going to pay for his crimes – real or imagined. But for now he was free and that would allow Aaron the time to devise a definitive plan to keep him that way.

His appointment with Anthony Delgado and Paulie Vincent was scheduled for noon, a lunch meeting to be held at Vincent's home. The three men sat around an imported table in the dining-room while a fire crackled in the fireplace. Vincent sat at the head in his motorized wheelchair, tethered to the oxygen tank that hung surreptitiously over the back. Tony Delgado sat with a glass of red wine and a cigar. Aaron Green had red wine too.

"Aaron," Vincent said, in a voice raspy from the flow of oxygen, "how is Peter doing?" His words came slowly, his sentences broken by deep gasps.

"He's home, Mr. Vincent."

Vincent nodded. "He is giving you trouble."

"He has. But it isn't a problem that cannot be resolved." He grinned collegially and spread his hands. "Kids. Do they ever grow up?"

"He is not a kid, Aaron," Delgado said. "He's thirty years old."

The alderman fought to suppress a flash of anger. "Not everyone matures as quickly as they should. But I think this last episode with the police has made him aware he is traveling down the wrong road. I know he is prepared to take the necessary steps to alter his course and I am ready to help him."

Delgado inhaled on the cigar then nodded in acknowledgment. "I am sure he will do well, Aaron. You are a good father and a good man. The city and your son are fortunate to have you."

Delgado was patronizing Aaron and the implicit sarcasm was not lost on him. His anger intensified.

Vincent turned slightly in his chair to face Delgado. "This witness is no longer a problem? Our interests are protected?"

Delgado nodded. "Yes sir. They are secure."

"Good. Thank you, Tony. Aaron, I think it is time to look at future options for our partnership. Would you agree?"

Vincent's use of the word "partnership" was euphemistic. The partnership was dictatorial, though always in a way that was meant to stroke Aaron and make it appear as though any of the decisions made had been his alone. Vincent was kind that way; a true politician who could take the taxpayer's money from him and then give a portion back in a government subsidy while making the poor schmuck think he was fortunate to have Big Brother protecting his interests. Green knew about such things. He had built a very successful career and an impressive power base doing the same thing.

"Challenges exist everywhere, Mr. Vincent. Business thrives best when periodic reassessments are done."

"I couldn't agree more," Vincent said, puffing between words. "Tony, perhaps you can tell Aaron of our plans?"

Green sipped the wine, watching as the enforcer nodded gently at Vincent's request, tapping ash off his cigar.

"Certainly," Delgado said. "Aaron, we've enjoyed a productive relationship. The transport and facilitating of…" he paused, clearly searching for the right words, "those who would come to our shores for a chance at freedom, the chance for the kind of life we too often take for granted, has been genuinely satisfying while also being financially rewarding. But as with any business, the opportunities are dwindling, particularly in the face of the shifting political climate in this country away from the very heart of its founders. It's a pity, to be sure, but one we must accept as a reality." He paused to sip his wine. Vincent's oxygen tank hissed.

Delgado continued, "To that end, I've taken the liberty of preparing a brief overview of where I think we need to head and how we can get there in the most expeditious way possible." He reached to the floor, at a briefcase that was near his feet. Outside, on the terrace, the wind whipped violently as the sky opened and rain began to pound the city.

Delgado extracted copies of a prepared summation, stapled and bound in a colored folder, and handed one to Green and one to Vincent. The alderman knew the latter was strictly for show. Delgado knew who buttered his bread and would not have drafted the proposal without Vincent's express orders to do so, and certainly would not be dropping the presentation on his employer this way. Vincent would have instigated it and signed off on it prior to the meeting.

Green pulled a pair of reading glasses from his inside breast pocket, perching them on the end of his nose before opening the folder and reading Delgado's assessment.

The men read in silence, punctuated only by the click of the oxygen machine and the pounding onslaught of rain. The report ran the numbers of the last quarter versus the costs of doing business. Revenue had fallen as the flood of illegal immigrants found other routes into the US. Although others were also seeking to come to America, it was the Mexicans that generated the greatest revenue, funding the operation and making it a profitable venture. Now, with new fences going up and a sharper focus by the US government on a growing problem, all of that had begun to unravel. Delgado's new proposal centered on the distribution of weapons, a matter that had always raised the rankles of the government as well as larger portions of the populace. When he was done reading the report, Aaron could feel his anger begin to rise again and the power to suppress it growing weaker by the minute.

"Guns?" he said, moderating his indignation as he closed the folder and lifted the wine glass.

"We… Mr. Vincent and I," Delgado said, with a deferential nod to the crime lord, "feel that the security threat to our way of life that has arisen from the influx of illegal immigrants presents an opportunity for profit. I am not talking about *all* illegals, of course, but certainly, as in all businesses, we get the bad with the good. But beyond that, since we live in an increasingly violent age when the number of groups that would do us harm is rising sharply, it seems only prudent that we arm ourselves and our friends. Wouldn't you agree, Aaron?"

He swallowed the wine and set his glass on the table. He was aware that Vincent had shifted his large head toward him and was awaiting his reply.

"Of course. It is hard to live in these times and not be aware of the escalating threats against our liberty and our safety."

"Yes," Delgado said enthusiastically, nodding in agreement, "that is exactly what I am talking about."

"Of course," Green said, choosing his words carefully, "there are inherent risks with this."

"There are with everything," Delgado said.

"Naturally," Green said, peripherally aware that Vincent's gaze was moving back and forth between them like a man at a tennis tournament. "But in our previous venture we had the support of a large segment of the public. Safe houses, protected routes… these all came into play and gave us a support base extending beyond the one afforded by our customers. In this instance," he tapped the folder lying on the table, "we have a diminished base of support and the increased threat of the state and the federal governments as well. Offering a chance at liberty to people desiring to flee their poverty was, at the very least, a humanitarian cause. But this," he tapped the folder again, "increases our risk for exposure, and with exposure comes trouble."

Vincent's head was focused on Delgado. The rain continued to pound the brownstone.

"These weapons are small and easy to conceal," Delgado countered. "They are inexpensive and various groups in and around the country are vying for them. These groups are no threat to us. They only pursue each other and that in itself presents an opportunity. As for the government, it has its own problems. Did it not ship arms to a group of Mexican drug gangs? Can't we do the same? Do we care who kills who, so long as we are not in their sights?" He shook his head. "I think this is a venture that we cannot afford to neglect. The timing is right and the opportunity is at hand, and if we don't seize it someone else will. And I might add, this is a business that has extended possibilities. There are nations all over the world who have their own problems, internal or external, and they require a steady flow of weapons and ammunition. The federal government has shipped arms to various warring factions for years and has reaped an enormous profit from it. Why should they have unfettered access to such a rich market and the profits it generates?" He paused, puffing on the cigar, waiting for Green's reply.

Aware that Vincent was listening, and that he had already put his seal of approval on the plan, Aaron sighed and said, "Of course, Tony. You are right, of course. I merely wanted to point out the risks. The plan is fine and I'm sure that my staff and I can implement it with little difficulty. When would you like to begin?"

Delgado smiled a humorless smile. He glanced briefly, but noticeably to Vincent. "We have to close down the current operation, but as soon as that is done, we can receive our first shipment."

The alderman acceded flatly, "I'll be ready."

CHAPTER 53

Christy smiled when she saw the call was coming from Campello. During their dinner meeting, he had proven to be a pleasant conversationalist and on the drive home, had been deferential to her, even protective, when she got into her car, waiting to be sure it started and that she was on the road safely. Maybe it was the cop in him. Maybe not. But she had to admit she liked his concern and had been touched by it.

"Hi, detective."

"We need to talk. Are you free?"

"Shoot."

"I mean face to face. Somewhere secluded. We've got a problem."

"What kind of a problem?"

"Not here. Not over the phone."

Nothing in the amount of time she had spent with him had given her any hint that he might be an alarmist. In fact, most cops were restrained and Campello was every bit a cop's cop. But the tension in his voice betrayed his concern.

"My place? Thirty minutes?" she asked.

"Tell me where and I'll be there."

She gave him the address and left the newsroom to meet him.

The drive to her near North Side apartment took no more than ten minutes, leaving an urgently needed twenty minutes to tidy up the place. Her home was a single-bedroom apartment, and her tendency to put off until tomorrow anything she could ignore today had left a pile of undone laundry, unfolded clothing, unwashed dishes and other debris of life lying about. Campello's apartment had been nearly immaculate, at least on the surface, with everything in its place. She did not want him seeing how the other half lived, and scurried about restoring the chaos into some semblance of order. For reasons she couldn't define, Campello's opinion had become important to her.

She slid the clothing, laundered and unlaundered, into the hamper, compacting it with enough force to close the lid. Next, she turned to the dishes, rinsing and scraping them, before packing them into the dishwasher where they would at least be out of sight. With a quick application of a duster and the tucking away of some loose notes and other things, the apartment was nearly presentable just as the knock came at the door. She stopped long enough to smooth her hands down her agitated form and took a deep breath. When she opened it and saw him in the doorway she felt a rush she had not felt in years.

"We've got to talk," he said, entering the apartment, not waiting for an invitation.

"OK," she said, taking in his gray button-down Oxford shirt, black slacks and black leather jacket. Christy appreciated the quiet formality of his style and when she stepped aside to allow him to enter, his scent was clean, masculine.

He looked around the apartment. "Nice place. You spend a lot of time on it."

She had not been prepared for the slur, but when she saw genuine appreciation on his face, she knew the comment had not been intended as an insult.

"Thank you," she said hastily, feeling every bit the phony as she gestured to the couch.

He shrugged his jacket off and sat. She asked him if he would like a drink and he suggested a beer. She brought him a bottle, setting it in front of him along with one for herself.

"Now, what's the pressing news?" she asked, sounding almost clinical.

"Longhorse's death wasn't a suicide."

"How?"

"Someone hanged him. I talked with my contact in the coroner's office. She confirms that he was murdered, based on her initial impressions. She won't know until she does the autopsy, but that won't be until tomorrow morning."

"So he was silenced?"

"Looks that way."

"But why? He turned on Polanski, so surely he wasn't a threat to anyone other than him. Why would anyone want him dead now?" She drank from the bottle.

"Think about it. His testimony before the board was radically different from his admission to Polanski."

"Right. I think we already knew that."

"And now he's dead. He was a threat to someone and they eliminated the threat."

"We still don't know who 'they' are for sure."

He set the beer on the table. "Undoubtedly someone under Vincent's influence. We may not know the 'who' with certainty, but here's the how." He began ticking off the fingers of one hand. "One, it could've been done by a cop. Unlikely, I'd like to think, but possible, so we need to consider it. Two, a visitor. I've checked the visitors' log and there's no one registered. Since he was held in segregation for his own safety, there are no witnesses."

"How convenient. But how could a visitor even be considered as the killer if no one visited him?"

"Again," Campello said, "it goes back to a cop. I said that there were no visitors logged in. I didn't say he didn't have visitors. And then there's possibility three: he actually did kill himself and the post-mortem evidence will show that."

"So if he was murdered, it leaves us with cop involvement, regardless."

"Correct." He took a long swallow of the beer. "And my commander is suspicious of me."

"You? Why?"

Campello shrugged. "Probably because Longhorse tried to kill

233

me. And during an earlier interview, I told him he was a dead man, even in jail, if his cohorts could get to him." He sighed and crossed his legs. "And Julio is under pressure. No doubt he's getting heat from the brass on Peter. We've arrested him twice and he's walked twice and his father holds sway over the department." He paused to swig the beer, then clearly hesitated.

"What? What is it?" Christy asked.

"My partner. Not Polanski, Rand. After he was killed I began running his case load. We had worked some of the cases together and I wanted to have a say in what cases were parceled out. I didn't want the ones I invested time in to disappear. I wanted to see them through to completion, for his sake as well as mine."

"Sure. I can understand that."

"The cases are classified by a number. But when I was running through the list, I saw a classification that doesn't exist."

"Meaning?"

"Meaning that it doesn't exist. It's a dummy. He was working something he didn't want anyone to know about, but he wanted to leave a record in the event something happened. It was something important to him that he wanted known if he wasn't around to see it through."

"What was it?"

He shrugged. "I don't know. I made a note of it, but when I went back to check it out, it wasn't there. It had been deleted out of the computer."

"The note?"

He shook his head. "No. It was gone. I ran through his list of pending cases again, but this time the case number was gone. It's like it never existed."

"Do you still have the file number?"

He nodded. "Yeah, but I can't retrieve it because he kept it as a private memo. The case number was his device, his way of keeping it safe. It has no official relevance. Now that it's gone, I don't know where to look." He drank the beer. "There's a much bigger conspiracy than I imagined."

"But you must have some idea who is working with Peter. You work with these people day in and day out."

"Yes." His eyes searched hers. "But it was different today. They were... distant."

"Your boss? Can you go to him?"

He finished the beer; played with the bottle. "He's the most distant of all. Hostile, in fact."

"Then you're in the same position Polanski was."

"I know. And that's why I need your help."

Christy exhaled slowly. "I'm in. I told you that last night."

He ceased playing with the bottle and focused his eyes on her. "There's something else."

She arched an eyebrow.

"Would you want to have dinner again, sometime?"

CHAPTER 54

Peter Green did not like Bobby Longhorse, but the DJ was loyal. Now that he was gone, Peter had to find a new source of support.

The warehouse had provided an opportunity to show the old man that he had what it took to be a success. The club had given him a chance to make a name for himself, securing the necessary political connections to keep it up and running, safe from the prying eyes of the police.

But Polanski had ruined everything by questioning him and then arresting him, jeopardizing the business behind the business. The customers Peter serviced were power brokers in their own right, requiring total anonymity. In large measure due to the quality of the stock he employed, his database of customers and their preferential desires had grown quite large, very quickly. His table of women had grown too, a heady list of Chicago's movers and shakers developing with it. In all his years as an alderman, his father had yet to wield the type of influence that Peter had been busy accruing. He may not be able to raise funds and slash budgets, but he could raise and slash reputations and the careers that went with them. Like any powerful man, Peter would do what was necessary to survive. But he also had enemies and if he was to remain successful, his enemies would have to be dealt with.

He had tried to explain that to Longhorse one evening while the DJ enjoyed a lap dance, but the dummy took action in a way that would've been better left to the professionals. A highly visible attack against a highly visible cop who ended up not being at the site of the ambush anyway. When Peter learned of the attack, he knew he urgently needed a conduit into the 28th district headquarters to ensure that Longhorse kept his mouth shut. But the problem soon solved itself. Longhorse's big mouth made him a big liability to others as well. Someone, most likely Peter's father, and probably through Delgado, had managed to convince the man to fall on his sword and recant his testimony. Fortune smiled again when Baranova was appointed as chairman of the IPRA in time for the hearing. But someone still saw Longhorse as a threat and had him eliminated. That left Peter to address the next threat on his own and through his own contacts, which gave him a sense of accomplishment.

Baranova agreed to meet with him at the club. The man was far more brazen than most of Peter's other clients, and his willingness to risk being seen coming in and out of the club spoke volumes about his audaciousness. And that was exactly what Peter needed most.

Baranova arrived twenty minutes late. He was his usual pompous self, offering no explanation or apology for his tardiness. Instead, he requested a specific girl, one whom he had gotten to know and appreciate. Peter told him she would be available later in the evening, and assured him she was looking forward to it as much as Baranova. But business needed to be done first, and he had a request of the IPRA chairman.

"I need some help with a particular police officer," Peter said. "He's becoming a huge problem."

Baranova was sitting on the couch, a drink in his hand. "Let me guess. Frank Campello."

Peter winked and shot at the man with a thumb and forefinger. "You guessed right."

"His partner is being investigated by Internal Affairs. If IAD finds against him, and it's certain they will," he paused to drink a bit of the martini, "they will inevitably open an investigation on Campello as well."

"And how long will that take?"

Baranova paused to think. He shrugged. "Five, six months, I should think."

"That's too long. By that time my problems will have escalated."

"I see. Is there some other way to alleviate the strain?"

"I was hoping you could tell me."

"There are rumors that he has become quite close with his partner. If that is true, pressure from his fellow officers could be all it takes to drive him out. Or perhaps it could lead to a transfer."

Peter shook his head. "I had something a little more definitive in mind."

"Like?" Baranova asked, his eyes narrowing.

"Like seeing that he's gone now."

"That was already tried once, and unsuccessfully, I might add."

He shook his head. "No, no, I'm thinking along political lines. Surely you have some idea, some connection that could help me eliminate this threat."

Baranova set the martini glass on the nearby table and folded his hands across his belly. "I am not without resources within the department. There are some ways we could defuse the threat, even if we can't eliminate the man."

Peter grinned. "Now that's what I'm talking about."

CHAPTER 55

Campello and Christy dined that evening at Fogo de Chao's, a premier Brazilian steakhouse on North LaSalle Street, a half mile north of the Chicago River. He quit work early and took an unusual amount of time preparing for the evening. He had been attracted to her the first time he saw her photo, but her persistent need to be right, her reputation as a journalist who wouldn't quit, had dampened his earlier feelings. He decided he had never been that much into her, and opted to stay out of her way, leaving her persistent questioning to others. But now that he had spent some time with her, talking to her, even seeing her in her own element, the initial attraction had begun to grow. He felt pleased when she accepted his invitation.

He picked her up at her apartment in his prized Corvette. He was hesitant about taking the Vette at first, but when she smiled on seeing it, even running her hand along one of the polished fenders, he knew he had made the right choice.

He promised himself, and her, that he would not discuss the job. He was convinced that his passion for his work and his loyalty to his colleagues had been, in part, to blame for his previous marriage failures and he didn't want to make that mistake again. Christy seemed to be everything the others weren't. She was smart, independent, sassy to a fault, but nevertheless she had the temerity to do what was right and reassess her feelings in light of new information. Her willingness to work with him, despite her mistrust of the police, spoke volumes to him.

They arrived a bit early but were ushered to the bar. She ordered a caipirinha and he had a Brazilian beer. Although they had already spent time together, had even argued, their time at the bar was a bit awkward for him. This was a date. A true date. And that fact alone complicated the situation, bringing new stress into the evening. But by the time they were called to their table and had visited the salad bar, he was beginning to relax and enjoy their time together.

"Are you from here?" he asked.

She pushed the salad around on her plate. "Born and raised. My Dad drove a truck and my Mom was a domestic diva." She smiled broadly. "How about you?"

"Oh yeah. Chicago through and through. My Dad was a cop, but you already know that. My Mom died early and Dad and I had a time to bond before the women started passing through his life. You know, lonely man meets lonelier woman?" He shrugged. "At any rate, none of them took a liking to me so none of them stayed very long." He ate a bit of salad. "But I've told you all this already, haven't I?" *Way to go, big boy. Impress the lady with old gossip.*

She smiled. "Did you have many friends?"

He nodded. "Yeah. I was always a popular kid. Good at sports. But that's not the same as family."

"No grandparents? No extended family?" She ate a crouton.

"No. Just Dad and me. He's an only child like me, and Mom's family never cared for him, so when she died they pretty much walked out of my life too. I think that's why the department is so important to me. It's the only family I have."

She grinned. "We weren't going to talk about work this evening, remember?"

They finished the salad and began the main course with a broiled rib-eye. After the steak was served he told her a joke – one of four he knew – and she laughed, holding her hand to her mouth in a way that he found endearing.

"I heard that one a long time ago." He cut the rib-eye into smaller pieces. "So why journalism?"

"I like the idea of searching out the story behind the facts. In what other career can you do that?" She ate a bite of steak.

"Then you should've been a cop. Searching out the facts behind the story is what I do all day."

She shook her head, holding her hand to her mouth while she chewed. "No, that's backward. You search out the facts behind the story. You're looking for the cold hard truth. Just the facts, ma'am," she said, mockingly. "But I want the *story*. You want to know how someone was murdered and who did it. That's your job. But I want to know why? Who was she? What's her story?"

"But we're both into finding the truth. Whether it comes from the facts or the story, we want to know what happened," he said.

She nodded. "I guess. But law enforcement wasn't an option for me. First, as I told you, there is my brother. That alone precluded me from ever looking at police work as a career opportunity. But there's also my love of writing. I like putting words on a page in a way that makes sense. I could never do that as a cop. But as a journalist…" she shrugged, "it seemed like the only real choice for me."

"When did you decide to pursue journalism? You must've had some influence along the way. Some encouragement from someone."

She rearranged a fried banana on her plate. "Oh yes. When I say it was the only real choice, I mean a *practical* option, because I wanted to write fiction. I started out in college as an accounting major, if you can believe that. *Numbers.*" She smiled in disbelief. "I don't even like to balance my check book. But I like to write. My short stories seemed to capture the professor's attention. When I decided I was pursuing the wrong course of study and expressed a desire to write, my lit professor advised me to look into journalism. Like you, I was a big fan of Edgar Allan Poe, but Poe died broke. When my professor told me nearly all writers die like that, it didn't take long to figure out that writers need a second source of income to survive. Very few make a living from writing novels, and virtually no one does from writing short stories – which is where my interests lie." She shrugged. "That's the extent of it, I'm afraid. Nothing earth-shattering in my story. I changed my major to journalism and things took off from there. One of my journalism professors was a great source of encouragement and now he's my editor."

"How convenient."

"Sometimes fate intervenes."

He shook his head. "I'm not a big believer in fate. I think we make our own way, for better or for worse, and I've not always done well there. I've been married four times. And I can assure you that each time I married them, I was confident I was doing the right thing. Clearly, I wasn't. So if I took the position that my experience was fate, I wouldn't be able to get out of bed in the morning. What would be the point? My life would have already been decided by forces greater than me and I would simply be along for the ride." He shook his head. "No, ma'am. I couldn't live like that."

"Four times?"

He had let it slip and from the look on her face, he wished he hadn't told her. But she needed to know and she might as well know now. "Yeah. Four failed marriages. How about you?"

She shook her head. "Never. I've never been married. I haven't dated all that much. I've kept my nose in my work. It doesn't leave much room for a personal life."

"Well, there's that too," he said. "Work, family. There's always something."

She gave him a puzzled look. "I thought you said you didn't have family."

"I don't. Except for my Dad." He glanced at his watch. "In fact, I need to see him on the way home. You interested?"

"In what?"

"In going with me. You might as well see the whole story."

She smiled. "Stories are what I'm all about. I wouldn't miss it for the world."

CHAPTER 56

They left the restaurant and took the Vette north along LaSalle Street, reaching Marimar in less than twenty minutes. Along the way, as always, Campello stopped to pick up his father's favorite treat.

"How long has he been here?" Christy asked, as soon as they drove into the parking lot.

"Dad was diagnosed with Alzheimer's five years ago, but he's been in Marimar for the last two. I had to put him here. I couldn't take care of him anymore."

She looked at him with admiration. "You took care of him?"

"What else could I do? He's my Dad." He put the car in park. "I had some help. My neighbor is a retired nurse and she would sometimes sit with him when I was working."

"You didn't consider putting him in here before that?"

He pocketed the keys. "I thought about it. But in the end, I just couldn't do it. I was capable of providing for him and seeing that he was clean, safe... fed. But my job is a lot like yours in a way. I don't have nine-to-five hours. That was OK at first, but as he started to decline, his care was more and more difficult to manage." He shrugged. "I had to do something and that was Marimar." He got out of the car and she followed. They entered the facility and walked past the nurses' station. A nurse on duty smiled when she saw Campello.

"More raisins?" she asked.

"Always. I think he waits for them."

"Don't kid yourself, Frank. He waits for you. He may not always be able to show it, but he enjoys your visits."

Campello and Christy entered the old man's room and found him sitting in his chair facing the TV. A game show was playing, but his expression told them he was miles away.

"Dad? I've brought you some candy." He handed the bag to his father.

"Who are you?" the old man asked.

"I'm Frank, Dad. I'm your son." He said to her, "We go through this routine every time I come."

She smiled.

"Dad, I want you to meet someone."

The old man fished a raisin from the bag and turned toward her with eyes that were vacant. "Who're you?"

Before she could speak, Campello said, "Her name is Christy."

"Christy?" He refocused on her. "Are you going to marry my son?"

She started to laugh, putting a hand to her mouth.

"Sorry," Campello said. "He's not very diplomatic."

"You *should* laugh, sister," the old man said. "You'd be another one in the bunch."

Campello's face reddened.

"Well, look at you," she said to him, laughing. "Big tough cop embarrassed."

"Yeah, well, like I said, he can be pretty blunt sometimes."

"So how about it?" the old man asked. "You going to marry him or what?"

"I don't know," she said. "Do you think I should?"

"Sure. Why not? Everyone else does." He ate another raisin.

"Good God," Campello sunk onto the bed.

"He doesn't stay married for long?" she asked, deciding the opportunity was too good to pass up.

The old man studied his son. "No. Who would want him?"

Campello dropped his face in his hands as Christy laughed all the harder.

"Is he hard to live with?" she asked.

"Well, yes. I ought to know. Why do you think I'm here?" He reached for another raisin.

"This wasn't a good idea," Campello said. "Maybe we ought to—"

She held up a hand, stifling another laugh. "Do you want him to get married again?"

The old man turned to his son with eyes that seemed to see him for the first time since he entered the room. "Yes. I want him to be happy. He deserves that much."

She didn't laugh anymore.

CHAPTER 57

Tony Delgado returned to the brownstone for a dinner meeting with Paulie Vincent. The discussion with Aaron Green had gone as expected, but it was clear the alderman wasn't enthusiastic about the new plans.

The evening had grown considerably warmer, despite the rain, but Vincent was sitting under a blanket in front of a raging fire. His pallor had worsened and his breathing was becoming increasingly labored. Delgado knew Vincent was dying and that his death would provide an opportunity to lead the business if he was persistent in his loyalty to the man who would choose his own successor.

Delgado removed his leather coat and folded it, laying it neatly on the nearby sofa. He pulled a chair nearer the old man and placed a hand on his.

"How are you feeling, sir?"

Vincent nodded his answer. "We have a problem with Aaron." As before, his words were punctuated with gasps for air.

"Yes," Delgado said. "He'll go along with the plan, but he's reluctant."

Vincent began to drool and dabbed at his lips with a folded tissue. "Yes. He needs to be on board." He inhaled deeply, fighting for air. "Do you have a plan?"

Delgado always had a plan. Although he was seen by several in the hierarchy as nothing more than hired muscle, his approach had always been one of brain over brawn. His ability to reason through a situation was legendary with most of his colleagues. *Do what you've got to do* if necessary, but opt for persuasion over force when possible.

"I may have, sir." He shifted on the chair, leaning forward so that Vincent would not have to strain to hear him. "Aaron is a proud man. He doesn't like to be told what to do, but we can't afford to ignore him."

Vincent nodded his agreement.

"We need to give him a boost. Give him something he can fix so he can be appropriately lauded for doing it. He is a politician, after all, and there's nothing they love more than praise."

A feeble grin enlivened Vincent's face.

"The plan I'm going to propose will serve two purposes. It will give Aaron a reason for continuing, while giving us the cover that will be critical in transitioning the business."

Vincent coughed and dabbed frothy blood from his lips.

"Since detective Polanski's arrest, the violence in the jurisdiction of the 31st has calmed down significantly. Many people saw the shooting of the young black man as racially motivated, and when Polanski testified that the two officers in question had planted a gun on the man to cover their tracks…" he spread his hands, "their suspicions were raised and their worst fears ignited. That has helped contain Peter Green to some extent, because the officers of the 31st and the 28th have been inordinately preoccupied. At the very least, it gave us time to run the interference that kept Aaron on board. Losing him would be quite costly and it would take several years to align another alderman with our efforts." He paused, allowing Vincent time to catch up. When the frail old man nodded, Delgado continued.

"Now, if the officers of the 28th had their own preoccupation to deal with, they would be less inclined to be concerned with our activities at the warehouse. My first thought was to hand them Peter and the club as a token, but also as a way of tying them up. Manipulating illegals into prostitution could have extensive repercussions that would reach well beyond the 28th district and into the federal government. Undoubtedly, it would also ignite a firestorm among a variety of civil rights groups."

Vincent shook his head, trying to avoid speaking in order to conserve his energy.

"Yes, I know. Bringing the feds into this would eventually raise questions about the warehouse. I've thought of that. And it would inevitably bring some of our government contacts into the spotlight, and that would be helpful to no one. So I have devised another plan. A much simpler one that will give Aaron something to do, while diverting attention away from Peter and aiding us as well."

He leaned closer, putting both hands on the old man's wrist. "I am suggesting we arrange for some of our union friends to begin a campaign of inflaming the passions in the 28th district. If we are successful in igniting the kind of unrest there that we had in the 31st, I think we can accomplish both objectives. It shouldn't be too difficult. With the death of the DJ occurring in their jurisdiction, and with Polanski and his partner focused on harassing Peter Green, we could sway opinion toward a police cover-up of another kind."

He spread his hands again. "It may not work, sir. But it's certainly do-able and I think it's worth the effort. And unlike the rioting in the 31st, this would have little chance of spiraling down into simple looting. Our friends could see to that."

Vincent closed his eyes. The hiss of the oxygen machine punctuated his labored breathing. A moment later, he opened his eyes, his decision made.

"Do it," he said.

CHAPTER 58

Before heading into the office the next morning, Frank Campello drove to Rand Adams' house. He had made a promise to his late partner that he would take care of the man's family if anything ever happened, and Rand had made a similar promise, agreeing to look after Campello's father. But there were other reasons for visiting Rand's wife.

He drove to the nearby western suburbs in the tan squad car and parked in front of the Adamses' home. There were no children in place at the bus stop, meaning the kids were already in school, and that was a fortunate break for him.

The house was small but well maintained, with a curving concrete sidewalk leading from the asphalt-covered driveway and lined on each side with blooming crocuses. A soft rain had fallen in the early morning hours and the lawn and foliage were laden with moisture.

He rang the doorbell. Sharon answered and immediately hugged him.

"What brings you around this early, Frank?" she asked, pulling him into the house and closing the door behind him.

"Just checking on you, sweetheart."

"Well, aren't you the nice one." She gestured for him to follow her into the kitchen. "I just put on some coffee."

The house was quiet and Rand's influence could be seen. Cubs paraphernalia, including photos and a signed jersey, hung on the walls. Photos of Rand, Sharon and the kids sat on the end tables and atop the piano. It was the house of a once happy family. Rand was the only missing element.

"The kids in school?" He sat on a stool at the breakfast counter and accepted a cup of coffee from her. True to Adams form, the coffee was in a Cubs cup.

"They left a few minutes ago," she said. "It's awfully quiet around here without them." She sat on a stool next to his with a similar cup of coffee.

"Anyone else been by?" he asked, lifting the cup to his lips.

She nodded. "Yes. Angelo Silvio came around yesterday. And Julio Lopez."

"Social call?"

"Just like yours." She smiled and patted his hand. "Hey, where are my manners? Would you like some breakfast?"

He shook his head. "No, Sharon, I—"

She was already off the stool and moving when he gently grabbed her by the wrist and steered her back to the seat.

"You sure?" she asked. "It's really no trouble. I've already got things out for the kids and—"

"Sharon, did Rand ever talk about the office?"

A confused look crossed her face. "What do you mean?"

"Did he ever discuss anything with you? Cases we were working? Problems he might have been facing?"

"Sure. Who doesn't bring the job home from time to time?"

"Anything specific?"

She furrowed her brow. "What're you getting at, Frank? What's wrong?"

"I think Rand may have been working on something that I didn't know about."

Her frown deepened. "You think it may have had something to do with his death?"

He shook his head and held up a hand. "No. I'm not suggesting anything like that. I'm just saying he may have been onto something, and I wondered if he mentioned anything about it."

She cocked her head. "What's up? Angie and Julio were asking me the same kind of questions yesterday."

He reached for the coffee. "They were?"

"They wanted to know if he had mentioned anything to me that I thought was unusual. You know, different. They wanted to know if you'd been around lately and I told them you were here the other day."

He drank the coffee. It had grown cold. "And?"

She shrugged. "I told them Rand had been a bit stressed before his death, but I shrugged it off then and I still do."

"Did Rand have a problem with Angie and Julio?"

"You mean you didn't know?" She rolled her eyes in an exaggerated, dramatic fashion. "The last few months before he died, he couldn't keep quiet about them. He said he felt like they were smothering him." She refreshed her untouched coffee.

Campello shifted on the stool. "Anything specific?"

She shrugged again. "No. In fact, I asked him, 'Rand, is there something they're doing?' and he wouldn't tell me. But I knew something was wrong between them. He just couldn't focus on anything else. I figured it was a personality conflict and let it go."

"Did Rand keep anything here at the house? Any files, documents, anything like that?"

She paused to think before shaking her head. "No."

He rose off the stool and glanced around the dining-room. Then he went into the living-room and saw the computer and printer on a desk at the rear of the room. "Sharon, can I take a look?"

"Sure."

He went to the desk and immediately sat and switched on the machine. After it booted up, he opened a folder and saw a file containing pictures of Rand, Sharon and the kids posing languidly on the beach.

"Those were from last summer," she said. "Surely you aren't interested in our vacation photos."

He didn't answer her. Instead, he continued to open folders and when he found nothing, he opened Rand's documents. A long list of titles appeared on the screen and he scanned them. He was halfway down the list when he found it. It was the same dummy classification that was listed at the office, but the file on Adams' personal computer was many times larger.

"Can I copy this?"

"Sure," she said. "What is it?"

"Answers, I hope."

CHAPTER 59

C ampello met with Christy and Polanski at Polanski's house an hour after leaving Sharon's. The morning continued to be warm, and they sat on the patio in the back yard. The lawn had thickened under the spring rains and flowers bloomed along the patio's edge. A large maple tree stood in the yard, its branches reaching over them like protective arms.

"Rand was onto something." Campello unfolded the printout and laid it on the table. "He has listed some names here, including Hoppity T's. And it looks like he was meeting with Juanita, regularly."

"If he was on to something, it was exclusive of his regular duties," Polanski said. "Otherwise, this would've come to light much earlier."

"I think it did," Campello said. "The morning you started with the 28th I was looking through Rand's old files. I was making a list of the cases I wanted to keep. I ran across a dummy file and wrote down the number. But then Lopez distracted me, and I forgot about it until now. That number has been deleted from the system, but showed up on his personal computer at home, and that's where I found this." He tapped the printout.

"If this is so hush-hush," Christy said, "why did he keep it at work?"

"He didn't," Campello said. "At least not in its entirety. We're trained to record the case numbers of the files we're working so that our replacements can recreate them in the event of our death or a sudden departure from the department. That happened in this case. Rand's case load was recorded as it should have been, so it's possible he did this automatically, reflexively, without thinking. Of course, he could've had a file and it's been compromised, or he may not have had time to complete it."

"If it's been compromised, then someone at the 28th knows its contents. That gives them a leg up on us," Polanski said.

"I'm afraid someone there already has. Bobby Longhorse is dead and it wasn't suicide. I called Barbara at the coroner's office this morning. She just started the autopsy, but had enough to confirm Longhorse was murdered."

"But wasn't it Juanita who set up Andy?" Jenny asked.

"It looks that way, but our thinking is that it was under duress. Either way, she's gone. Vanished."

"Why was Rand meeting with her?" Jenny asked.

Campello shrugged.

"If you can find her," Christy said, "you may have the missing link."

"What can we do to help?" Polanski asked.

Campello shook his head. "Nothing for the moment. You're on suspension, remember?" He turned to face Jenny. "And I owe you an apology."

"For what?"

"For doubting your husband. I've been entrenched in the CPD – the system – for so long, I've forgotten why I was there."

She shook her head. "A lot of men doubted Andy. You're not the only one. But unfortunately for you, you may now find yourself on the receiving end of some very nasty attacks."

Polanski nodded his agreement. "You're going out on a limb, Frank. You may find that the people you thought were friends really aren't. You could lose the only family you've ever known."

"But you'll have a new one," Christy smiled.

"You may be in a bit of trouble, too," Campello said. "I may need you to do some stories on certain people as we go through this. Shake them up a little."

She shrugged. "I can do that."

"Your editor won't get upset?"

"Sure. He'll make a scene, scream, things like that, but in the end he always goes with my instinct."

"OK. Then here's what I need for the moment. I need you to do a story on Juanita Delaney. Dig up what you can and make sure she appears to be the center of our investigation into the ambush. Make clear that she's the link, the *femme fatale*, whatever. She has to look good for it."

"Why? What'll that do?" Jenny asked.

"If she set Andy up, it'll hang a target on her back and she'll have to come in. If she was under duress, it'll smoke out the people who used her and give us a lead while bringing her in. Either way, she'll have no place to hide and she'll have to contact us."

Polanski shook his head. "It's a calculated risk, Frank. You're endangering her life."

"I know. But right now, I don't know who I can trust. Bringing her into the open is the only way I know of getting to the problem." He crossed his legs. "And there's something else."

"What?" Christy asked.

"Gloria told me that Peter is always trying to live up to his father. That he can never find the old man's approval. I need for you to go after him in the article. Portray him as the loser he is. He's been arrested twice, after all. It shouldn't be too hard."

"That could expose the paper to liability."

Campello nodded. "It could."

"So what do we do in the meantime?" Christy asked.

"Nothing. For now, I'll try to smoke out the traitors in the department. And I'm going to start by ringing some bells."

CHAPTER 60

Aaron Green arrived at the Board of Trade office to meet with Tony Delgado at Delgado's request. Such a request was never a good thing and nearly always spelled trouble of the political kind.

Delgado was already behind the desk, a signal that he was in charge. He wore a black turtleneck over black jeans. His iconic leather jacket was draped over the sofa.

"I helped myself to a drink, Aaron. I hope you don't mind." He raised the glass.

"No, I don't mind. In fact, I think I'll have one myself." He slipped behind the bar and prepared a scotch and soda for himself. Once he had the drink in hand, he took a seat in one of the two chairs that stood in front of his desk. "To what do I owe this honor, Tony?" He fought valiantly to prevent sarcasm from seeping into his voice.

"Mr. Vincent and I have made some necessary plans and we want to pay you the courtesy of keeping you informed."

"I see." He sipped his drink. "You're here to inform me." This time, he allowed the sour note of sarcasm to slip through. If it was noticed by Delgado – and surely it was, for the enforcer was not as dumb as he looked – he ignored it.

"There have been some changes, the result of new obstacles, and we are initiating efforts to contain them. As we have said before, we value our alliance with you."

Green ignored Delgado's patronizing words.

"We will need for you to hold back on your efforts to resolve the strike."

"What? Why?" He was truly dumbfounded.

"It's a bit delicate, Aaron, but with Polanski's troubles, it is necessary to move the unrest to the area of the 28th. Our union representatives assure us they can aid us in this, and we assured them that if they did, you could gain a better contract offer when the time came."

"I have a great offer for them now. They were happy with it, Tony, and we're about to close the deal."

Delgado held up a hand. "We're aware of that, Aaron. And we truly appreciate your efforts and can certainly sympathize with your situation. And it's important to us that you understand your efforts in this instance will cost us also. But sometimes we all have to give a little with one hand in order to receive with the other. But I assure you, as soon as our needs are met, they will sign the new contract. Of course, it will need to be better than the current one." He waved a hand back and forth. "Not huge, of course, but better."

"Why are you doing this?"

"Our reasons are our own. But they are necessary, I assure you."

"And how much larger does the package have to be?"

Delgado shrugged. "Not much. But enough to make it clear to all involved that the union acted in good faith and their efforts in holding back on the contract were genuine. You will also need to be certain they are not cast in a bad light. It is critical the City be seen as the hold-out in this case."

"That's impossible!"

Delgado spread his hands. "We have faith in you, Aaron. You've done excellent work over the years and we see no reason to doubt you now." He finished the drink. "There is also the matter of Peter."

"What about him?"

"He is becoming a liability, Aaron."

"He's my son."

"We know. But he's still a liability. He has arranged for Baranova to quash Campello's hearing. We have no problem with that, of course, but he's running on a track that is entirely separate from our own and he's doing it without checking with us. Could you talk to him, please?"

Green gritted his teeth. Delgado's tone carried an implied threat.

"I will."

"Excellent." Delgado rose from behind the desk and then marched briskly to the sofa where he slid into the leather coat. "I know that Mr. Vincent appreciates your efforts, Aaron. I certainly know I do."

"That's what it's all about," Green said, refusing to check his sarcasm.

CHAPTER 61

Campello arrived back at the Castle mid-afternoon. A voicemail message from Barbara confirmed their earlier phone conversation. The autopsy was complete and revealed that Longhorse's death was indeed a homicide. In addition, it appeared he was drugged before he was hanged, although she would not have the tox screen results for a few more days. There was no longer any value in being covert. If he was going to unravel the tapestry of corruption that had enveloped his world and smoke out the perpetrators, he knew he might as well begin now.

Most of the detectives were out – not unusual, given their work and the time of day. Lopez was in his office, of course, and Tertwiller and Hughbanks were present.

Campello asked the others to meet him around his desk as he gathered Lopez from the office. Once they had clustered around him, he dropped himself into his seat.

"Longhorse didn't commit suicide. The coroner's office confirms he was murdered and I think he was murdered by one of our own."

For a moment, the others stood in stunned and passive silence. Then Tertwiller spoke.

"That's a pretty heavy allegation, Frank. Do you have some proof?"

He leaned back in his chair and placed one foot on top of the desk while he crossed his arms over his chest. "Not yet. But I will. I think we have a snitch in the district and I think he's working with Paulie Vincent."

The group exchanged looks.

"Are you accusing one of us?" Lopez said.

"You all but accused me earlier, Julio." He shook his head. "No, I'm not accusing anyone, yet. I'm informing you, because I think we need to be more discreet. Someone in this building is on Vincent's payroll and it could be anyone."

"In my office," Lopez said.

"No."

"No?"

"No. This is something that everyone needs to know, Julio. Someone killed Longhorse and it was to keep him quiet about the sudden change in his testimony."

"And how do you know this?" Hughbanks asked.

"Why would the man kill himself? In fact, why would he change his testimony at all?" Campello asked.

"Changing his testimony doesn't mean he was lying. Maybe he was lying before and he changed to the truth?" Tertwiller said.

"Maybe. But he changed nevertheless and that means someone got to him."

"You're making a leap here, Frank, and you have no basis for it," Hughbanks said.

"You're starting to sound a lot like Polanski," Tertwiller said.

"Maybe he wasn't all wrong."

Tertwiller's and Hughbanks' expressions fell.

"Whose side are you on, Frank?" Hughbanks said.

Lopez interrupted before he could answer. "Let's not accuse anyone of taking sides. Polanski has done enough damage to the department."

"I'm not saying Andy did the right thing," Campello said. "But I am saying he may not be all wrong."

"About what, Frank?" Tertwiller asked, setting on the edge of Campello's desk.

"That Peter Green murdered Trina and that he is in league with Paulie Vincent. After all, we know that a guy like Vincent doesn't remain a player unless he's greased the right wheels, and that means someone on our side of the fence is taking money to pervert the system. When you consider the fact that Vincent's number-one thug, Tony Delgado, is spending an inordinate amount of time with Peter, it's a cinch that Vincent has an interest. Delgado and Peter are together all the time, whether it's at the club or the warehouse."

"And you think all of that means that Longhorse was murdered and that one of us had a hand in it?" Tertwiller asked.

Campello shook his head. "I'm saying that I believe Longhorse was murdered to keep him quiet and that it could not have happened without support from the inside. Whether that's one of us or the guys at county or the guys downstairs…" He shrugged. "It makes no difference. Vincent has got someone on the inside."

She looked at the others and shook her head with pity. "And that's it?"

He spun the monitor around so that everyone could watch as he booted up the machine. Within minutes, Rand's case file came on the screen. "Rand had a dummy file. He kept it separate from the others and from me. I think he knew something and was killed for it." He began scrolling down the list of case files.

"Rand was killed by a suspect in an ambush," Tertwiller said. "You were there. You saw it go down."

"Did I?" He scrolled to the bottom of the list. "When I returned after Rand's death, I reviewed his cases. He had a dummy file number right here." He pointed to the screen. "And now it's gone."

She leaned forward and examined the list. "This is just a list of his cases. Where's the secret file?"

"It was deleted," he said.

"All right, that's it. In my office, Frank," Lopez said. "And I mean right now."

CHAPTER 62

The newsroom was alive with activity; reporters were answering phone calls and typing on keyboards, making last-minute edits before the rapidly approaching deadline. Christy sat in Demille's office with the door closed. The man had a pained and skeptical look on his face, but was not as contrary to her suggestions as she had anticipated.

"So let me get this straight," he said. "You think that the shooting involving this cop—"

"Rand Adams."

"Rand Adams… was not what it appeared and that the killer's girlfriend may have been involved with the cop as an informant."

"That's correct."

"And where are you getting this?"

She laid it out for him and when she was done, it was clear he was impressed.

"It sounds like you're on to something."

"You think?" She smiled.

"How do you want to play this?"

"An exposé. Like we have something the police don't. Embarrass them a little. If she's in town, it'll drive them to find her and give her a reason to surface."

"It could put her in danger if half of what you've told me is true."

"It's a calculated risk, Clarence," she said, echoing Polanski's statement of earlier that morning.

Demille paused in thought, stroking his chin. "When do you

want the story to run?"

"Tomorrow morning. Lead on page one."

He snorted. "There are riots, Christy. A strike."

"I know. But if I'm right, they're linked."

He went to the window that looked onto the Chicago River six stories below and stood with his hands clasped behind his back. Low-lying clouds seemed close enough that he could touch them. "If this girl gets killed we could be in trouble. Especially if you're wrong."

"I'm not wrong, Clarence."

He continued gazing out the window, across the cityscape. "You could be, you know. You just said it's a calculated risk."

"It's calculated in our favor. Besides, we've made them before."

"Not with an individual whose life was in the balance."

"You said yourself the rioting is continuing. Even though it's slowed, there is still risk for innocent civilians."

He nodded, continuing to look across the city.

"I'll do my research, Clarence. I'll be fair, but I think we need to find this woman. If she can corroborate half of what we think she knows, she will expose the corruption in this town like no one since Eliot Ness."

He chuckled. "What about you?"

"Me?"

He turned from the window and stood with his arms folded behind his desk chair. "You've been my protégé. I've cared about you and your career since I discovered you. I don't want anything to happen. No story is worth that."

She was taken aback. He had never been so open, so tender with her before. "Nothing is going to happen to me, Clarence. I'm a big girl. I can take care of myself."

"The girl at the pier couldn't. These people you're trying to expose are unknown to you. And they're rough customers. It's difficult enough to protect yourself when you know who you're up against. It's downright impossible when you don't know who they are. You'll never see them coming."

"Clarence, it's a risk I'll have to take. I knew what this business entailed when I signed up. It's never stopped me before."

"You've never done anything like this before."

"Have you forgotten already? I did a story on Polanski and the cover-up at the CPD just a few weeks ago. And last year I covered the embezzlement at City Hall, and then there was—"

"I know what you've done, Christy," he said. "I'm not questioning your ability or your tenacity. And I'm certainly not questioning your judgment." He grinned. "What I'm saying is that the people you're going after will make the politicians at City Hall seem like boy scouts. And the story on Polanski did no harm to anyone in particular. Remember, you won't be writing about an amorphous thing – a corporate or government entity. You'll be writing about a *person* who has information on people powerful enough to stop her. You'll be writing about the shadow people. And if your story rings true, they won't be in the shadows for long."

"That's what I'm hoping, Clarence."

CHAPTER 63

Campello met Christy for dinner at an out-of-the-way location to avoid any chance of being seen by members of the department. It was likely that their developing relationship would soon be discovered, but given the tenor of the times and the task at hand, it was important to keep it under wraps for as long as possible.

They met at an Italian restaurant ten miles outside the loop on the city's South Side just as the sun descended against the western sky. Christy ordered linguini with clam sauce; Campello decided on lasagna. They were learning that in addition to their taste in literature, they both enjoyed Italian food.

"So he was OK with it?" Campello asked.

She set her wine glass down. "It was sweet, actually. It was the first time he hasn't been patrician with me in months. Like he was more colleague than mentor."

Campello smiled. "I don't think the department is going to be so kind to me. Lopez laid me out pretty well in his office this afternoon. Told me point blank that I was looking at a suspension if I kept pursuing my theory on Longhorse."

"Did anyone back you? Give you a hint of who might be on the up and up?"

He shook his head. "I don't think I need to find who's on the up and up. I need to find who isn't. There'll be fewer to find that way."

She rotated her fork in the linguini. "You know my stance on that."

"I do."

She ate slowly, taking time to think. "I heard that the state's attorney's office is dropping charges against Caine and Dorchester. Their case was resting on Andy's testimony, and now that charges against him have tainted their star witness, the whole thing is unraveling."

"They're guilty," he said. "And you know, six weeks ago I would've probably covered for them. I would've talked to them about it, maybe been upset by what I saw, but I would've interceded for them."

"My, how you've grown." She smiled at him over the rim of her glass.

"Yeah, well, don't push your luck, lady. I'm still a cop."

"I think I can iron that wrinkle out of you."

He laughed.

"So what, exactly, did Lopez say?"

He cut into the lasagna. "Just that he was disappointed that an officer of my stature would allow himself to make wild accusations against other members of the department."

"Did you?"

He shook his head. "No. I didn't. That's just it. I wanted to rattle some cages. Try to gauge their reactions. But I took pains to not point fingers at anyone specifically."

"But he says you did."

He nodded. "He certainly implied it."

"Do you think he's in the tank with Vincent?"

He set his fork down. "I certainly hope not. I've known Julio since I went on the department." He opened his mouth and started to say something, but closed it and picked up his fork.

"What?" she asked. "What is it?"

He set his fork down again and rested his elbows on the table with his hands folded in front of him over the still nearly full plate. "He's been pushing me to work the murder and not Peter Green. Every time I discuss the case with him, he steers it back to Trina."

"It sounds like he wants you off Green's back."

"And at the same time, he's willing to go along with me if I have enough to raise his suspicions. Like when Rita was killed and

I told him I wanted to interview Juanita. I told him point blank that I thought Peter killed Rita and that Juanita could be a lead, and he agreed to my request. Even took some heat for it, but stood by me."

"Listen," she said, "there's something you need to know."

His eyes narrowed.

"Before that day at the pier, when you found Trina, I called my source at the department. That's how I found out you and Andy were working together. My source said that he didn't know for sure that Andy would be transferring to the 28th, but that the scuttlebutt said he would. When I asked who the commander of the district was, my source said it was Lopez and that he's as straight as they come."

"Who's your source?"

She rested her elbows on the table and her chin on her folded hands.

"Come on, Christy. If your source is placed, he would know if Lopez is legit or not. My life is on the line."

She hesitated, with her chin still resting on her hands. "It's Silvio."

CHAPTER 64

Campello drove home in the Vette, gliding through loop traffic with unusual grace. He replayed the conversation with Christy. Her revelation that her source was Silvio had not been a total surprise. Angelo had always been a bit aloof, rarely associating with his fellow officers, unless it was a trip to Jeep's.

But nearly everyone liked and respected Silvio, including his new partner, Shelly Tertwiller. As soon as her transfer to the 28th had been initiated, Silvio volunteered to work with her and she accepted.

Campello had never taken issue with Silvio, but would have as recently as two days ago if he had known the man was a snitch for the press. But now, with all that had happened, Campello wasn't sure about anything anymore.

He turned into the condo's parking garage and deftly guided the classic car to his reserved spot near the elevator. As usual, the sodium-vapor lamps that were suspended throughout the facility cast the garage in a mix of light and shadow, and the Vette's headlamps did little to discharge the uncomfortable feeling of parking in an isolated garage.

He pulled nose-forward into the stall and killed the engine. When he climbed out of the car, he saw two figures standing in the shadows.

His hand slipped under his jacket and rested on the butt of his pistol.

"We trusted you, Frank." It was Shelly Tertwiller. She stepped into the light. The other figure remained in the darkness.

"I was wondering how long it would take before you'd come

forward," he said, keeping an eye on her hands.

"How could you do this, Frank? How could you turn on your own?"

"I haven't turned on anyone, Shelly." Campello stepped away from the car, out of the overhead light and into the shadow opposite her. He peered into the darkness, but could not identify the other figure.

"Polanski's career is over," Shelly said. "He's stuck his nose where it doesn't belong."

"In Vincent's business?" Campello asked. "How much is he paying you? How much does a detective go for these days?"

"Save it, Frank," Shelly said. "You know the score. You have to give a little to get a little. It's how the world works."

"It's not how I work."

She laughed. "Isn't it? Are you telling me you've never accepted a freebie? Never taken something from someone who gave it to you just because you're a cop?"

There had, in fact, been times when he had accepted items from citizens and others. A free dinner here, a bottle of wine there… tickets to a sporting event.

"What's the matter, Frank? Cat got your tongue?" she asked, while the other figure remained silent. "It's so much easier to point fingers at others, but a whole lot more challenging to measure up to the same standard. Tell me, do you think Polanski accepts freebies?"

"I'm not Polanski's keeper, Shelly."

"And you're not ours either, Frank," she said, her voice rising, echoing in the concrete canyon. "We don't need more oversight, we need more support. We're engaged in a war out there." She motioned to the skyline visible through the open areas of the garage.

"And that gives you the right to become part of the problem? To join Vincent and his crew?" His hand tightened on the butt of the pistol.

"Give it a rest," she said. "People don't care if Vincent rigs a few elections or runs some girls. All they care about is that no one breaks into their home and steals their television. Crime is personal, Frank.

Their only concern is that the bad guys stay away from them. No one gives a rip if points are shaved at a basketball game. That doesn't matter to them. It's not *personal*, Frank."

"What Caine and Dorchester did was personal. Personal enough to trigger rioting."

She laughed again. "Those riots may have started out with a political agenda, but they're something far different now and you know it. It's entitlement, Frank. Those people think they're *entitled*."

"And how does that make them different from you?"

She chuckled and pointed her finger at him, while turning to the silent figure. "He's good with the comebacks."

"I'm a good cop, Shelly. I thought you were, too."

She moved closer to him, closing the distance. Her hands were free so he shifted his gaze to the figure in the shadow.

"I'm a realistic cop," she said. "I see things as they are."

"Me too, Shelly. And I don't like what I see."

"Then you'll have to do something about it. And let me warn you. You have no idea just how big a problem we can be."

She stepped back into the shadow and the two of them climbed into her car, pulling away with a squeal.

Campello exhaled sharply, allowing his hand to slip from the pistol.

CHAPTER 65

Christy's story broke the next morning on page one as Clarence had promised, pushing news of the previous evening's rioting to page two. By the time she had showered and dressed, her story was being picked up by local broadcasters.

She was not a typical breakfast eater, often preferring a latte from Starbucks or a breakfast roll over more traditional fare, but she decided to take the time for a brief breakfast before leaving the apartment since it was unlikely there would be time for lunch. The tone of her article had highlighted Juanita Delaney as the chief person of interest and had been accusatory toward the CPD with special focus on Peter Green. That meant the fur would soon begin to fly and there was little doubt that she and Demille would be reprimanded by Morgan Tower, the owner and publisher of the paper. It wouldn't be the first time, of course. She poured herself a bowl of cereal and had just gotten a container of milk from the refrigerator when there was a knock on the door. Her watch read 7 a.m.

She set the milk on the table and went to the door. Opening it, she found Frank Campello standing in the hallway.

"Can I come in? I've got something to tell you."

He told her about the event of the previous night, right down to the direction they left when driving out of the building.

"They confronted you?" Her hand trembled slightly as she poured milk over her cereal.

"Most brazen thing I've ever seen, and I've seen a lot."

She held her hands to her mouth in wonderment. "This puts a whole new color on things."

"It does for me. I've got to go in there today and work with them like I don't know a thing." He shook his head. "I'm starting to feel like you. Who do I trust? Where do I go?"

"You can trust me. You can trust the people."

He couldn't stifle his laugh. "The people? You sound like some hippy revolutionary from the sixties. People don't care, sweetheart. Shelly was right. Crime is personal. No one cares what the cops or politicians do until it affects them directly. Let some snippy senator take a bribe to fix a transportation bill that puts hundreds out of work and no one says a thing. But let a local alderman arrange a garbage strike and everyone's up in arms."

"Your choice of example is apropos."

He shook his head. "You keep using big words around me and I'm going to have to get a dictionary."

She laughed. His humor eased her tension.

"I didn't mean to suggest that Green or the garbage strike is pertinent," he said.

She crossed her arms as a frown creased her face.

"What?" he asked.

"Why now?"

"Excuse me?"

"Why now, Frank? Why did they confront you now?" She ate a bit of the cereal and pushed the box across the table to Campello. He shook his head.

"It's pretty obvious that they've seen the difference in me," he said. "I shook them up yesterday. I'm sure that didn't help."

She pursed her lips and nodded. "Maybe."

"Do you think they could've gotten an early edition of the paper?"

She shook her head. "Anything is possible, of course, but that would be very unlikely. It was rushed to press late last night. Other than Clarence and me, no one else knew about it."

Campello raised an eyebrow.

"No. Don't, Frank. He's above reproach. It wasn't even his idea and he's going to take a lot of heat over this."

Campello kept his eyes fixed on her and she held his gaze, determined that he not bring Demille into the swill that was Chicago politics.

"OK, OK," he said, relenting.

"Besides, we now have a bigger problem," she said.

"Juanita." He had already thought of her.

"Exactly. How will we know if she decides to come in?"

"It's a cinch she won't contact me. And since I'm *persona non grata* with the boss, and since I don't know who's in league with Shelly, I'm going to have to keep an eye on everyone."

"If she doesn't come in, it could mean she's out of town, and in that case our efforts were for nothing," she said. "Or she could be dead. The end result is the same."

He shook his head. "I don't think she's dead. The baby was missing and so were its clothes. It's more likely she's on the run."

"Is there any chance that someone she knows might reach out to you? Does she have any close friends?"

He rubbed fatigue from his eyes before glancing around the kitchen. "Do you have any coffee?"

"Sure." She left the table, started up her coffee maker, then came and sat back down.

"She does have at least one friend," he said, giving her Gloria's name. "So far, she's been resistant to helping me other than some background information."

"The stakes are higher now. Different," she said. "Maybe she'll be more willing if she understands that."

"Maybe."

She pushed the box of cereal, the bowl, and the carton of milk aside. "What're you going to do, Frank?"

He stroked his chin. "I think I'll go to Gloria's. It's worth a shot. Besides, I don't have a lot of options."

"No, I mean, what are you going to do about your job?"

"I'll just have to do it." He shook his head in exasperation. "Now I know how Polanski must have felt. Except he had his wife for support."

She looked at him, aghast. "And *you* have *me*!"

CHAPTER 66

Peter Green was livid. He was sitting at a circular glass-topped dining-table with a bowl of Fruit Loops, wearing striped PJs. The article in the *Chicago Star* painted him as a no-good son of his father; portrayed him as someone who lived off the fat of the land without making a useful contribution. At best, he appeared as the inept operator of a second-rate strip joint that was given to a wayward and incompetent son by his rich daddy. According to the article, the club was intended as a means of provision, given his multiple failures at virtually everything else, and could hopefully sustain him when he would one day be on his own. But Peter was a loser and the paper even quoted one of the dancers as saying he was "in it for the lap dances". To top it off, the reporter had researched his academic record and then raised questions on how he gained admissions to the Ivy League schools in the first place. The entire thrust of the article, as far as he was concerned, was to demean and belittle him.

He flung the paper across the room and banged his fist against his forehead, cursing wildly. Tears formed in his eyes as he shook with rage. Everything he'd built was in jeopardy. Powerful clients would not do business with him if there was a risk they'd be exposed in the news.

"It's not true, it's not true! I can do things, too. I'm not like you said."

He slapped at the bowl of cereal, knocking if off the table and onto the floor, and shot upright out of his chair. He began to pace the length of the room before coming to rest in front of the window that looked down onto the city his father had ruled for decades.

His father. The old man couldn't do anything without a battery of lawyers.

And Vincent. The story had been accurate about that. The old man was in servitude to Vincent.

He chuckled. Then just as suddenly, he recalled his portrayal in the paper. And the rage rose again.

"What do I do? What do I do?"

His voice echoed in the spacious condo. There was no one to ask for help; nowhere to turn. Baranova had done all he could do and Campello would be dealt with. But there was that reporter. That…

The paper was lying on the floor where he had flung it. He knelt to pick it up.

"Christy," he said, unfolding the first page and studying the byline. "Christy Lee."

He marched to the window again and looked across the overcast sky. Several buildings away, across the street from the Wrigley building, stood the offices of the *Chicago Star*. That was where she worked. That was where she had made a fool of him for all Chicago to see. She had destroyed, with one article, everything he had taken great pains to build. He would not be able to enter the club without hearing the snickers, and wondering who among the dancers had such little respect for him that she would slander his name. And that other chick. The one who was with Hoppity.

He quickly scanned the article.

"Delaney. Juanita Delaney." He couldn't remember her. There had been so many. But she would remember him. So would that skank in the office across the river. They would remember him for as long as they lived.

CHAPTER 67

Campello left his apartment for a run along Michigan Avenue. He was dressed in a blue vinyl coat, a red toboggan cap, and New Balance running shoes. The chilled brisk air was invigorating. It had been a while since he'd been able to exercise and his stress level reflected it.

His route took him past the fabled Golden Mile, across the river and as far south as the art museum and the diner where he and Christy shared their first real time alone. He went round the next intersection and was on his way back when his phone rang. He paused running long enough to answer it, but continued to jog in place. It was Gloria.

"I've heard from Juanita."

"Where is she?" he asked, stopping to focus on the call.

"She's afraid."

"She should be. She's caught in the crosshairs of warring factions." A bus drove past and he put a finger in his free ear to better hear the conversation. "All of Chicago has read the article by now."

"She didn't set you up. Not willingly."

"I figured that. But I also know she's expendable and when she becomes a liability they'll kill her."

There was silence on Gloria's end of the line.

Campello said, "I can help her. Where is she?"

"I need to call her first."

"By all means, but do it quickly. Time is running out."

He hung up and resumed his northbound run toward home.

When he rounded the corner to his apartment, his phone rang. Juanita was willing to come in.

They drove to the far northwestern suburb of Arlington Heights and to an apartment complex on the Southwest Side. The place was nice, several notches above the apartment that Juanita had occupied in Chicago. Gloria got out of the car with Campello.

"Let me ring her first. When she sees me, I'll motion for you."

He agreed to wait while she made the initial approach. Within minutes, Gloria returned to the open doorway of the apartment building and motioned for him.

He followed her to a second-floor apartment that overlooked a courtyard that lay between the two buildings of the complex. The space was small, with a living-room, a dining area and a galley kitchen between them. Juanita was pacing the floor, holding the baby tightly in her arms. She looked squarely at Campello before glancing back to Gloria.

"You need to talk to him," she said to Juanita, reaching to take the baby.

The woman handed the infant to her friend. "I didn't want to set you up. They thought they were getting Polanski. All they knew was that he was driving the burgundy-colored car."

"I know," Campello said. "I was able to put that together. Who are they?"

"Peter Green and Bobby Longhorse." Juanita's answer supported the testimony that Longhorse had given Polanski prior to the hearing. She was telling the truth.

"Did they threaten you?"

She nodded.

"How did you get out of town?"

"Peter's friend, Tony Delgado, told me he would see to it that I was safe. He said that after the ambush failed, I would be a target for the police."

"Did he set you up here?"

She wrapped her arms around herself. "No."

"This is my place," Gloria said. "I sometimes do business here."

He was getting the full picture. "Do you work for Gloria?"

Juanita cast an eye at her benefactor and employer.

"She has to make a living," Gloria said, gently bouncing the baby.

"I'm not here to judge. I'm here to help. Where did Delgado send you?"

"He put me up in an apartment in Elk Grove. When I saw the article, I knew I had to run. That's when I called Gloria."

"And I told her to come here. I keep a key in the flower-pot out front."

Green had already killed one girl; killing another would've been no problem. It was more likely that Delgado intervened by playing it smart, and had simply paid for her to leave town, never to return. It was less likely to attract attention than killing her.

"Juanita, I need to go back to that night with Hoppity. Did detective Adams contact you prior to the shooting?"

She seemed both startled and relieved by his question. "Yes, but he spent most of his time with Peter."

Campello was confused. "Most of his time?"

She glanced at Gloria then back to Campello. "Yes. But when they found out I was seeing Hoppity, they asked me to talk to him." Her eyes became pleading. "I don't know anything about any of that, detective. I really don't. I just want to take care of my baby and make a living. I—"

"You don't know anything about what, Juanita?"

"About Hoppity's problems with Peter and detective Adams."

Campello had a sinking feeling. "What do you mean?"

She cast a nervous eye toward Gloria again. The woman nodded, encouraging Juanita to continue.

"Hoppity was getting big. He sold everything from meth to pills. But Peter wanted to cash in. The escort business was growing, but not bringing in the cash he'd hoped. Hoppity was his main rival and Peter wanted to manipulate him. When he found out I was seeing him, Peter asked me to talk to detective Adams."

Campello felt sick. "Did you?"

"Yes. The detective said that Hoppity was a bad man and would kill me and Clarissa if he thought we were in his way. At first, I thought he was just concerned. You know? Like a cop ought to be. But then he wanted me to set Hoppity up. I refused."

"And a few nights later, he showed up and Hoppity was ready." She began to cry.

"I told him about detective Adams and he said not to worry. But when both of you showed up he said, 'This is it', and then he told me to get down and that he'd take care of it."

"He thought it was an ambush and reacted."

"If he hadn't, you guys would've killed him." Her voice broke.

"Us guys? You think I'm part of this?"

"Aren't you?" She wiped her eyes with the heels of her palms. "Peter started leaning on me and when you came to the apartment, I thought I could offer them something that would get them off my back. They know you, you're with them, so I couldn't offer them you. Then they told me about a cop who was snooping around and they wanted him. They said his name was Polanski and said if I didn't call him, they'd make sure my baby never knew her mother. I called him and covered for you."

"Covered for me?"

She nodded. "During the trial."

"Trial? You mean the board review?"

"I guess. Detective Adams was going to kill Hoppity, so Hoppity came at him first. He'd have killed you too if he could have, but you shot him. They used me to lead them to Hoppity, so they figured they could use me to lead Polanski to them. That's why I didn't tell you anything that day. I had already called the station to get him and left a message. I thought you were coming instead, so I kept quiet. If he didn't show, I would be dead."

"There was no one with you at the apartment that day?"

She gave him a confused look before shaking her head. "No. But I couldn't tell you anything, because you're with them. They wanted Polanski. Not you."

He collapsed on the sofa. Her revelation explained a lot.

"I covered for you, detective. I covered for you and I didn't set you up. I just want to be left alone. I want to take care of my baby."

He was no longer listening. He had already heard enough.

CHAPTER 68

Anthony Delgado entered the brownstone and found Paulie Vincent before the fire. A breakfast tray of soft-boiled eggs, bacon, toast and coffee sat untouched before him. He was as pale as anyone Delgado had ever seen, and the guards standing watch around the house exchanged glances with the enforcer, signaling their belief that Vincent's time was short.

Delgado took a seat opposite his employer's motorized wheelchair. "We have a problem, sir."

The old man nodded slowly. A tube in his nose had replaced the mask and his eyes were bloodshot, the eyelids heavy.

"This morning's paper carries a significant story about us, and the Greens, and our liaison with the PD. If they make a connection, we could be looking at serious damage." He paused to wait for a response from Vincent. When none came, he continued.

"I believe that such a connection is unlikely and even more remote if they are seeking evidence that ties us to the operation. But I am concerned about Peter. He's volatile and I fear he may make an attempt on this reporter or the officers involved, or may go to the cops and spill everything."

"Where is he?" Vincent mouthed silently.

"In his condo. I have taken the liberty of stationing a couple of men outside the building. One in a car and another on foot. Regardless of the route Peter takes, they will be with him. They will keep me informed."

Vincent closed his eyes and nodded again.

"I would like your permission to resolve the issue with Peter."

Vincent opened his eyes.

"I don't want to concern you with this sort of thing, but I do believe it is in our best interests and that time is closing down." He paused, then continued, "And I'd like to erase the girl, Juanita. She's the subject of the article and if she feels the need to go to the police, she could be a conduit to us. She certainly knows more than she should about Aaron and Peter and could use that as leverage. That would create problems for us."

Aaron? mouthed Vincent.

Delgado glanced at the men stationed in the house. "Aaron will be hurt. It is possible we will have to sever our relationship with him too."

The old man closed his eyes and Delgado paused, allowing him time to assess the situation. It was deteriorating and any attempts by the hotheaded Peter to solve matters would only worsen the situation. He had been allowed to conduct his business on the side so long as he didn't interfere with Vincent's plans, and so long as he didn't bring undue attention on himself. That had all changed with the murder of the girl at Navy Pier and the subsequent attack on the detective. Delgado's efforts to usher Juanita out of the city had been the least costly way of solving a problem that had been partially created by Peter. Repeated efforts to have Aaron rein in his son had not been fruitful and it would fall to Delgado to clean up the mess that others had created. But that was as it should be. After all, Vincent was near death and Delgado was the most likely to succeed him. The enforcer was best prepared to rally the organization after Vincent's death and take it to new heights. That couldn't happen with the old way of doing things and certainly not with the childish Peter hanging over their heads. He and the girl needed to be dealt with, and if the alderman had to be excised as well, so be it.

The hiss of the oxygen and Vincent's labored breathing overrode the crackling of the fire. But then the crime lord opened his eyes, and by doing so, gave Delgado the green light.

CHAPTER 69

Christy arrived at the *Chicago Star* newsroom at half past ten. Clarence was already surrounded by suits, all of them looking toward her as she stepped off the elevator that fed directly into the room.

"I wouldn't want to be in your shoes," Ted said, under his breath.

"They wouldn't fit." She set her purse and coat on her desk and went directly to Demille's office.

"Have a seat, Ms. Lee," said one of the men – a tall, thinly built man with white hair. He was Morgan Tower and he was standing casually next to Demille's desk, hands in pockets. His poker face was tanned.

She sat and crossed her legs.

"Please tell us you enjoy working here," he said, getting directly to the point.

"I do."

"And you enjoy working with Mr. Demille?" Tower asked as the others stood passively watching her.

"Yes." She smiled at Clarence. He sat behind the desk keeping his eyes on her and a half-smile fixed on his face.

"Then for the love of God, could you please tell us what you were thinking when you wrote that story in this morning's paper?"

She exhaled sharply and looked at Clarence. He gave her the best "might as well" shrug he could muster, and she opened up, telling Tower and the others, presumably his attorneys, everything she knew, including the visit from Campello that morning and his planned attempts to find Juanita.

"If you have told me everything, Ms. Lee, it is likely that you have endangered this young woman's life as well as exposing this paper to a significant number of lawsuits."

"Yes, sir."

His face remained stoic. "That's it?"

"I believe in what I'm doing, sir. This city is as corrupt as any in the country and more than most. The mob is in bed with politicians and the politicians are in bed with the cops, and that leaves the people out there," she gestured to the cityscape outside Demille's window, "caught in the middle."

"And you propose to fix all of that by endangering this Juanita Delaney and us?"

"That was never my intention, sir."

He rolled his eyes. "The best-laid plans…"

"What would you have done?" she asked him, turning the tables.

"Me?"

"Yes, sir."

He grinned. "I would've done what you did, Ms. Lee." His eyes narrowed and focused sharply on her. "If I was your age with nothing to lose. Unfortunately, I have a great deal to lose and nothing to gain."

She glanced at Clarence again. The half-smile was still in place.

"You're toying with me, aren't you?" She stood face to face with Tower. "'Cause if you are, the game's over. If you're not, I can quit and take my exceptional skills to a competitor and do my story on the Tower empire and how it's unwilling to take a stand for the truth. I think the people of this city deserve that much."

He grinned again. "I do too, Ms. Lee." He gestured for her to have a seat and she sat again. "I am impressed by your story, but I'll admit I was angry this morning." He nodded to the men in the room. "I had our legal department go over the story and there are certainly some risks here, but I think you're right and I think the time is right to tell the story. The people are sick of lawlessness and rioting. This town has seen too much of that kind of thing over the years and the one thing it needs from time to time is a good cleaning out. Your story just might do the trick."

Clarence smiled.

"So, I can continue?"

He nodded. "Yes. But I want you to understand there is a downside to all of this."

She braced herself.

"If you make an untrue allegation, I will dismiss you and Mr. Demille here. I am tolerant, but I am no patsy. I expect solid journalism without sensationalism and unsubstantiated rumors. Understood?"

"Yes."

"And one more thing."

"Yes?"

"Be careful, Ms. Lee."

CHAPTER 70

Peter Green pulled out of the parking garage in his metallic-blue BMW M3 convertible. The top was up and he floored the pedal, speeding the roadster onto Lake Shore with no regard for anyone who might have been crossing in the car's path. The stereo was at full tilt, playing the heavy metal music he preferred, and he drummed his fingers on the steering-wheel, bouncing his head to the tune.

He drove south, glancing briefly to Lake Michigan on his left, which was as gray and colorless as the sky. The dense and choppy water lashed against the shore.

He zoomed south to Randolph and turned right toward south Wacker. He followed the road north toward the river and to north Wacker Drive and the *Chicago Star* building. It was nearing noon and it was likely he would see the woman coming out of the building or the garage and he wanted to be there when she did. It was a gamble, but if he was right the payoff could be huge. If not, he would try again at another time. He had researched her on Google and found an updated photo. She would not humiliate him again. No one would laugh at him. Everyone would know he had talent and could get things done.

He drove as quickly as the dense traffic would allow, weaving between lanes and taking only minimal care to avoid other vehicles and pedestrians in the pursuit of his goal. They were inconsequential – just like the tramp on the boat who had started this whole messy affair. If she had only said "yes", had only surrendered to him what she had undoubtedly given to men all over Chicago, she would be alive today and his business none the worse for wear. And that angered him. Trina hadn't taken him seriously, even when he told her he would kill her if she resisted him. And what good did that do her? Was it better to be dead than to have been with him? Didn't it make more sense to give in and live than to resist and die?

He stopped at a traffic light one block from Wacker Drive. The Merchandise Mart was visible ahead, standing watch on the north bank of the river as it had for decades. Throngs of pedestrians, tourists and natives alike, milled past him, aware only of their own petty problems and locked in their own little worlds. He had better things to do. And if he could remove the woman from his life, he would be taken seriously. Maybe even by his father and the men who ran him. They would see that Peter Green was an astute businessman in his own right and a force which they would have to acknowledge.

The light turned green and he floored the accelerator, nearly killing a young man who had been foolish enough to get caught mid-intersection.

Peter turned right onto north Wacker. The *Chicago Star* was just ahead and there was a curbside opening, normally reserved for cabbies. He took the spot and parked the Beamer. His watch read ten minutes after twelve.

They had followed Peter in an older-model Chevy, staying several car lengths behind. His driving had been erratic and it had been difficult at best to maintain a discreet distance while not losing him. But they managed to stay with the BMW, and followed him to Wacker Drive. He parked in front of the *Chicago Star* building, confirming their fears.

The man driving the Chevy pulled alongside a cab that was parked curbside and then phoned Delgado. When he received confirmation, he let his passenger out of the car. The passenger – a tall, solidly built man with shaved head, jeans, and dirty tennis shoes – moved to the middle of the sidewalk and paused to light a cigarette. With his hand cupped around the smoke, the man kept his eyes on the BMW and its driver, puffing gently until the cigarette was fully lit. Shaking out the match, he tossed it to the ground, and nodded to the driver of the Chevy before he began walking east along the sidewalk, toward the M3 convertible. His hands were thrust into the pockets of his jacket.

The driver of the Chevy revved the engine and searched the surrounding area with a nervous eye for the driver of the empty cab.

Peter waited in the BMW for his prey to appear. Under his jacket, in a shoulder holster under his left arm, he was packing a .357 magnum with a 2-inch barrel. The large-bore handgun was loaded with high-velocity rounds and would ensure she would be taken down for good. He wanted to leave no room for error.

He crouched down in the seat to better peer at the car's rearview mirror and kept an eye on the revolving door. No sooner had he lowered himself, than he saw her coming through the entrance on her way to the sidewalk. She matched the photo he had seen on the internet, point for point. She was an attractive woman. She would have brought a premium on the open market.

He pulled the revolver from its holster and pushed the button that lowered the passenger's-side window.

The man from the Chevy was less than twenty feet from the car when he saw the right-side window come down. He briefly paused, midstride, and then crouched to peer into the BMW through its rear window. Peter Green was looking toward the *Star* building and directly at a woman who was coming through the revolving doors.

The man on the sidewalk pulled a Glock from the small of his back and motioned with his left arm for the driver of the Chevy to pull into traffic.

The car separated from its double-parked position and began to creep alongside the BMW.

The hit man charged toward the convertible as effortlessly and quietly as he could. He did not look at the pedestrians on the sidewalk, or at the passing vehicles on Wacker, or even at Christy. He kept his eye trained on Peter Green and the convertible's open window.

Peter cocked the hammer and called out to Christy.

She turned her head in his direction.

The tall man reached through the open window of the Beamer and thrust his pistol inside. Without saying a word, he fired four shots and then tossed the weapon into the car where it landed on the lifeless body of Peter Green.

CHAPTER 71

The open attack on Christy gave Campello pause. Peter Green was dead. Whoever killed him had probably not done it to protect the reporter. Instead, they were rolling up the rug to protect their own interests. That meant Juanita, Gloria, the Polanskis, Christy and Campello himself were potential targets. They knew too much and that was something the forces arrayed against them could not tolerate.

They met at Campello's apartment without Andy and his wife, who were being scrutinized by the press. Reporters from all over the Midwest were gathered in front of their home with TV cameras, microphones and radio equipment, making it impossible for anyone to get in or out without all of Chicago knowing.

Campello gathered the crew together in the living-room and began to lay out the scenario as well as a possible way out.

"We've got to get you three to safety," he said to Christy and Juanita, who was holding her baby.

Christy shook her head. "The attack on me was isolated. It was Peter being stupid."

"You're a liability to the crew that hit Peter," he said.

"I don't think so. Think about it, Frank. I'm the reporter who wrote the article. Any attack on me is an attack on an open press. They – whoever they are – aren't that stupid. They could've let Peter finish the job and then taken him out at another time. But they didn't. They stopped him."

"But you know too much," he said, while the others watched the give and take like spectators at a Chicago Bulls game.

"They're the real targets of this," she said, nodding toward the others.

"Agreed. But I couldn't concentrate on them if I thought you were still out there, an open target for whoever might want to draw them out."

She smiled. "You're sweet. You really are. But I can take care of myself."

"I'm a cop," he said. "I'm not sweet. And I know you can take care of yourself. But not against people like these. Especially when you can't see them coming."

"I don't know as much as they think," Christy said. "And what little they think I know can be eliminated by eliminating her." She nodded toward Juanita who sat wide-eyed with Clarissa on her lap. "It's more important to protect her and let me stay on the job."

"She has a point, detective," Gloria said. "If we can get out of town, she can go to work on the other end."

Campello shook his head. "It's no good. They'd use her as leverage against me – *us* – and that would put her in danger."

"It's a chance we'll have to take," she said.

"We don't have to take any chances at all," Campello said.

Christy looked at him, dumbfounded. "Yes we do. These people," she gestured to the others, "have put a lot on the line trusting us. We can't leave them now."

She had him. He knew it. And so did she.

"If we leave town, where will you be?" he asked.

"Here."

He shook his head. "If this is going to work, I need to know you're safe."

She paused to think. "Maybe Andy could—"

Campello shook his head. "Andy can't stay in town. He's being too closely watched. If anything, he's going to have to go with me or stay put. If he sticks his head outside the door, someone will see it. If he were protecting you, he'd be no protection at all. He's got his hands full trying to avoid being a target himself. And then there's his family. He can't watch them and you."

"Frank, I don't need protection," she said. The others shifted uncomfortably.

"You take protection or this doesn't fly. We end it right here."

She attempted a stare-down, but this time he had *her*. "OK, OK," she sighed. "Do you have a suggestion?"

"For now, you stay with Demille at the office. You trust him?"

"Completely."

"Then stay at the *Star* building. They have a shower there, right? Kitchen facilities?"

She started to speak.

"We don't know who we can trust, Christy. I don't know him. But you do so I'll go with your instinct on this. I may have someone else, and I'll call you to let you know if I can get it arranged. But for now, on short notice, stay with Demille."

She looked at the others, searching their eyes for support of her position. She found none. "OK, OK, I can go along with that if Clarence will."

Campello spread his hands. "He does, or it's over and they win."

"They're not going to win this one, Frank. They may have control of the city and the police, but they don't control me. They don't win this one!"

CHAPTER 72

Andy Polanski liked the plan. It was the first time he'd felt useful since getting arrested. In fact, since going public with his allegations against Caine and Dorchester. After hanging up from Campello, he told his wife everything.

"I don't like it, Andy," Jenny said. "It's risky and it separates us." They were upstairs in the bedroom. Polanski had two suitcases opened on the bed.

"Everything I've done has been risky," he said. "But God has always provided for us. This may be another case of His provision."

"Going into hiding?"

"Didn't David have to go into hiding even though he had already been anointed as King?" He put both hands on her shoulders and looked intently into her eyes. "This is better than sitting around, don't you think?"

"No. We're safe here. We can——"

He released her and went to the window that looked directly down on the front of the house. He opened the blinds and gestured to the media that had been posted outside their window. Vans with antennae, radio broadcast trucks and trailers full of reporters from newspapers and magazines from across the Midwest were gathered outside the house.

"Look at them, Jenny. They're like a bunch of vultures, just waiting for us to die."

She crossed her arms and turned her head away from the window. He closed the blinds.

"I have to do this. *We* have to do this. I don't want to die in this house, hiding from them." He pointed toward the window.

"What about the kids?"

"They'll do fine. Surely you can't be suggesting that going to school and passing through that crowd out there is any way to live."

She sat on the bed. He knelt in front of her, putting both hands on hers.

"They'll have a good time."

"You won't be there."

"I will soon. This won't last forever. Nothing does."

"Where am I supposed to go?"

"It doesn't matter. Just away from here." He nodded over his shoulder to the window behind him. "They'll think that I'm still here and you're coming back. They're used to seeing you take the kids to sports practice... piano lessons. Except this time, we'll all be leaving."

She shook her head. "I don't like it."

"I know. You said that already."

She sighed, lowered her head, pausing to think. He rose to his feet and went downstairs, giving her time and space. It was important that she follow the plan, but it would be far better if she were fully on board.

He was sitting quietly in the living-room, reading the story of David's flight, when he saw her at the base of the stairs twenty minutes later.

"OK," she said. "I'll do it."

Polanski stood at the upstairs window, watching as the kids arrived home from school, maneuvering their way through the pressing throng of reporters who attempted to badger them into answering questions on topics they knew nothing about. He ran downstairs to be there when they entered the house and watched as Jenny put a finger to her lips and motioned for them to follow her upstairs. They seemed confused at first, but quickly adapted to the game she was playing, a typical Jenny attempt at lessening their burden.

While they were changing clothes and getting their suitcases, which Jenny had already packed, he went to the hallway closet and extracted his personal weapon, a 9mm Beretta, and two fifteen-round magazines that were fully loaded. He also grabbed an extra box of shells and dropped them into the bag he had packed. Prior to the kids arriving home, he had dressed in jeans, a flannel shirt, and sturdy boots. He had already tossed a jacket and gloves into the trunk of the car, along with a flashlight, matches, reading material and a disassembled sniper rifle with scope. He kept the latter in an aluminum suitcase lined with pre-molded padding designed to accommodate the weapon's various components.

The cabin would be empty of foodstuffs, but these could be purchased as soon as everyone had arrived. He was making a last-minute check when the kids came bouncing down the stairs with Jenny in tow.

"Everyone ready?" he asked.

"All ready, Captain," Jenny said, playing along despite her misgivings.

"Time's a-wastin'."

Jenny and the kids shuttled past him to the garage and he checked that the lights were still on, the blinds were closed, and the TV was blaring. He then followed them to the car, where the kids were buckling up and Jenny was behind the wheel. He leaned in through the open driver's-side window.

"Don't use the cell phone unless you absolutely have to," he said.

"I know."

"Pick up a pre-paid phone as soon as you can. They're harder to track."

"I know," she said, her anxiety slipping through.

"And stay with your parents until I call."

"I know, Andy."

"I love you," he said, kissing her. "I'll see you in a few days."

He waved at the children, buckled in their seats, before climbing into the trunk and pulling the lid closed.

CHAPTER 73

Campello and the women arrived at the cabin in the waning daylight hours. He found the key exactly where Polanski said it would be, and they went in, setting their suitcases on the floor. The place was musty, but clean, and adequately furnished. They were standing in a central room that held a rustic-looking couch and several chairs, a rack of books, a wood-burning stove and a large oval-shaped braided rug. A small kitchen was located in a sequestered portion of the living area and had a stove, a refrigerator, and a few cabinets. Campello strode across the cabin and inspected the two rooms that fed off the living area. They were bedrooms, each with two twin beds. One of them had a bathroom and shower.

"Whose cabin is this?" Juanita asked, holding Clarissa.

"It belongs to Polanski's in-laws," Campello said, returning to the living-room.

Gloria opened the refrigerator. "It's empty."

"We'll get some food as soon as he arrives. I don't want to leave you alone and I sure don't want to risk exposure by driving into town." He nodded to the baby's travel bag. "She should have enough for a few days. We'll get more when we go into town. You and the baby can have the bigger bedroom with the bath, and Gloria can take the other. Andy and I will sleep out here."

Gloria picked up her bag. "Sounds like a plan, chief." She went into the bedroom and dropped her case on the bed. "But I want to freshen up, first." She went into the bathroom in the larger bedroom.

Campello told the women to get comfortable. He had thought

about collecting their cell phones, too, but since service wasn't available in the area surrounding the cabin, he decided against it.

"I'm going to take a look around. Stay inside, but if you need anything, just open the door and call me. I won't be far."

He left Juanita standing alone, looking confused, while he went outside with his pistol in hand. The area surrounding the cabin was heavily wooded, with a small stream nearby. A dirt path led to a small driveway that was partially covered in gravel and that led to the main road that took them directly into town. Electrical power fed into the cabin from a single line that could be easily cut if their attackers decided to isolate them. There were no crawl spaces, no out-buildings or other places to hide. If their attacker found them, they would be in a world of trouble.

He was finishing his inspection of the cabin's security, when a car pulled off the main road and onto the driveway, heading for the cabin. He clutched the pistol tightly and squinted into the developing darkness. It was Polanski.

Because Polanski had a high profile, he remained with the group while Campello went into town and purchased the food and supplies they thought they would need to sustain themselves for several days. That evening, Campello prepared dinner, and after eating, they gathered in the living area of the cabin. It was warmed by a glowing fire that Polanski had built in the wood-burning stove.

"The bedroom windows lock," Polanski said, "but of course, that's no security in itself."

"We'll take shifts," Campello said, nodding toward his partner. "When this thing is over, Christy will send a friend for us. I gave him the location of the cabin before I left. He is the only one who knows where we're at, and for the moment, the only one who seems to be above the fray."

"But you told Christy to tell no one, to trust no one," Juanita said, fear dripping from her.

"I know. I don't know her friends or their connections. I don't know if I can trust all of mine. But I have to trust someone, so I took it out of the department."

"Does Christy know where we are?" Gloria asked.

Campello shook his head. "The less they know, the better," Campello said.

"So what happens next?" Juanita asked, holding the sleeping baby in her arms.

"We wait. Christy is going to go after Aaron Green. Since his son is gone, he might be willing to roll over on the others. If so, she wants to know. But I suspect the department will begin rounding people up, one way or the other, even though we don't know who that is, exactly."

"How are they going to catch everybody?" Gloria asked. "If half of what I've heard is true, the best they can hope for is to get the snake's tail."

Campello shrugged. "We do the best we can."

"But what happens if they get us?" Juanita asked, anguish building on her face.

"We're not going to let that happen."

"But what if it does?"

"Then they win."

Clarissa stirred and began to cry, and Juanita left the room to change her diaper and prepare for bed. Campello, thinking about an additional source of support, decided to take a chance. He made the call, talking in hushed tones over the cabin phone. The evening had worn thin on all of them and Polanski glanced at his watch as soon as Campello rejoined the group. It was nearing eleven thirty.

"I'll take the first watch," Polanski said, rising from his chair.

"Call me in three hours," Campello said. "Sooner if there's trouble."

Polanski agreed and opened the metal case.

CHAPTER 74

Delgado was finally able to reach Aaron Green. Multiple attempts to find the alderman at his home and various offices had not been successful and he did not respond to the enforcer's emergency page. Finally, after several phone calls to his home and cell, contact had been made. Aaron agreed to meet with Delgado, but only in a public setting. They met at midnight in the lobby of a hotel. The place was crowded. Patrons were drinking in the adjacent bar, the restaurant was filled to capacity, and people jammed the revolving doors, coming to and from the outside cab stand. Green was tearful, and Delgado tried to assuage the alderman's grief while keeping an eye on the people in the lobby. This was not the scene he wanted.

"Aaron, I am truly sorry. But you must know we had nothing to do with this."

"Who else?" Green asked, blubbering. "Who else?"

"Peter was living life his way, Aaron. You know that as well as anyone. You did the best you could. But we cannot control everything. Sometimes not even those who are closest to us."

"They killed him. *You* killed him."

"No," he said, lowering his voice, a signal for Aaron to do the same. "I had nothing to do with it, nor did any of my crew. This kind of talk is foolishness. This is why I'm reaching out to you, Aaron," he said, using the man's name as a means of building a bridge, "and it's why I'm going to help you find the man who did this."

"How?"

"I have my men on it now. I didn't want to tell you this, but I believe that detective Campello was the one who killed Peter. I have made a phone call to the police to report my suspicions. They have been quite receptive. Campello has been harassing Peter, as you know, and so has his partner. The partner has been sequestered and is no longer a threat. But it is critical that you remain calm. We cannot replace Peter, but we can find the individual responsible for this." He placed a hand on Aaron's arm, only to have him pull away.

"Aaron, it's important for you, for me, for Mr. Vincent, and for Peter's legacy, that our partnership not be affected by this tragedy. I know you're upset. I would be too. But we will help you find justice on this. Real justice. Not the travesty of the courts."

"It won't bring Peter back." He dabbed at his swollen eyes.

"No, it won't. But it will give closure." He reached again for Green's arm. The man did not shirk him this time. "Aaron, you must trust me. This is the time when friendship means the most. It's when the rubber meets the road that true friendship stands tall. We won't let you down." He looked earnestly into the alderman's eyes.

Green sighed heavily and nodded.

Delgado smiled and patted the man's arm. He was about to speak when his cell phone rang. "Excuse me." He flipped open the cell and stood, walking a few feet away.

"We've got a handle on them," the voice on the other end of the line said. "They've taken the girl to a cabin. Our guys are on it now. And get this. Polanski is with them. You want us to finish this?"

Delgado glanced at the despairing Green. "No. We will need this buffoon a little longer. Have the others handle this. It's too hot and I don't want any more of our guys involved."

"I'll make the call."

CHAPTER 75

C ampello slept fitfully and woke with a start at the crunching sound of gravel. He glanced at his watch. It was 3 a.m. Polanski was to have woken him at 2:30.

He cursed and rose to his feet, running a hand over his face. Through eyes that were bleary with sleep, he peered through the living-room window by standing to one side and gently pulling the window-shade aside. In the moonlight he could see a sedan creeping up the driveway, but he couldn't tell who the occupants were.

He pulled the pistol from its holster and immediately went to the bedrooms.

Gently pulling the door of the first bedroom partially open, he was able to see that Juanita and her baby were sound asleep. In the second bedroom, Gloria was an immovable mound under a stack of blankets. The windows in both bedrooms were closed and secured and the shades were pulled down.

Campello went back to the living-room window and pulled the closed shade aside. Three occupants climbed out of the car. The vehicle's dome light did not illuminate the interior of the car when the door was open – a clear sign that its occupants were professionals and did not want to be identified.

He bolted to Gloria's bedroom and opened the door, being careful to close it behind him. He left the lights off, but gently shook her awake.

"Get up and get down on the floor. Stay under the bed. We've got trouble."

He left the room and went into Juanita's. He told her the same thing and she immediately climbed out of bed and gently carried Clarissa with her as she slid onto the floor and under the bed.

Campello closed the door behind him, and glanced through the living-area window again. He could see only one occupant now. The other two were likely moving to the back of the cabin.

He picked up the cabin phone and called Silk 'n Boots. The phone answered on the first ring. "We have trouble. Call—"

The line went dead.

CHAPTER 76

The crashing sound of broken glass came from the rear of the cabin. He turned and immediately saw Jerry Hughbanks poised at the window. For a second, their eyes locked. Then Hughbanks raised a pistol.

Campello fired, striking the window-frame and forcing Hughbanks to duck for cover. Juanita screamed and Clarissa began crying.

Campello moved for cover behind one of the chairs that stood in the living-room, off to the side of the direct line that was formed by the front and back doors. No sooner had he taken cover than a shot came through the window from which he had been looking earlier, perforating the window-shade and striking the wall next to Juanita's bedroom door. She screamed again and he repositioned himself farther along the wall and into a corner of the living-room where he would be out of the line of fire that was likely to come through one of the windows.

From outside the cabin, he heard Polanski's voice.

"Drop it."

A second shot was fired, but from the sound, it was not directed at the cabin. A third shot echoed in the night, but this time it came from a high-powered rifle.

Campello crawled to a position near the bedrooms. If the cabin was rushed, he wanted to be near the women. He gently pushed open both bedroom doors. Clarissa was crying, but Gloria and Juanita were under the beds as instructed and there was no evidence that the windows in their rooms had been breached.

"Stay down," he said, trying to sound as calm as possible.

From outside came the noise of another shot, followed again by the report of a high-powered rifle.

"Frank," it was Polanski's voice. "There are three of them. Two are down. The other one is around back."

Campello rose to his feet and inched along the wall to the rear door. Shards of glass crunched under him as he moved with the pistol held in both hands. His heart was pounding and his palms were sweaty.

When he reached the door, he knelt and gently turned the knob, opening it to the outside.

"Give it up!" he called out to Hughbanks. "You've got nowhere to go."

He was answered by a gunshot that struck the wall overhead, raining debris on him. The muzzle blast had come from the woods beyond the cabin. Hughbanks was less than ten yards away and to the left.

Campello dove through the open doorway and rolled on the ground, through the wet grass, to a position that was to his right and behind the bushes he had scouted earlier in the day. Hughbanks fired again, but this time the shot went wild. Campello was aware of rushing footsteps from the front of the cabin and drew a bead on the approaching figure.

"Whoa, whoa! It's me," Polanski said, holding a .30-06 Springfield rifle with a night-vision scope. He crouched with Campello behind the foliage. "It's Hughbanks, Tertwiller, and Chin."

"Where are they?"

Polanski looked at him. "Tertwiller and Chin are dead."

"Jerry!" Campello yelled. "Tertwiller and Chin are dead. Give it up."

Another shot hit the wall of the cabin directly overhead.

"I've got him," Polanski said, drawing a bead with the rife. He fired and the shot echoed, before the night grew suddenly quiet.

CHAPTER 77

Christy arrived with Jimmy Small. Campello had hoped that his phone call to the bouncer would prompt him to go to her, even though the signal had been disrupted when the line was cut.

Their car moved up the gravel driveway and Campello, sitting with Polanski on the porch, rose from his chair to greet her as she stepped out of the car.

"I'm so glad to see you," he said, hugging her.

"I called the local police. They should be on their way."

Jimmy shook Campello's hand, then surveyed the area. Tertwiller's body lay face down, motionless in the dew-soaked grass, ten feet from the porch. Chin was lying face up, less than twenty yards from her, and Hughbanks had been left where he fell, several yards from the rear of the cabin in the dense woods from where he attacked.

"You OK?" she asked.

Campello nodded, still holding Christy close. "Let's go inside. It's warmer in there."

The three of them moved toward the porch, avoiding looking at the two dead detectives, and joined Andy Polanski there before going into the cabin. Once inside, Polanski stood the rifle in one corner and Campello removed the holster from his belt and set the weapon on the small table in the living area, glad to be free of it. The women were in the bedrooms and a pot of coffee was gurgling to its finish on the counter in the kitchen. The fire in the wood-burning stove had burned itself out long ago, but everyone had been too busy and too disrupted to build another fire. The cabin had grown significantly cooler.

"I'll get some wood," Jimmy said. "Be back in a sec." He left the cabin, closing the door behind him.

Campello, Christy and Polanski poured coffee. Christy added creamer and sugar to hers and then joined the men around the table. Juanita came out of the bedroom looking disheveled, but upbeat for the first time since Campello had met her. Gloria remained in the other bedroom, packing.

"Baby asleep?" Christy asked.

Juanita nodded, running a hand through her hair. She poured a cup of coffee and sat at the last vacant seat at the table.

"The locals will be here soon," Campello said. "Then, and only then, can we call Lopez." He still wasn't sure who he could trust and he didn't want Lopez in the cabin until the local police had a presence.

"There's going to be a lot of media over this," Christy said. "In fact, it's already started." She grinned.

"What do you mean?" Campello asked.

"Aaron Green called me. He's turning on Paulie Vincent and his crew. He's prepared to give names, dates, transaction history… everything." She sipped the coffee. "Clarence and I have already started the series of articles on it and the first will run…" she paused to glance at her watch, "in approximately two hours."

"Is he willing to testify?" Polanski asked.

She nodded. "More than that. He's already begun working with the state's attorney and the FBI. He will announce his resignation as alderman in a press conference this morning."

"That's one conference you won't want to miss," Campello said, smiling.

The door opened and Jimmy came in carrying an armload of wood.

"When are we leaving?" Gloria asked, coming out of the bedroom with her hands tucked in the rear pockets of her jeans. "I'll be glad to—" She looked squarely at Jimmy. "You!"

CHAPTER 78

Before Campello and the others had time to react, Jimmy Small dropped the wood and drew a revolver from the waist-band in the small of his back.

"I didn't want it to end like this, Frank," he said. "I really didn't." He took Campello's pistol from the holster and held it in his free hand. Polanski's rifle was across the room and did not pose a threat.

"Jimmy?" Campello said. The name hung in the air like acrid smoke.

"He works for Delgado. He's the one who worked me over," Gloria said.

Campello looked from her to the bouncer.

Jimmy motioned with the revolver for her to sit in the living-room chair. "I'm sorry, Frank," he said again. "But I've got to get out of here. If she hadn't been here," he pointed with the gun to Gloria, "everything could've went on without problems."

"Jimmy, what…?" Campello said.

Gloria answered for the bouncer. "He's an enforcer for Delgado. He was hired to watch Peter and the club when Delgado couldn't be there. He's the one who probably killed Rita. Delgado never likes to get his hands dirty."

Sirens could be heard in the distance.

"Into the living-room. Now!" Small motioned with the revolver again. Clarissa began crying in the back bedroom and Juanita rose to tend to her.

"Don't!" Small said. "Get over here, now! All of you!"

The group at the table rose with their hands elevated and began moving to the center of the room. Polanski closed in on the women to his right and simultaneously moved in front of Campello, revealing the 9mm pistol jutting from a holster behind his back.

"You're the one who killed Longhorse, aren't you?" Christy asked, having seen the gun in Polanski's back and trying to divert Small's gaze away from the men.

"I never liked that guy."

"Who covered for you?" she asked. "You had to have help from within the department."

"That's none of your concern," he said, still motioning for them to move into the living-room. "When they find this place on fire, you—"

Campello pulled the pistol from Polanski's waistband, just as the detective dove sharply to the right, tackling Christy and Juanita and driving them to the floor. Gloria was too far away for him to reach her.

Small fired.

Campello fired.

CHAPTER 79

Radios squawked from squad cars parked on the gravel drive; their blue lights cut a swathe through the cabin. Gloria lay dead, several feet from Jimmy Small's body. Juanita held Clarissa close to her breast, sitting between Polanski and Christy. Campello was talking to one of the local uniformed officers when he heard a familiar voice.

"Is everyone alright?" It was Julio Lopez. He was standing in the doorway with his star pinned to the collar of his jacket.

Campello, driven by rage, grabbed Lopez by his jacket and drove him into the cabin wall. The officer Campello had been talking with grabbed both of his wrists.

"Detective! Let go."

"You," Campello said. "You've been at the heart of this since it began." He repeatedly slammed Lopez into the wall despite the officer's attempts at restraining him.

"Let go of me, Frank! There's a lot you don't know."

The officer tried to pry Campello's hands free of Lopez's jacket but Campello resisted him. "Leave me alone. Don't you know who this is?"

"I'm Julio Lopez and I'm the commander of the 28th district. That means I'm your boss."

"Shut up!" Campello said, driving the man harder into the wall.

"Frank, there's a lot you don't know," said Lopez again. "There's a lot *I* didn't know."

Slowly, deliberately, Campello eased up on Lopez, allowing him to stand erect, but keeping a focused eye on him.

"Sit down, Frank," Lopez said. "I have something to tell you."

Campello glanced at the uniformed officer, and then slowly took a seat next to Christy. She gripped his arm.

"Frank, you're a good cop. Polanski is a good cop and whether you believe me or not, I'm a good cop. But there are some who aren't and they've been in bed with Paulie Vincent for a long time."

"Tell me something I don't know, Julio."

Lopez sighed and shook his head. "We... the brass, have known for a long time that Aaron Green was being manipulated by Vincent and his crew. Willingly manipulated. His warehouse has been a conduit for all sorts of contraband and activities that have been essential to Vincent's business. Most recently, the warehouse has been importing illegals from Mexico and a few from Central and South America. They do it for a fee and then they help these people find employment for an additional fee. But there have been other uses of the warehouse, including drugs, counterfeiting... you name it. Their plan now is to import automatic weapons for sale and distribution all over the world. It's been in the works for a long time, but Vincent only recently informed Green about it. We've been monitoring the situation with ATF." He paused, glancing at Christy. "Christy's article sped the timetable up considerably and her personalizing of the thing into Peter Green's lap drove him over the edge. We think he was taken out by some of Vincent's men, probably Jimmy," he nodded to the dead enforcer, "and that it had nothing to do with Peter's planned murder of Christy."

"You're saying I was saved by happenstance?" she asked, gently squeezing Campello's arm.

"Probably," Lopez said.

"And where does that leave me?" Campello asked. "And was that you with Tertwiller in my garage that night?"

Christy frowned and then looked at Lopez.

"A large number of the officers at the 31st are on Vincent's payroll. That includes Shelly and her husband. So, yes. I was there that night. They had taken me into their confidence, so I played along until I could iron out who else was involved. At the moment, it includes Hughbanks." He glanced at his folded hands. "And I know this'll pain you, Frank, but—"

"Rand."

Lopez nodded. "Yes. Rand was the leader of the group. He's the reason I had Polanski transferred to the Castle and assigned to you."

"To keep an eye on me."

"Yeah, that's pretty much it. I didn't know for sure if you were working that closely with Rand or not. So I figured if you were, Polanski might be able to draw you out."

"Was he aware of this?" Campello looked to Andy, who appeared stunned.

Lopez shook his head. "No. But Silvio is. He's a righteous cop."

"So why have you been blocking me? Telling me to lay off Peter?"

"For the same reason I kept telling you to focus on the murder. You were getting too close to an investigation that Internal Affairs started months ago. We were concerned you'd muck it up and we'd lose months of work. We have taps on Aaron Green's offices and phones, and on Vincent's. We just couldn't take a chance."

"Who let Jimmy in to kill Longhorse?"

"We don't know. No logs were made, of course, but you can bet that we find who did it. By the way, the tox screen on Longhorse came back. He was definitely drugged before he was hanged. It's a matter of running down the shifts." He approached Campello. "Frank, I know this is hard. But you'll have to trust someone. Start by trusting me."

CHAPTER 80

ndictments were handed down by the grand jury against seventeen officers in the 31st, including detectives Caine and Dorchester. Charges were dropped against Polanski when Aaron Green testified how the bogus claims were arranged and who arranged them. His resignation did not meet with the outcry he had hoped, signifying that the citizenry of Chicago was far more adept at recognizing fraudulent politicians than he had thought.

Two weeks after the incident at the cabin, Campello and Christy met with the Polanskis at a local pizzeria known for its deep-dish Chicago-style pizza.

"I've been given my choice of districts," Campello said, lifting a heavy slice of sausage-laden pizza from the pan. "But I'm staying at the Castle. I've been there too long to quit now. Besides," he shrugged, "better the devil you know than the devil you don't."

Christy grinned. "You're phraseology is apropos."

"There you go again with those big words."

"Not me," Polanski said. "I'd just as soon not work with the devil at all."

Campello shook his head as he bit into the large slice. "It's a figure of speech, Andy."

"Maybe. But he's real and he's all about corruption. It doesn't matter if it's individuals, cities, town, nations, or personal morals. He's all about destruction. Slow, methodical, incremental, but destruction nevertheless." He lifted a slice from the pan. "I'm resigning."

Christy looked at Campello, who stopped mid-bite.

"No, Andy, you can't mean that!" she said. "Not now. Not when everything has been cleaned out."

He shook his head. "I was never a cop, Christy. I was trying to clear my father's name."

"You succeeded," Campello said. "You're everything he wasn't."

Polanski shrugged and Jenny held tightly to his arm. "I'm a businessman. It's what I was made to do. I'm going back to it. Besides," he said, looking at Christy, "corruption is never fully flushed out. The police will never win, and they will never lose. It's a war that is fought one battle at a time. And I don't have the stomach for it anymore." He nodded to Campello. "But you two make a great team. It'll be fun to see how it all works out."

She kissed Campello on the cheek and ruffled his hair. "It will, won't it?"

Across town, in the brownstone once occupied by the late Paulie Vincent, Anthony Delgado was being installed as head of the family. His first act was to telephone the resources that made his ascension possible and that would herald future success. The people he depended on to nullify the institutions that stood in his way had been loyal. He would need their support and he wanted them to know he valued their input.

"Paulie is gone," he said in one of these phone conversations. "But I am certain we can continue our long and prosperous relationship. I trust you've cleaned up your position and will remain a valuable asset?"

"Count on it," Silvio said.

Below is an extract from *Chicago Knights*, the sequel to *The Sons of Jude*

CHAPTER 1

3:00 a.m.
Tuesday, June 9
Chicago

Officer Tom Dowd was sitting behind the steering-wheel of his cruiser, parked curbside on Rush Street, just south of the intersection with Delaware. His partner, Jessica Crowley, was typing the report from their last run into the car's laptop when Dowd suddenly cocked his head.

"What's up?"

"Did you hear that?"

"Hear what?"

The night was unusually warm and the car's windows were rolled down. He put a finger to his lips. "Just listen."

The overhead streetlamp partially illuminated the interior, revealing Dowd's furrowed brow and thin lips. He was fifteen years her senior, wiry and fastidiously neat. He had combed his evaporating hair backward along the sides, giving him an eerily similar appearance to a younger version of the actor Robert Duvall.

"You're hearing things," she said, redirecting her attention to the computer just as the sound of breaking glass wafted through the canyon formed by the buildings.

"There," he said. "Hear that?"

She paused with her hands poised over the keyboard. Within seconds, the sound of crashing glass emanated again from somewhere around them. She looked slightly to her right, northeast of their position. "It sounds like it's coming from over there."

Dowd started the car and pulled away from the curb, creeping northward along Rush Street. Because the cluster of buildings rendered the acoustics unreliable and made it impossible to pinpoint the exact location of the sound, they visually scanned their respective sides of the street as they advanced. It wasn't until they were in the intersection that a revving engine drew their attention.

"There!" Crowley said, pointing at a red Porsche Boxster parked along the south side of Delaware.

Dowd stopped and directed his spotlight on the car. A tall man stood amid shards of glass on the passenger's side of the Porsche, holding a crowbar. He tossed the tool aside and jumped into the car.

Dowd put the cruiser in reverse, aligning it with Delaware before shifting into drive and accelerating around the corner. He flicked on the light bar and siren just as the Porsche rocketed from the curb, heading east. Crowley immediately radioed the dispatcher, giving her a description of the car along with the tag number and the direction they were heading.

"Two suspects," she said. "One is a tall black male wearing a dark shirt and pants. The other is unidentified and behind the wheel."

The dispatcher acknowledged the information and immediately put a call to all units in the area.

As Dowd chased the suspects along Delaware and into the intersection with Michigan Street, the Porsche suddenly turned to the right, nearly flipping from momentum, before racing southward along the famed thoroughfare. They flew past the restaurants, shops and bars for which the Magnificent Mile was known. All had closed hours earlier, and the street was largely deserted.

The cruiser's radio came alive with chatter as other officers began detailing their efforts to head off the suspects and thwart yet another car theft. The city had seen a sharp upswing in thefts over the last two months.

Dowd stayed with the Porsche, keeping his spotlight focused on the car's cockpit. The suspect in the passenger's seat appeared to be giving directions to the driver, pointing excitedly and unintentionally telegraphing to Dowd the direction the thieves intended to go.

He pursued them south along Michigan, past the Wrigley building and over the Chicago River. Both cars hit a sharp dip when they crossed Wacker Drive, causing the suspects and the pursuing officers to bounce in their seats. The Boxster's tailpipe struck the pavement as the car hit the low-lying area, sending a shower of sparks into the air.

Dowd glanced peripherally at the intersection. There were a few pedestrians on the sidewalks, most likely late-reveling tourists, but they posed no threat to the pursuit nor were they endangered by it. Had the streets been more congested, Dowd would have been forced to abandon the chase. The department's vehicular pursuit policy had been revamped in 2004 following the death of an innocent civilian in a crash with a fleeing suspect.

Crowley pointed ahead to a bevy of cruisers. Officers were laying Stop Sticks across all of Michigan's southbound lanes.

Dowd slowed his speed, anticipating that the suspects would turn in an attempt to avoid the barrier. He was right. The Porsche's brake lights glowed suddenly as the car veered left, heading east on Monroe.

"They're working their way towards Lakeshore," he said.

Crowley radioed the change of direction. Officers from other districts would begin anticipating the direction of the chase in an effort to thwart the fleeing suspects.

Dowd glanced at the speedometer. He was keeping pace with the Porsche by hovering close to eighty miles an hour. In the adrenalin-soaked moment, he became aware of his intense grip on the steering-wheel and the pounding of his heart.

The suspects tapped the brakes again, slowing considerably before turning right onto Lakeshore, just as Dowd had anticipated. The thieves and the pursuing officers were heading south.

Crowley relayed the new information, yelling over the whine of the siren and the wind whipping through the open windows.

The Porsche shot across the southbound lanes to the far left, increasing the speed of the chase. Dowd's speedometer climbed to 100.

The dispatcher radioed Crowley, telling her the name and owner of the stolen car. He was a local.

"Probably working late," Dowd said.

"Trying to pay for that car."

The chase continued until they reached the Hyde Park area, south of the city, where a new roadblock had been formed by other officers who were laying Stop Sticks across the roadway. Again anticipating the suspects' next move, Dowd slowed his speed. The Porsche broke to the far-right lane and raced along the shoulder of the road, in an attempt to circumvent the officer's efforts, but failed when the Boxster rolled over a Stick, shredding all four tires. Dowd followed the Boxster, maintaining his speed and distance, occasionally swerving to avoid the flying debris that came at him from the Porsche's disintegrating tires. But as they reached East 57th, the sports car's brake lights suddenly glowed and the Boxster veered sharply to the right, sparks flying, as the suspects fought to maintain speed on bare wheel-rims while exiting Lake Shore Drive.

"They could be heading for the Museum," Crowley said. The Chicago Museum of Science and Industry had a surrounding park and underground garage in which the thieves could abandon the car.

Dowd shook his head. "They're not heading anywhere. They're looking for a place to land. I'll bet it's going to be Washington Park."

The Porsche sped past the Museum with the cruiser in tow, working its way in a haphazard fashion westward, before confirming Dowd's prediction by entering the park. The thieves reduced their speed but on the bare rims were unable to navigate the sharp turn and flipped the car end over end several times before coming to rest upside down against a tree. Dowd stood on the brake, spinning the cruiser sideways and coming to a stop twenty yards from the overturned sports car.

Steam rolled from the crumpled Porsche as one of the suspects climbed from the driver's side of the car and began running.

"I've got him," Dowd said, leaping from the squad with his pistol and flashlight in hand.

Crowley radioed the dispatcher with their location and requested an ambulance.

As Dowd increased the distance between himself and his partner, the sound of arriving units grew increasingly faint, replaced by his own labored breathing and the jingling of the keys on his belt. Although he kept in shape, running and lifting weights several times a week, he was nearing fifty. It wasn't long before the thief was out of view.

Dowd stopped running and leaned against a tree, resting his hands on his knees. He gasped for air. Beads of sweat formed on his forehead and perspiration trickled down his spine under his shirt and bullet-proof vest. He had lost the suspect, so he extinguished the flashlight to prevent the thief from locating him. Fighting to subdue his breathing, he strained to listen. Hearing nothing, he slid the flashlight into the ring on his belt and tucked the Sig Sauer pistol in its holster, retracing his steps. The accident scene was now awash with the blue light of emergency vehicles.

Jessica was standing near the overturned Porsche, talking to another officer. She motioned for Dowd to join her as he came into the clearing.

"You OK?"

"I'm fine. What've you got?"

"Take a look at this," she said, kneeling alongside the demolished car.

Dowd knelt, resting one hand on the car and one hand on the ground as he peered into the vehicle. The suspect they had seen with the crowbar was lying askew on the passenger's side, his eyes open and fixed.

"He's just a kid," Dowd said.